COCKY CHEF

J.D. HAWKINS

Paperback formatting by Shanoff Formats
www.shanoffformats.com

TABLE OF CONTENTS

This book is dedicated to Chris Cornell, who passed away while I was writing it and whose music has been the soundtrack of my life. Rest in peace.

"The minute you start compromising for the sake of massaging somebody's ego, that's it, game over."

Gordon Ramsay

CHAPTER ONE

COLE

Hunger can drive a man crazy. That emptiness inside that twists and stabs until the only thing you can focus on is filling it. Power, money, women...food.

Some men have appetites that can never be appeased—hungers so big, so powerful, that they can never stop. Men like me.

"We're here, Mr. Chambers."

I look up from the invoices and work orders in my lap and see the driver glance at me in the rearview mirror. I nod to him as the Maybach pulls up in front of the restaurant.

Usually I'd drive myself—God knows I own enough cars to run a grand prix—but today's been a busy one, and I've spent every moment I could poring over paperwork for the new spot in Vegas.

"Thanks, Derek," I say as he opens the door and I step out into the canopy lights of Knife: the hottest restaurant in L.A. I hand him a hundred bucks. "I'll get a cab back."

He smiles in gratitude, spins back into the car, and drives away, leaving me to stand for a moment in front of the place. It still looks beautiful after all these years. A grand entrance; glass so fine you'd swear there was nothing there, framed by woodgrain hand-picked from Portland logs. A deep red canopy modelled after Prohibition-era movie theaters looms over the doors. Above that, the word 'Knife' in understated steel lettering. Through the glass on either side of the entrance, glowing in the gold of candlelight against the exposed brickwork, I can see the diners sitting at their tables.

The music of their chatter, laughter, and clinking cutlery is faint, as faint as the aroma of garlic and white wine sauce on mussels, the sweetness of a newly caramelized soufflé. Sensations that compel you like a woman's flickering eyelashes, urging you to draw closer, close enough to devour what you've set your sights on.

The place is clean, elegant, modern. And on a night like this—even after a day like today—when the Pacific breeze moving through L.A. jostles the palm fronds like they're conjuring a dream, it's almost magical.

What you don't see are the blood, sweat and tears embedded in those bricks. The struggle and hardships that glued them together. The betrayals and broken friendships, the burning drive and resilient determination that laid its foundations. Only I can see those.

I walk up and enter, greeted by the maître d' standing behind his podium.

"Evening, Mr. Chambers," he says.

"Evening, Charlie."

He's worked here for six years, and is still the best in the business. The joke goes that Charlie is so good at making people wait that it's only a matter of time before the DMV hires him. The job is in his blood. So much so that he still won't call me Cole no matter how many times I've told him to.

"What'll it be, sir?"

"Well, I've just spent a whole day dealing with the morons in

Vegas, I haven't eaten since this morning, and I'd like to get home in time to see the Clippers highlights. As long as it comes with a side of the most alcoholic wine we have, I don't care."

Charlie smiles wryly.

"Very good, sir."

Most restaurant staff would start sweating at the idea of picking something off the menu themselves, but like I said, Charlie's of a different breed. His party trick is knowing what people are gonna order while they're still standing in line.

I've just told him that I'm tired and pushed for time, which means I won't bother with an appetizer. The most alcoholic wine we have is a Zinfandel red, which is recommended for the beef dishes. And besides, it's a Tuesday in May, so we've just had a fresh delivery of ribeye cuts.

"Will table four suit, sir?"

I nod appreciatively and move inside. It's a relatively quiet night, which means most tables are full but there's no line outside. Instinct immediately draws my eye to the three attractive women at a table across the room. Specifically the demure blonde facing me in a green dress so thin you could blow it off. She catches me looking and immediately reaches for her wine glass to hide the upturn in her lips.

Seconds after I take my seat, the wine is brought and poured at my table. I lean toward the waiter and point subtly in the direction of the blonde.

"What are they drinking over there, Ryan?"

He glances over nonchalantly, then back at me.

"The house rosé, sir."

"Send them another bottle of it, on me. Tell them—but look at the blonde when you do so—that it's for dressing so elegantly this evening."

"Yes sir."

The waiter leaves and I wait for the blonde to glance over at me again before raising the glass in her direction. She smiles more broadly now, then whispers to her friends, who all look over. Just a quick glance before they turn back to themselves, leaning in to giggle amongst each other like conspirators.

Maybe they recognize me from the TV show I had a couple of years ago, where I taught a bunch of ex-convicts and young offenders how to cook professionally. It was a fun time, but I quit the show when I realized the production company kept trying to stir up drama between the cast members. In reality, most of them took to the kitchen like ducks to water, and the heat of it left none of them with enough energy to cause trouble. So the producers thought it would spice the show up a little to instigate some fights, get the cooks wound up. Well, I don't like drama—especially in my kitchens. So I quit. Swapped the chef whites for fine suits, started combing my hair in the mornings, and decided to get back to the business side of things since Knife seemed to be running well on its own with limited supervision from me. That's when I started my plans to open up another restaurant, this time in Vegas.

The wine arrives and I enjoy the show, the women still all shocked mouths and slight blushes. The waiter points back at me and I raise an eyebrow, keeping my eyes on the blonde as I bring the glass to my lips, savoring the sweet taste of the wine and the elegant curve of her cleavage at the same time. She's smiling now, bashfully hiding behind that hair and stealing glances at me. Her slender fingers delicately holding the fork that plays around her plate. Gentle and careful. I won't say getting this woman into bed tonight will be easy, but the truth is, it's not gonna be hard. And after the week I've had, I could use the distraction.

"Your steak, Cole."

I turn away from the blonde to see Ryan, the waiter, place the large plate in front of me.

“Thanks,” I say, a little growl edging into my voice as I look down at the marbled meat. It’s all juicy softness, outlined by the prickles of peppercorns and grill lines, the red wine sauce glistening so that it seems almost alive. The blonde’s gonna have to wait a little.

I slice a piece—pleased to find the knives have been sharpened as I like them—and reveal the center; red as lust. I spear it, take a piece of the crisp potato like an afterthought, and put it in my mouth.

It takes about a second for my brain to get the messages my tongue is sending it, but when I realize it I slam the cutlery back on the plate loud enough to make the diners around me turn in my direction. Ryan rushes over, his Ken-doll eyebrows shooting upward as he sees my tightened jawline, my fixed expression.

“Something wrong?” he says tentatively.

“Who’s working the vegetables tonight?”

“Um…Willow.”

“Willow?”

“Yeah…the new chef. We hired her last week, remember? While you were in Vegas.”

I frown. “Bring her out here.”

Ryan hesitates for a split second, forcing me to look at him and erase any doubt that I’m being 100% serious. Then, he bolts. After tapping my fingers on the fine tablecloth for a few moments, Ryan returns, the chef in question following close behind him.

She walks elegantly, proud. Shoulders back and chin high. The chef whites and baggy black slacks hiding her body, dark blonde hair twisted up and buried under a hairnet, but the long neck and delicate features of her face all the more striking for the outfit’s plainness. Doe-brown eyes set in an oval shape, lips that pout like they’re mid-kiss, and a slightly upturned nose so demurely imperfect that only an artist could have made it.

"Is there a problem?" she asks, glancing from me to Ryan and back again. Her hand is on her hip, exhibiting a flash of attitude.

I take a second, frowning at her. She clearly has no idea who I am…

"You cooked these potatoes?"

"Yes…" she says, frowning back. "And?"

"Can you tell me which herbs go into them?"

"Uh…sure," she says, shooting a confused look at Ryan. "There's a little sage, some thyme—"

"Thyme."

There's a slight tilt of her head when I interrupt. Enough to show me that she knows where I'm going with this, but the fierce defensiveness doesn't leave her expression, or her voice.

"Yeah. Thyme."

"The menu says thyme," I announce, then point contemptuously at the potatoes on my plate. "But this? This is lemon thyme."

She sighs quickly, a slight admission, but there's not an ounce of regret about it.

"We're out of regular thyme, sir."

I can tell she's trying to appease me, using her soothing 'customer service' voice. Unfortunately for her, it won't work on me. Because I'm the boss, and this is my recipe.

Ryan leans toward Willow and murmurs, "It's probably at Leo's station, he always forgets to put stuff back when he's done."

"I didn't know that," Willow answers under her breath, then looks back at me as if expecting it to satisfy. "Honestly, I think the lemon thyme makes the dish work better anyway."

The smile that cracks on my face, an incredulous chuckle, is involuntary. Even if this girl doesn't know who I am, that's a ballsy thing for a cook to tell a customer.

"Do you, now?" My voice is like ice.

"I do," she says firmly. "The citrus clears the palate a little better. Since the steak sauce has a strong aftertaste it brings out the flavor a little more with each bite. Especially when it's served that rare."

"Willow," Ryan cajoles quickly, "I can handle this now, maybe you should—"

"You don't just throw whatever you think works into a recipe," I say, my smile gone now. "If I want a mystery plate I'll go to the jambalaya place down the street. This is a three-star restaurant. If I order something I expect it to be exactly the same as it is on the menu." She's gritting her teeth now, her fake smile gone tight. I don't let up. "If you were out of mussels would you give me pistachio nuts and tell me they're the same because they come in a shell?"

"Wow," Willow says, folding her arms and shaking her head detachedly. "You really are a special kind of asshole."

Ryan's face goes white. "Um, Willow—"

"*I'm* an asshole?" I interrupt.

"Yeah. So you don't like the lemon thyme—does that mean you have to bring me out here to ream me out and try to embarrass me in front of the other diners?"

"Willow, stop—" Ryan reaches for her arm but she brushes him off.

I'm out of my chair and staring her down now, drawing myself up to my full height of six foot two. "It's not a matter of whether I 'like' lemon thyme or not, it's a matter of you doing your job properly."

"And what's your job? You some kind of big shot actor? With your attitude and your fancy suit and your massive…jawline? What do you do that makes you so big-headed you think you can just come in here and speak to me like that?"

"*Willow!*" Ryan says, with just enough force this time to draw her attention. He points at me and looks at her. "That's Cole Chambers. He owns this restaurant."

CHAPTER TWO

WILLOW

So this is it. This is how you fuck up your dream job. By serving the wrong ingredient to your boss, one of the best chefs on the west coast, an infamous perfectionist, before calling him an asshole to his face.

And now his narrow blue eyes are fixed on me like searchlights. That broad, handsome face that I suddenly, and all too late, recognize with full clarity. I've seen that face too many times to count, pointing at me from the covers of cookbooks or celebrity gossip magazines, or twisted with hellish anger as he chewed out chef trainees on TV—and now that same face is staring at me with judgmental amusement. I feel even more ridiculous and exposed for not realizing it was him, but that tailored suit and combed hair makes him look more like a laid back movie star than the sinewy-armed force of nature that spins and shouts around the kitchen on TV or escorts the hottest models and actresses all over L.A. on dates.

My heart sinks, my blood runs cold, and the realization that there's no turning back now stretches the moment out to an eternity.

Cole looks at me blankly, making it clear that it's my move, so I do what I always do when the chips are down and I've made an idiot of myself: I turn my chin up, put my shoulders back, and stop giving a fuck.

"Well," I say, pulling off my hairnet and letting my chin-length bob fall down around my face. "At least I can say I met the 'great' Cole Chambers."

Before either Cole or Ryan can say anything else, I spin on my heel and march back toward the kitchen, already unbuttoning my chef whites. Striding through the plumes of steam, confused looks tossed at me by my fellow ex-colleagues, I grab my bag and take the rear exit like the building's on fire.

For a moment, as I'm closing my car door and then reversing out into the street, I wonder if I'm being rash, running out like this. Then I remember the stories of how uncompromising Cole is, his insufferable attitude on TV, how many sacrifices and how few concessions he makes in search of great food. They say he fired somebody once for over-salting a whitefish filet, that he kicked out a customer who asked that his bouillabaisse come with the mussels de-shelled. There's even a story that he ran seven miles in the rain so that he wouldn't have to serve the wrong kind of apples in a tarte tatin.

I didn't believe those stories, to be honest, but seeing him face-to-face, those keen eyes that sear through you like a cleaver, that hard, commanding face, those broad shoulders—it's clear Cole is a guy who knows what he wants, and doesn't settle for an inch less.

Besides, I've tasted failure too often now to mistake it.

Imagine the most exquisite, vibrant restaurant you can. Upscale, unique fittings built of reclaimed barnwoods, colorful works by local artists across the walls, gold embossed menus, a kitchen at the back just open enough to allow the rich aromas of seared meat and sautéed onions to fill the space. A restaurant that assaults your every sense with delights—touch, sight, smell. A rotating menu of seasonal ingredients and the freshest cuts. Hearty, savory soups where a handful of perfectly paired flavors fight for prominence in your mouth, peppercorn steaks that explode on your tongue, mint lamb chops so tender and aromatic you feel like you're dreaming them.

Now imagine that restaurant's elegant, frontier cabin design, sitting in the middle of nowhere at the end of a long, winding dirt road in Idaho. Just off a main road that has four drive-in fast food joints. Invisible for miles, so that even the locals wouldn't find it unless they plugged the exact address into their GPS. Think about who would be naïve enough to put that restaurant there.

Well…me.

To be fair, it was the only location I could afford after spending so much on the restaurant itself. I figured people would pilgrimage there once word of how awesome the place was got out. But even the food critics couldn't be bothered to come out and see it. We had a few loyal customers, since most people needed to visit only once before they became regulars, and my sister Ellie and her husband made sure to stop by at least twice a week with their friends and colleagues, but it still wasn't enough to keep the business going. It didn't help that I kept the food cheap, stubbornly trying to prove the point that good food didn't have to be exclusively expensive, that for the price of a processed burger meal you could eat something twice as fresh, twice as healthy, and ten times tastier. Principles that strong can be hard to carry, though.

By the end of the second month there was so much food left over each day that even the staff didn't want to take any more home. By the fourth I had to decide whether to pay the suppliers or the waiters. When the head and the sous chef told me they'd work for free if I told them I believed I could turn it around, I knew I couldn't lie to them. We shut the place down the next day, and I felt like a part of me had been cut away, leaving behind just another woman in her mid-twenties with no job, bad credit, and the nagging thought that I might not be cut out for this business.

The whole thing left a scar that not even weeks of moping around started to heal. I had to couch surf at my sister's while I figured my next move out, and the huge debt of my cooking education weighed on me like a bag of stones. I wasn't helped by the fact that my boyfriend at the time, Nick, decided that a day after the closure was his cue to send me a break-up text. In hindsight, it was probably a blessing in disguise—it was clear Nick basically saw me as a meal ticket, and that what I thought was love was really just the comfort of having somebody around, though Nick couldn't even provide that in the end.

It's difficult not to define yourself by a failure that big. I started to wonder if maybe I really was just another average chef who needed a reality check. If maybe my ideals and ambitions should remain just ideals and ambitions. I remember seeing an ad for a fry cook at a cheap steak house and actually considering it, then crying my eyes out once I realized how desperate I'd gotten. I felt like my entire life plan had imploded, leaving me with nothing.

It was Tony who convinced me to move down to L.A. We'd met while studying under Guillhaume de Lacompte in France. As the only two Americans we clung to each other for support as the grumpy, pockmarked Frenchman ranted and criticized his students in what was more like a boot camp for nuclear war than a prestigious gourmet cooking course. During every lesson we'd approach the stations with the trepidation of a bomb defusal. We should have known it was going to be near-traumatic when Guillhaume's first words to us were: 'Food is not a matter of life and death. It is more important.'

Returning to the US, while I spent a year preparing the most ambitious culinary industry failure in Idaho's history, Tony worked in L.A. at some of the hottest restaurants, switching between them and working his way up the ladder with the mercenary aptitude of a gun for hire.

"Listen," he had told me over the phone, just days after the shutdown of my restaurant back home, "come down to Los Angeles. Chefs can't walk ten steps here without being offered a job. Pay off your debts, make use of those God-given talents you've got, and *then* figure out what you wanna do with the rest of your life."

"I dunno, Tony…"

"What are you afraid of? Getting a tan? Working with the best chefs in all the nicest places? Serving food to celebrities and actors and singers? The great tips? The gorgeous men? You're right, it does sound scary."

"Ugh. Men are the last thing on my mind right now. Like…the very last thing on the list of things I want."

"I get it. You're a country girl—hate the city. You wanna spin across the meadows like Julie Andrews every morning—and one day you will, I'm sure. But if you wanna make something of yourself, you've got to go to the city, and L.A. is the one to be in right now."

His words had tumbled through my mind for days afterward, leaving a bitter aftertaste that I could only cleanse by admitting they were probably true. Finally I realized I had nothing left to lose but the little bit of pride I still clung to like a comforter. So I packed up some clothes, books, and all my anxieties and then left my dusty hometown for good. But as I drove down to L.A., I felt more like I was leaving all my dreams behind unrealized than heading toward them anew. Struggling and just about managing to suppress the feeling that I was heading for another personal disaster, that L.A. would chew me up and spit me out.

Karma decided to start cashing itself in when I arrived though.

Within days I found a great apartment with an awesome fitness instructor roommate named Asha, Tony had me taking on open shifts at the sushi place he worked at, and after just a couple of months I landed an interview at the hottest place in the city: Knife. I didn't expect to get it, being one of the most inexperienced of the candidates, but it turned out to be more of a cooking test than a formal interview, and I got the job. Martin—the manager who was looking after the place while Knife's owner set up his new spot in Las Vegas—said it wasn't even close.

That was just over a week ago, and things couldn't have gone much better…until about twenty minutes ago when I decided to fuck it all up because I didn't ask anyone in the kitchen if we had any plain thyme. So here it is. Smacking me in the face. Rock bottom. Now I'm pushing open the door to my apartment, struggling not to cry in case I find I can't stop.

Asha's sitting on the couch watching TV, her long, powerful legs propped up on the coffee table. She turns moon-like brown eyes in my direction as I enter, and with the kind of perception that only someone who genuinely cares can show, asks, "Is something wrong? It's not even ten. I thought you were finishing after midnight tonight?"

"So did I," I say, letting myself slump onto the loveseat beside her.

She keeps those eyes fixed on me, and I know she wants the whole story. Asha used to be an MMA fighter, so she's good at staring people down.

"Spill it."

I take a deep breath. "I just fucked up the job at Knife. Royally."

"*What?*" Asha cries, pulling her legs from the table and facing me directly, toned muscles twisting in my direction. "How? Everything was going so great."

I rub my eyes and sigh deeply as I replay the scene in my mind.

"I used a *slightly* different ingredient for the potatoes than what's listed on the menu. It was the first time I've ever done that, and ninety-nine point nine percent of people wouldn't have even been able to tell the difference...so—of course—the plate was going out to the one guy who could."

"Who?"

"Cole Chambers. The owner. My boss."

Asha breathes in through her teeth, and puts a hand on my arm. I can tell she's already thinking of how to soften the blow.

"So...he fired you? Just like that? I mean I know he's supposed to be a jerk, but—"

"I didn't give him the chance. Once he started yelling, I walked out."

"*Willow...*" Asha says, shaking her head.

"What was I supposed to do?" I say, frustration and anger at myself seeping into my defensive tone. "Just stand there and let myself be embarrassed?"

"Come on now," Asha says, her tone gentle but firm. "You shouldn't have just walked out like that. He might not have fired you."

"No, he would have," I say, shaking my head adamantly. "It's not like I haven't seen him fire somebody before. I recognized the look on his face. He was pissed, and he wasn't giving me any second chances. I was just saving my pride."

Asha sighs and tilts her head in disappointment, braids falling over her shoulder.

"Would he really fire you over that? One ingredient out of dozens, out of a hundred dishes? You could have explained it was a mistake, that it won't happen again. Surely he would understand that."

"No, you don't get it. Cole's whole thing is that he's precise, meticulous. His recipes are like paintings, every brushstroke matters. For me to just throw something else in there—"

I stop myself to drop my head in my hands, my own stupidity sounding even more ridiculous when I'm forced to articulate it out loud. Asha reaches out and rubs my back.

"Whatever," she says, in a voice as soft and soothing as aloe. "It'll be okay. Los Angeles is full of restaurants."

"And all of them are a step down from Knife," I say. "It's not like I can just coast much longer. I'm still paying off my debts, and I'm not even sure I've made rent this month."

"Leave all that for the morning," Asha says, standing up with a sudden burst of vitality, enthusiastic defiance in her voice. "Look, the night's still young. Let's go get a couple of drinks—maybe a few too many. My first class isn't until tomorrow afternoon. We'll get dressed up, we could dance a little," she says, swaying her hips, "and I guarantee you it'll all seem much less like the end of the world when you wake up with a hangover."

I look up at her, forcing a smile to show how much I appreciate it.

"Thanks, but...I don't really feel like going out. All I wanna do right now is make a gigantic batch of the sugariest, chocolateyest, meltiest fudge brownies and eat myself into a sugar coma."

Asha raises an eyebrow mischievously as she considers it, and I can almost hear her stomach growl.

"Well. That works for me."

CHAPTER THREE

COLE

I turn up at Knife early the next morning. Early enough to smell the jasmine still lingering in the coolness of the night air. Insomnia can be a real problem, but in the restaurant business it's virtually a necessity. So here I am, in the only area of Knife that I allow to be a mess: the back office.

I'm sitting behind the desk, among the filing cabinets and piled-up receipts, a few crates of wine in the corners (I let the staff use the room for storage sometimes). The sound of the dish washers hosing down the last of the pans a satisfying background music as I run through the accounts and figure out the pricing of some seasonal menu items.

As a couple of the chefs start arriving for the lunch shift, I hear a knock on the open door and look up to see Leo's bald head in the doorway. He's wearing a buttoned-up checked shirt and creased slacks that would have been out of date even in the sixties. He's one of the few chefs for whom the chef whites are a step up. Even though he's forty two, he still has the smooth, puppyish skin of a baby.

Clean scalp reflecting even the dim light of the office, skin pale enough to make you wonder if he commutes from Alaska.

"Hey boss," he says, in his gritty, quiet voice. "Willow just turned up. Should I tell her to leave?"

"Why would you tell her to leave?" I ask, my voice firmly dismissing his assumption.

"Ok, ok," he says, holding up his hands. "I didn't know you wanted to fire her yourself."

I lean back in my chair, cross my arms, and shoot him a look like I'm about to challenge him to draw.

"Who told you I was going to fire her?" I'm feeling defensive about her all of a sudden, and I don't know why. Especially considering that her behavior last night was unacceptable.

Leo looks at me a little nervously, as if performing a dozen calculations at once. He glances back into the hall, looking each way, then steps inside the office, leaning forward so he can lower his voice.

"Of course you're going to fire her. Right? I mean, she fucked up a main dish and made a scene in front of the customers, then bailed in the middle of a dinner shift. We were a man down for half the night."

I look at him for a few seconds and he waits expectantly, oblivious to my intent.

"Come see me after your shift, Leo," I say calmly, returning my attention to the computer screen.

I don't want to hear anything else—and Leo's just about smart enough to realize that, so he turns on his heels, rubbing his bald head as he leaves the office.

Shortly after that I hear another light rapping on the door, and look up to find Willow there. Except this isn't the Willow from last night, a pretty face poking out of that shapeless chef's uniform—

there's nothing shapeless about her now. Tight, ripped jeans hug her toned legs, her shirt struggling with the combination of her round breasts and that tight stomach, leaving a mouthwatering strip of flesh around her navel that reveals itself only a little as she moves.

"Shut the door," I tell her, growling the command, then watch with focused eyes the balletic movements of her body. Delicate fingers on the door handle, swish of her hair against the nape of her neck, turning just enough for me to study the jeans-filling roundness of her ass.

She turns back to face me, big, brown eyes looking up from that angelic face, and I stand up to walk in front of my desk. I need to move, partly because I've been sitting down for too long, and partly because the sight of her in street clothes has got my blood pumping a little too hard, a shot of adrenaline unexpectedly slamming through me.

"I'm surprised you came back," I say, leaning back onto the desk and folding my arms.

Her cheeks color a little but her gaze stays fastened on mine. "I came to say I'm sorry. I shouldn't have used the lemon thyme. I get it. And you're absolutely right. That's not acceptable for Knife, and I hold my hands up to that. I shouldn't have changed the recipe. It was a momentary lapse of judgment, and I thought I could get away with it. But I'm not here to make excuses. I just wanted to explain and to say I'm sorry."

I nod at her. There's something down-to-earth and genuine about the way she talks, the way she looks me in the eye. Perhaps I've spent too long in the upper echelons of Los Angeles' nightlife, but her straightforward manner disarms a little of my anger.

"You don't get to make mistakes when you work for me," I say firmly.

"Which is why I wanted to apologize."

"Apologies don't change the past. I don't make them, and I don't accept them." Willow simply nods before turning back to the door, that gentle hand already on the handle. "Did I say you could leave?"

She turns back to me, the regret in her eyes replaced by a hard pride. It's the kind of look people usually build up for decades before they feel they can direct it at me.

"Am I supposed to just stand here so you can shoot negative platitudes at me before I get fired?" she says. "Because I can watch one of your shows if I want to see you cut somebody down."

If those tight jeans made me second guess whether I should fire her, the way she stares me down like I'm not the best chef in the country, and she's not just some new hire, is piquing my interest enough that I want to keep her around at least a little longer. She'd make a hell of a poker player.

"Give me one good reason I shouldn't fire you," I challenge.

"I'm not going to beg you for my job."

"Most chefs would, in your position."

"Well, I'm not most chefs."

"Clearly," I say, allowing myself a little smile as we stare each other down.

Willow breaks her gaze, hanging her head a little, but I don't miss the way her eyes flicker over my body, lingering for a half second on the biceps of my folded arms.

"Neither are you," she says, though her tone (and my rampaging imagination) makes it more innuendo than retort. Our eyes lock.

The electricity crackling between us is almost audible. A charge less like that of manager-employee relations, and more like the sexual ambiguity of two people swapping looks across a bar. There's no doubt in my mind there's something between us—and the fact that I wanna find out what it is makes it almost impossible for me to fire this girl out of my life.

"It's your first week and Michelle tells me you've been handling it like a champ apart from this...*faux pas.* We've had chefs who couldn't even make it through a second shift."

Willow shrugs, and I can see she's relaxing a little now, her hand no longer on the door handle.

"Well, I won't pretend it was easy. But I'm not afraid of working hard."

"Obviously not," I say, picking up her resume from the desk and waving it. "You don't make it through Guillhaume's course without having some steel in you."

"Oh yeah," she grins. "I think I actually learned more about my emotions than about cooking under him."

I glare at her intensely once again, freezing her with a look.

"Regardless. That was the first and last time you walk out on a shift. If I give you another chance, are you gonna fuck me over?"

There isn't even a flinch, not even a quivering lip as Willow looks right back at me and shakes her head, "No. I won't. You're the boss."

"That I am. And you'll do well to keep that in mind." I nod and smile a little, making it clear that the issue's settled for now.

Willow seems to relax, and I find myself calming in her presence.

"So what did Guillhaume call you?" I ask, in a more easy tone.

Willow lets out a quiet laugh; she knows what I'm talking about. Everyone who studies under the Frenchman gets a specific nickname, an insult designed to demean and break one's spirit through repetition, but which most chefs carry like a badge of honor —that is, if they're able to survive the boot camp that is his training course.

"Well, as soon as he found out where I was from he stuck me with 'the Idaho Potato.' Said my talent was making everything taste as lifeless as mash," she says, smiling wistfully at the memory. "*'Curse ze farmer zat pulled you out of ze ground!'*"

I smile along with her. "You got off lightly. He used to call me the Hollywood Assassin. Said I cooked like I was trying to poison somebody."

She laughs again, gently. Her face showing a few more phases of beauty. I let the moment settle, enjoying the sight of her a little more, that smile, those eyes...

"Well," she says, glancing at the clock above the desk. "I really should get on the lunch shift."

"No you shouldn't," I say, stepping out from behind the desk. "I had Mark come in to take your spot. Wasn't sure if you'd even show up today."

"That's fair." She frowns and nods, as if disappointed that she won't get the chance to work today.

I don't know whether it's because I've been too busy to take a woman in weeks, the cramped intimacy of the back office, or the delicious curves of her body, but I'm struggling to find a way to end this conversation that doesn't involve pulling her over the desk and tugging her jeans down to her ankles to bury my head between her thighs and find out what she tastes like.

I check the time, and realize I should have left the office about two minutes ago.

"What do you think about kids?" I say, packing my pockets as I prepare to leave the office.

"Um...as customers? In the restaurant?"

"No," I say. "I mean, are you good with kids? Do you like them?"

"Sure. Actually, I used to volunteer teach a cooking glass for an elementary school in Idaho. And I have two nieces back home, and either they're mature or I'm not, 'cause we always have a great time together. Why do you ask?"

I move toward the door and hold it open for her.

"Because I'm gonna need your help," I say as she moves through, and I steal one more look at her peachy ass. I talk as we move through the restaurant, toward the front. "I signed up for this Young Chef mentoring program—or rather, Martin signed me up for it. He thought it would be a good bulletpoint to the publicity around me, and the new restaurant. Said I had gone too far down the 'hard-edged food perfectionist' route, and needed to show a more humane side."

Willow nods as we push through to the tables.

"I can see that," she says, without sarcasm.

"Yeah…well, I'm not exactly sure I have a more humane side. Last time I spoke to a kid, I was one." I push open the front doors and scan the street. "There they are."

The mousey woman with a warm smile who I assume to be Chloe's supervisor is standing next to the small girl. The kid has dark hair, tied back into a ponytail, and dusty, tan skin. I wasn't exactly sure what nine year olds look or sound like, but she's a little more upright and tough-looking than I imagined. Less a waddling toddler and closer to the kind of savvy kids you see in movies, not least because she stares at me with a judgmental gaze.

The supervisor waves and we start moving toward them. If I thought this was a silly idea when I heard it, then I think it's outright stupid now that I'm actually doing it. What the hell am I going to do with this kid? Teach her how to make a red wine reduction? Make her a cheesecake and sit her in front of a TV to watch cartoons? I suppose if worse comes to worst we can use an extra pair of hands peeling garlic cloves.

What I'm feeling right now is probably the closest I'll ever come to empathizing with guys who have no confidence going on dates;

concerned about doing or saying the wrong thing. I don't even know how to greet her, whether I should shake her hand, tousle her hair, or lower myself to her eye level and make baby noises.

Luckily, Willow wasn't lying when she said she liked kids, and does exactly what I needed her to do—help me.

"Hi there, I'm Maggie," the supervisor says, shaking my hand.

"Cole Chambers. Great to meet you."

"Hello, I'm Willow," she says, shaking the supervisor's hand with a smile before directing a huge smile and happy eyes at the girl. "Hey you! What's your name?"

"Chloe," the girl says, and immediately I'm struck by the way Willow's infectious smile seems to compel the kid to do the same. Guess it works on kids, too.

"That's a gorgeous name," Willow says.

"I like yours, too," Chloe replies, shedding any shyness instantly under Willow's warmth. "It's also the name of the tree."

Willow laughs easily.

"What do you think?" she says, wryly. "Am I like the tree?"

Chloe sizes her up, her smile showing her gapped teeth now, enjoying the game.

"No…well, you're tall. But a lot less droopy."

We all laugh, and I turn to Maggie to ask, "So what are we doing today?"

"Oh, that's on you. I'm leaving her here now," Maggie says, in the slow, clear tones of someone who often addresses large numbers, "and I'll be back to pick her up in a couple of hours. Does that sound ok? My cell number is in the email we sent you, just in case."

"Wait, but what am I supposed to do?" I say, getting a little frantic now. "Just give a cooking lesson, or lecture her on matching appetizers to mains, or—?"

Maggie eyes me, a little puzzled.

"Nobody told you anything?"

"Nope."

"Well, Miss Chloe is involved in a cooking competition, and she's made it through the first rounds already but the finals are in a few months, and most of the contestants—as well as being experienced and having attended cooking courses—are being mentored by various chefs from California. None of them as big as you, though, I must say," Maggie smiles.

"Oh, that sounds awesome!" Willow says, glancing from me to Chloe to share her excitement.

"So," Maggie continues, "you can do whatever you want, whether it's refining her skills or working on her mental game—anything you can think of to try and help her be a better cook. It's not about the winning, of course, but it should be fun for both of you."

"Say no more," I assure her, finally feeling like I have a handle on the situation. "I might not understand kids, but I definitely understand competition."

Minutes later, Willow, Chloe and I are walking toward the neighborhood farmers' market. Willow and Chloe are getting on like a house on fire, and I'm spending more time marveling at how good Willow is at this than I am thinking about the kid.

"Are we going to cook after this?" the kid asks.

"Hell no," I say. "I don't let chefs get anywhere near a flame until they prove they can understand the principles. Produce, plan, and prep."

Willow squints at me a little.

"Isn't that exactly what you used to say on your show? The one where you showed convicts how to cook?"

I glance at Chloe, then back at Willow.

"I don't see how this is any different—with less swearing, perhaps."

Willow nods, a smile as if humoring me, and we enter the farmers' market, passing through stall after stall where I drill into Chloe the importance of choosing good produce and providing consistent quality.

After about an hour of eyeing vegetables with a critical gaze and squeezing fruit, I turn to Chloe.

"You have any idea what you're gonna cook for the final round?" I say.

Chloe looks up at me, the smile she's been pointing at Willow turning into a pout.

She shrugs and says, "I dunno. The first round was assigned dishes, and after that one they gave us the ingredients they wanted us to use to make something up, but for the finals we have to pick our own dish. I have no clue. There's just too many things I could choose."

"Well," Willow says, "what do you like to eat best?"

Chloe thinks for a second.

"Pasta."

I shake my head and frown.

"You ain't winning a cooking competition with pasta."

Willow glares at me before turning back to Chloe.

"That sounds great," she says. "Let's see about selecting some ingredients to make your pasta the best."

I don't like the way Willow overrides me—if anyone pulled that with me in the kitchen, they'd be washing dishes for a month. Yet the combination of her being so disarmingly hot, and the way Chloe seems to respond by gaining a burst of energy, gives me no choice but to roll with it.

We continue walking on a little, buying agua frescas and a box of ripe, fragrant strawberries to eat while we check out the other produce. I give up on trying to add anything productive to the conversation, especially in the face of seeing how adept Willow is at it. It's hard to imagine the kind of women I usually spend time with pulling silly faces for a kid, or even putting that much effort into one, and if I suspected Willow was something a little different before, I'm absolutely sure of it now. Instead, I focus on complimenting Chloe's skills at choosing perfectly-ripe fruits and vegetables, and keep my mouth shut as she goes on and on about ideas for her competition-worthy pasta sauce.

Eventually, we make our way back to Knife and meet up with Maggie again at the curb. I send Chloe home with a bag of her farmers' market selections and she grins and waves at me and Willow through the departing car's window. When the SUV is out of sight, Willow turns to me and I can almost sense her sympathy.

"You weren't lying, huh? About needing help. I mean you weren't awful, but…"

I shrug. "Guess I'm never having kids."

Willow laughs.

"Never say never. Besides, I think she's going to be good for you. You need a kid around to keep you from taking everything so seriously."

I narrow my eyes at her, but for some reason it's hard to give that gorgeous face my tough-guy stare, especially when she's smiling playfully at me.

"You speak to all of your bosses like that?" I ask.

"To be honest, I never had a boss before."

"Figures."

Though everything about the moment signals she's about to leave, that we're about to part, I find myself wanting to spend more time with her, wanting to dig a little deeper beyond that captivating face, those doe eyes. Confident enough to handle me, headstrong enough to assert herself, yet down-to-earth enough to handle Chloe—there's something about her…

She turns to leave and something within me makes a snap decision.

"Listen, we should talk. Properly. Martin told me you were special, and Michelle does nothing but sing your praises—but I'd feel more comfortable knowing you a little better myself, especially since I wasn't the one who hired you."

"Sure. Now?"

"No. I have a full day that should have started about fifteen minutes ago. Tonight. My friend owns a place not far from here. We'll grab a bite, have a drink. You can tell me your story. Best way to get to know a cook is by eating with them."

"Sounds good to me," she smiles, and I wonder if she buys the idea that I'm being completely professional. "Though I'm not sure I have enough of a story to fill a whole evening."

"Then consider it the start of one."

CHAPTER FOUR

WILLOW

I crash out as soon as I get home, sprawling out on the bed around midday and telling myself I'll just rest my eyes a bit, then waking up at six pm feeling detached from reality and seeing a missed call from my sister that I'm too wrung out to return right now. It's hard to recognize how busy and exhausted you are until you actually stop for a second.

Since I started working at Knife just over a week ago, I've been surviving on power naps and soup fumes. Even in a city of four million people it feels like we've served half of them. Add to that the emotional climax of thinking you got fired, the relief at finding out you haven't, and the thrill of being invited out for drinks with one of the most famous chefs in the world. The whole city seems like a timewarp, where things happen on fast forward, and where everything can change in a moment.

It's satisfying, in a way. More satisfying than lingering around the back of a kitchen watching your chefs chain smoke through another empty day. But the more I experience the craziness of L.A., the more I feel like I'm still just a girl from Idaho.

And then there's Cole. I knew I'd meet him eventually, I just didn't expect it to be on such charged terms, and to be honest, I didn't expect him to be so hot. Sure, I'd seen his TV shows, and though I might work like a machine there's enough human in me to feel a heat in my chest when his eyes get all focused—but there's something more to him in reality. Those eyes are even more impressive, and all the masculine energy that made him the private fantasy of millions of housewives is still there, but that focus is even more intense when it's directed at you. He listens intently, like he's trying to read between the lines, and he never breaks your gaze, as if he's holding you with them.

Or maybe there's something about me that he…no. I'm not even going there. He's my boss, and he probably can't help the effect he has on women. No reason to think this is anything other than a slightly social but very professional business meeting.

Asha comes home around seven, while I'm in the bathroom moisturizing my face.

"Willow?" she calls from the doorway.

"I'm in here."

I hear her drop her sports bag and come to the bathroom, where she looks at me anxiously and leans up against the doorframe. Her brown skin glistens with sweat, glowing with the exertion of teaching another kick-boxing class.

"So how are you feeling?" she asks, in a voice as tenderly cautious as a therapist's. "Was he there this morning? Did you argue with him again?"

"Yeah, he was there. He didn't fire me."

She lifts a brow. "No?"

"No. We talked it over and I told him I knew I'd made a mistake, and he said he'd give me another chance. It's all good now."

"That's awesome!" Asha says, beaming a pearl-white smile.

"Yeah. Actually we're going out to get a drink together. Seeing as he didn't get to interview me for the job himself. Maybe we'll start off on the right foot this time around."

"Great! When?"

I check my phone on the sink.

"In about forty minutes."

Asha's smile drops, leaving a stunned incredulity on her face.

"So why aren't you getting ready?"

"What are you talking about?" I say, stepping back from the sink to show her my skinny chinos and tank top under the plaid shirt. "I *am* ready."

Asha steps back and looks me up and down, an expression of utter disbelief on her face.

"Did you say you were going for drinks? Or that you were going apple picking with him?"

I look back at the mirror.

"It's nothing fancy," I say. "Just a drink at his friend's spot. We'll probably just be talking shop a little before he has to run off and do something more important."

Asha steps beside me so that she can stare at me in the mirror.

"Girl, this is Cole fucking Chambers, *everything* he does is fancy. The guy's had his own TV show, he's been on the cover of GQ. You can't go on a date with him looking like someone who works in a hardware store."

"No," I say, turning to look at her directly. "It's not a date. This is just a work thing. Colleagues. There's nothing date-like about this, no 'dateyness' at all."

I don't want to admit that I'd half-considered the idea myself before pushing it away—but I've got a feeling Asha is going to admit it for me.

"Oh please. You're not in Kansas anymore, honey. Ain't no gentlemen here. If he's taking you out for drinks and it's not daylight, trust me: he's interested."

"Why would he be interested?" I say, almost laughing at the ridiculousness of the idea. "Like you said, he's 'Cole fucking Chambers.' He can—and does—date a different European supermodel every week. I'm just his new employee."

"I guess we'd better get you looking like a supermodel, then," Asha says, spinning so fast she almost whips me with her braids.

I follow her as she marches into my bedroom and yanks open my closet.

"Why do I get the feeling you *want* me to fuck Cole?" I ask.

Asha flicks through my outfits shaking her head and grimacing at each one.

"I just want you to get close enough to introduce me."

"Even though yesterday it sounded like you wanted to get him in a chokehold?"

"That's how all my relationships usually start. Here," she says, pulling a tight sweater dress from the rack and jabbing it toward me. "Let me see you in this."

"This?" I say, taking the dress from her and staring at it. "I've never even worn this before. My sister bought it for me before I left. I don't even think it'll fit. It looks like barely enough material to make a pillow cover with."

"Should be perfect, then," Asha says, as she starts foraging in the base of the closet for boots. "The heels on these are a little high, but you won't be driving anyway. You're taking a cab, right?"

I narrow my eyes. "Why would I take a cab when I have a perfectly functional vehicle of my own?"

Asha laughs, handing me the boots. "If this night goes the way I know it will, you're gonna be so full of lust and alcohol that you'll be in no shape to drive yourself home afterward. Trust me, you want the cab. I'll call one for you now. Don't argue."

Knowing that I'm not going to win this battle, I retreat to the bathroom to get changed, more concerned about the idea that this is actually a date than I am about the dress. Did I miss something obvious? Am I so frazzled from work that I didn't pick up on the signs? Surely if this was a date he'd have said so—Cole Chambers is not exactly the kind of guy who hides his intentions. He might be hard to read, but dating an employee you've only just met is too stupid a notion for anyone to entertain. Or maybe that's the way things go in L.A.?

If this *is* a date, though, I'm not sure I should be going. Cole's my boss, and I've spoken to him a grand total of two times. Plus, I've worked my ass off to put my failures behind me—the restaurant flop, the small town claustrophobia and overbearingly concerned parents, the ex-boyfriend who was more like an emotional leech than a romantic partner—so dating is not on the menu of things I'm looking for, and it's completely against my current philosophy of starting fresh and taking things one step at a time.

But then again, there *is* a part of me that I have to suppress whenever I think of those intense eyes, the hard muscles of his tattooed shoulder, the way his forearms bulge when he crosses them over his perfect chest…

"You done?" Asha asks from the other side of the bathroom door.

"Yeah," I call out.

She comes inside where I'm standing in front of the mirror again, turning this way and that to see how the dress looks. I glance at her and see that she's smiling, a fairy-godmother smugness on her face.

"Ooh, yes! How does it feel?"

I shrug and pull the dress up a little over my cleavage.

"It feels ok, actually. I kinda like it."

"Like it?" Asha says, as she steps forward to pull the dress down and re-expose the cleavage. "Girl, you should love yourself in this dress. That man is going to need an icepack when he sees you."

I laugh a little and look back at myself in the mirror.

"Aren't I a little overdressed, though? If he turns up in sweatpants and a T-shirt I'm going to die of embarrassment."

Asha looks at me sternly, like a protective mother.

"If he turns up in sweatpants *he's* the one who's going to die, trust me."

I laugh gently.

"He won't though," Asha continues, smiling with a lusty anticipation. "I'm sure he knows exactly what he's doing."

"Yeah. That's what I'm afraid of."

The cab pulls up at the address Cole gave me and I see him standing outside immediately. It's hard not to notice him, the tailored lines of his suit lending him a striking silhouette in the fading evening light, all right angles and good posture. I step out of the cab and walk toward him, suddenly feeling like the dress is way tighter under the focus of his gaze.

When I draw close he leans over and air kisses me. I almost swoon from his nearness and his subtle, masculine scent. It takes every ounce of willpower I have not to leap into his arms and beg him to show me the back seat of his car. Maybe I haven't been out with a guy in longer than I realized.

"You look amazing," he says, stepping back a little to cast his eyes down and up my body with admiring frankness.

"Thank my roommate," I say, before looking around at the long wall of solid brick behind us. "Where's the restaurant?"

Cole smiles and steps aside, holding out his palm toward a discreet stairway that leads down to a mezzanine door.

"Down the rabbit hole," he says.

I step forward, wondering if he's staring at my ass as I descend the staircase, and push open the door. The second I do I'm greeted with the soft groove of hipster music, the chatter of a few dozen diners, easy, buzzing, second-drink laughter. Old fashioned Edison lightbulbs hanging from antique fixtures fight against the darkness of the large space, casting their soft glow against the exposed piping and metallic tables. Sweet aromas fill the air, and I immediately start picking out the flavors: sweet and sour sauces, teriyaki, barbecue sauce that uses whiskey as a base, fresh cilantro and red onion and guacamole.

I take a moment to soak it all in. The fashionable diners, the clean, angular, rustic-industrial aesthetic of the fittings. Something touches the small of my back and I turn to see that it's Cole's hand. He smiles and urges me toward an unoccupied booth, waving and calling out a few greetings to the chefs operating the open-plan hotplates.

After settling into the booth I shuffle a little, picking at my dress to make sure it's still in the right place.

"Are you comfortable?" Cole says, leaning forward.

"Sure," I shrug. "Why wouldn't I be?"

"I was just wondering if you were a little too...'down-to-earth' for a place like this?"

His concern is obvious, so I don't take it as an insult. Instead I look around as if checking something, then smile back at him.

"Seems to me the people here are eating and drinking just like they do in Idaho."

Cole chuckles lightly then flicks a finger for a waiter to come over.

"You'll like this place," he says. "A buddy of mine set it up a couple of years ago. It's already a staple of L.A. It's a concept menu."

I raise a brow. "Oh yeah? What's the concept?"

"All the foods are hand foods. Continental fusion. Wraps, samosas. Sushi, antipasti. All of it's good."

I nod politely, quieting the voice inside of me that wants to express how much I hate the notion of a 'concept' bar. Trends like this come and go, but great food that's made well—that's something that lasts. I'm interested to see if this place is more the former or the latter.

When the menu comes I tell Cole to recommend a mix for us to share, and order a blueberry cider cocktail. Then I spend a while asking him about how the Vegas place is going, and what his plans are for the next time Chloe shows up for a lesson.

By the time the drinks come I realize that Cole isn't entirely the difficult, uncompromising, and reserved person that I—and most people—make him out to be. Sure, he's passionate about cuisine, but he's also funny and thoughtful and charming as hell. By the time the food arrives, he's actually telling me he agrees with what I said about the lemon thyme and that he's considering altering the recipe. And when the second round shows up, I'm telling him the awful story of my failed restaurant back in Idaho. I can't believe how at ease I feel, given how poorly our first meeting went and how turned on I am in his presence.

He listens intently, and I realize as I'm telling him how little I've actually spoken about my restaurant to anybody who wasn't there. All the while he asks attentive questions about my business plan (I didn't exactly have one) and day-to-day operations, nodding as he absorbs the information but never venturing an opinion, until I finish and find I've just recounted my spectacular failure to one of the most successful chefs in the country.

When I'm done he leans back and looks at me in a way he hasn't done yet, as if from some deeper part of him, his narrowed eyes glistening with some new perspective.

After a pause that's almost awkward, even after the second cider, he says cryptically, "I knew there was something about you."

Cole picks up a cannoli, looks at it for a second, then holds it out in front of my face. "This is great. Try it."

It's an intimate gesture, feeding me like this, and yet somehow it feels natural to lean forward, toward those calloused hands, and take a bite from the creamy treat, our eyes never leaving each other. I swallow it and smile, deciding to change the subject before the heat inside of me makes me say something embarrassing.

"What do you mean, 'something' about me?"

"Something different. Something unfulfilled. Hungry. I noticed it when you walked out the other night." He stops to spin his glass, frowning at it. "I'm curious though. What do you mean when you say you wanted to cook 'real' food?"

"Real food…you know, stuff that isn't so overelaborate. Pretentious food."

Cole turns his frown from his glass to me.

"Food like mine, you mean?" he says, a little challenge in his tone.

I hesitate for a second too long before saying, "What? No. No…I mean, Knife is basically a steakhouse at the end of the day, right? Forget I said anything."

"Come on, say it."

I look at him for a moment, my pulse racing under his gaze, like I just took a wrong turn somewhere and found myself trapped. Suddenly I remember that he's my boss, that I've only worked at his restaurant for a week, and that I was already inches away from being fired.

"Go on," he urges again. "We're both adults. I can take criticism. I'm curious to hear what you actually think."

I laugh a little nervously, hoping it'll break the stiff look on his face, but his expression doesn't flicker, and I know the only way out is the truth. There's something about how he's looking at me that makes it easy to forget he's my boss, that I'm his employee. It's easy to forget that he's a household name who most people in the restaurant keep looking over at, and that I'm just a girl from Idaho with a failed restaurant behind her and not enough free time to figure out the next step forward. He looks at me, and I look at him, and we're suddenly just a man and a woman, with all that entails. More intimate and trusting of each other than our brief introduction should make us, and somehow I feel like it's the most natural thing in the world to speak my mind.

"Ok. Well…it's not just your restaurant, I see it in a lot of places. Overcomplicating everything. Taking the simplest dishes and flavors, which are already great, and then dressing them up like they're going to a prom. Using three different cooking processes on a cut of meat just because it looks good on a menu. Fifteen different herbs so that people can't tell what they're even tasting. Covering everything in sauces as if we're ashamed of tasting something in its natural state. Using its French name, then sticking it on a menu with a five-times mark-up. Sometimes it almost seems as if the only way we can react to a culture of fast food is by going to the other extreme and making everything as difficult and as pretentious as possible."

After a pause, one in which I can't quite determine what Cole thinks of my emotional outburst, he says, "Is this the alcohol talking?"

"No. It's all me," I say, defiant with the sound of my own words.

"Even though you studied with Guillhaume?"

"*Especially* because I studied with Guillhaume."

Cole's blank face breaks into a laugh, and I watch him in confusion.

"You do realize that's why your restaurant failed, right?"

Indignant, I say, "My restaurant failed because of its location."

"No," Cole says, with a cockiness that annoys me. Slowly, he leans forward. "You're an idealist. You think too highly of the average diner—and that's why it failed."

I grit my teeth, genuinely weighing the option of telling Cole exactly what I think, and the alternative of keeping my job.

"You wanna hear a secret?" he says, taking my restraint as a sign to carry on. "I don't tell this to many people. It took me too long to figure out for me to hand it out freely, but you…I think you should hear it."

I fold my arms and ignore Cole's eyes flickering down to my cleavage for a second.

"Sure. Go ahead."

"It's three secrets, in fact. Three secrets that can make any dish taste infinitely better. Doesn't matter what it is. Starter, main, hell, even a fucking sandwich."

"I'm all ears."

Cole looks at me as if he's judging whether I'm worthy, then, after a dramatic pause, starts to talk.

"First one," he says, waving a finger, "make the dish look good. Lot of people underestimate how powerful the eye is, but the thing is…we *taste* with it. A great dish doesn't start at the first bite, it starts when the waiter brings it to your table and puts it in front of you. You see those Titian reds and Cezanne greens of a salad and you already taste the freshness—even if it isn't actually there. Never serve a potato that isn't golden brown and you'll never get a complaint. We *taste* with our eyes first. The way a dish looks is a promise, a prelude, it's like foreplay—"

I almost spit out my drink.

"*Foreplay?*"

"Exactly like it," Cole continues, without missing a beat. "Years ago, when I was starting out, working in catering with my partner, we perfected this recipe for ribs. Beer and honey cooked, *just* right. To this day I doubt anyone on the planet could do them better than us. But every time we put them out and waited for people to try them, all they'd say is 'they're good.' That's all. 'Good.' Well, 'good' wasn't good enough for us. These things tasted flawless, but nobody seemed to get it. Then we figured it out—they tasted exceptional, but they looked like any other rack of ribs you'd find at a backyard cookout. Uneven tones, congealing juices, streaky grill marks."

Cole shifts in his chair with the vividness of his story.

"So the next time we cook them, we fucking sculpt the things. We treated them like museum pieces, got those burn marks just right. Chopped them up a little to show off that texture, set them next to a chunk of golden cornbread and a pinch of cilantro to make those reddish-browns pop. And you know what happened the next time we brought them out?"

"What?"

"There were *gasps,*" Cole says, with a sense of aggressive satisfaction. "You bet your fucking ass people had more to say than 'good' after that."

I sit back and look over at the waiter, pointing at my empty glass when he looks over.

"I believe it. What's the second secret, then?" I say.

"The second one is simple: Charge ridiculous amounts of money."

Now I'm the one laughing dismissively.

“Come on, seriously?”

Cole’s stern expression leaves no doubt that he is.

“Seriously. You’re right that there’s a problem in the restaurant business—but it’s not the cooks—it’s the diners. You *seen* people eat lately? They taste the first bite only, and the rest is just filling a hole. Doesn’t matter how good your food is, if you’re giving it away cheap it’s just fuel. You charge a hundred bucks a head for a couple of lamb chops, though? People are gonna savor every bite.”

“I get what you’re saying.” I nod, running my finger around the rim of my glass. “But is it ethical?”

Cole just grins. “Ethical? Hell, I’m performing a service. They’re gonna sit for an hour talking with each other about how complex the flavors are, how aromatic it is, how perfectly cooked it is. They’ll try their hardest to figure out the seasonings like they’re solving a jigsaw puzzle. I’m giving them an experience they’ll never forget. You see, you gotta make people work for something to appreciate it, and if you hit them in the pocket, they’re gonna make damned sure they find something to appreciate.”

My fresh drink arrives but Cole doesn’t tear his eyes away from me, lost in the momentum of his own arguments. He doesn’t even need prompting for the third secret.

“And the last one,” he says, leaning over the table now, his voice low and directed, as if uttering a conspiracy. “You wanna leave your customers wanting more. Now I’m not saying leave them hungry, but you wanna leave them a couple of bites short of completely satisfied. The meal lingers then, so they don’t just forget it and start thinking about work or traffic or their taxes. Think about it: people will love a single bite of caviar more than they’ll ever love a plate of it.”

I nod a little and take a slow sip of my drink. Cole sits back, satisfied.

"And there you have it," he says, victoriously. "The three secrets."

"Bullshit," I say, calmly.

"Excuse me?"

"I could not disagree more with everything you just said."

He laughs. "Really now?"

"Yeah," I say, almost confrontational. "I think your secrets suck."

The laugh dies away and Cole glares at me, his face flickering between confusion and offense, as if he's never heard somebody speak to him about his craft this way before.

"Do they? How so?"

I take a deep breath, realizing that I'm well beyond the point of control, only my principles guiding me now.

"You talk about dishes looking good—well, what if I don't agree with your idea of what's attractive? What if I like my salads cut roughly and jumbled in a bowl instead of arranged and stacked like a flower arrangement? What if I like food that looks like food, and not post-modern art that's trying to guilt trip me into liking it."

"You don't underst—"

"And as for pricing stuff ridiculously just so that people take their time eating—I think that's awful. Maybe that works on the money-obsessed celebrities that go to Knife, but where I come from, people aren't so good at lying to themselves and they can't afford to purchase a plate of satisfaction. If a bad meal is expensive, well that just makes it worse. You wanna make people appreciate something you made, then you should make it with love."

"Whether you like it or not, it's the—"

"And small portions? Jesus! It's like you don't even know what food is *for* anymore! Great food is great food. It should make people feel happy and satisfied, not starve them into thinking it's better than it actually is." I gesture at the doll-sized tacos and one-bite samosas in front of us. "Look at this. It's like a child's portion size! Maybe that's enough food for supermodels and decadent actors, but for somebody who's drained after a nine hour shift, this is only going to leave them more hungry. What were these, thirty dollars a plate?"

I'm almost out of breath at the end of my rant, glaring back at Cole as if reflecting the dark irritation in his eyes. Before regret can set in, and the reality of where I am, before I remember who I'm talking to and how easily he can just hand me a pink slip. Before I start backtracking like crazy in order to still have my job tomorrow, he shakes his head, that infuriating grin back on his perfect face.

"You know that's why your restaurant failed, right?"

"My restaurant failed because of its location," I respond quickly, realizing I'm repeating myself. Instinct taking over again. "Nothing else. If I had half as good a location as Knife I'd have thrived."

"You think it's that easy, do you?" Cole smiles darkly, fully offended now.

"I never said I think it's that easy," I reply. "But I *know* that I'm that good."

He doesn't say anything after that. The silence is long enough for anxiety to set in, an awkward realization that I might have just fucked everything up—again. I sip my drink, looking around the restaurant to avoid Cole's calculating stare.

"Prove it," he says, eventually.

"What?"

"Prove it," he repeats. "You think you're so good, that you've got it all figured out, that I'm wrong—then show me."

I put my drink down slowly.

"How?"

Cole shrugs.

"Cook for me. Something great. Something you think is 'unpretentious' and 'real.'"

I shake my head. "You're hardly the best judge. My point is what would work in a restaurant."

Cole smiles, as if I'm balking at the challenge. I think hard, and eventually figure something out.

"Actually, you know what? I'll do it. But if you like it, you let me put it on the menu at Knife. It could be a special—just for a week. See what your customers think. Then we'll really see who's right."

Cole looks off into the distance for a second to consider it.

"Ok. Deal." He offers his hand across the table and I take it slowly, waiting for him to laugh and tell me this is a joke. "But I have to try your dish first. I'm not just going to let you put anything on the menu. You'll make it for me, and if I think it's acceptable, we'll add it to the specials menu and see if the customers agree."

"Sure. Just tell me when."

Cole throws me a look of confusion.

"Not when. *Now.*" He extends his arm to reveal his designer watch and checks it. "Knife's been closed a couple of hours now. So we'll have the kitchen to ourselves."

I down my drink like I'm heading to war.

"You're on," I say, already sliding out of the booth. "Let's go."

But as I march confidently toward the exit, I can't help wondering if this is the chance of a lifetime or the worst mistake I've ever made.

CHAPTER FIVE

COLE

In the back of the cab I manage to pull my attention away from the golden skin of Willow's legs just long enough to call ahead to the restaurant. It's late enough that the dish washers should be just about done, but I need to make sure. When they answer, I tell them to take an early night, that I'm bringing private guests. It's not an unusual request, so I know they'll be gone soon.

Willow stares out of the window intently, tapping her fingers against her lush mouth. She's probably thinking of what to cook. I don't mind her silence, since it gives me a chance to gorge on the sight of her body, to drink her curves in, get drunk on them. By the time the car pulls up outside Knife I'm woozy with lust. Irrational, alcohol-infused imagination doing all kinds of things with that taut body beside me.

"You figured out what you're gonna cook yet?" I tease, as the cab speeds away leaving empty air between us.

She gives only a tight, mystic smile as response. There's too much solid determination about her now to entertain me. The laid back, graceful elegance she's had up to this point now replaced by a directed poise, as much precise strength as it is focused determination. She turns and walks up to the restaurant with catwalk straightness, so fast that I almost have to quicken my gait to catch up to her.

"Are you going to be able to give me a hand?" she asks as I unlock the door.

I push it open for her.

"I'm not good at taking orders."

"That's ok," Willow smiles as she steps through. "I'm good at giving them."

Before I can even close the door behind me she's making a beeline for the kitchen, tying an apron on around that tight dress and somehow still managing to look just as hot. I watch her pulling pans from the rack, firing up the stove, moving around the kitchen like a whirling dervish. She rushes past me at pace, ferrying a few bottles to the counter.

"Grab me a couple pounds of mince," she calls out, her voice projected and sharp now, the kind of voice you develop working in a loud environment. "Red peppers—long enough to have some spice—and start chopping a sweet onion. Chopped, not diced."

I get an adrenaline rush at her words, pulse racing at being ordered about by someone so purposeful, hot, and focused. It's been too long since I actually cooked so hands-on, and even longer since someone told me what to do in a kitchen, or anyplace else.

I watch her, smiling a little as she chops a few cloves of garlic as fine as powder in a matter of seconds, only half-hearing. She stops a second to look at me sternly.

"If you're not helping, you're getting in my way."

There she goes again with that mouth. You don't spend your entire life fighting your way to the top, then fighting everybody who tries to knock you off, to be spoken to like that. But I somehow find myself grinning, wondering if this girl knows how hot she sounds, how badly I'd like to rip that apron off her and give her my own set of orders, orders that have nothing to do with food.

"Yes ma'am," I drawl agreeably, pulling off my suit jacket and rolling up my shirt sleeves to get to work.

For the next fifteen minutes she works the kitchen up into a storm of aromas. Grilling Mexican chorizo with the beef patties, baking rolls that smell as sweet as cake, flash-frying herbed potatoes. My mouth waters as plumes of spicy smoke rise and unfurl around us—so admittedly, she may have had a point about the tiny portion sizes. I tune into her working rhythm, watching her move from task to task amid a cacophony of sizzles, slammed oven doors, the rhythmic beat of knife on wood to the low rumbling of boiling water.

"Where is this chorizo from?" she asks, as she chops it carefully.

I stop mixing the minced meat with my hands—as per her instructions—to smile at her.

"A little place down in the Argentinian pampas. Beautiful place," I say, then lean in to her and lower my voice. "You'd love it."

She stops cutting for a second, looking up at me and noticing how close I am. For a second that professional demeanor breaks, a little smile, a slight blush, a little flick of the hair before she's back to business again.

"I'm sure I would, if I ever get the chance to go."

I think about telling her I'd take her, half consider my schedule and wonder if I can drop everything right now to charter a plane there for both of us. But before my mind wanders too far off-course, Willow pulls me back into the cooking with another command.

She's laser-focused on the food, switching between disciplines almost frantically, but always poised, always in control, oblivious to the way I'm eating her up with my eyes. An embodiment of my two favorite things: beautiful women and great food. The sight of her toned legs as she squats to check the oven, the red kick of grilled peppers in my sinuses, the arch of her back as she leans over to check the pot, the crackle of hot oil touching coriander seeds. A synesthesia of sensual gratification, stirring a heart-pounding hunger inside of me now, my blood hot as oil, muscles tensing in anticipation, this woman glorious enough to devour.

I'm so distracted by thoughts of what I'd do to her body on an impromptu vacation that I barely notice when she finishes, plating the food as I study the taut curve of her thighs.

We stand side-by-side at the counter, and she looks at me directly for the first time since we started, pulling off her apron and tossing it aside.

"It's a rush job," she says, suddenly looking a little nervous. "I would take a little longer with the buns—I know this great Eastern European way of making them super light. And if I *really* had time I might consider alubia beans—but I doubt it."

I tear my gaze away from those soft eyes to look at the plate, gathering some sense of civility about my senses as I see what it is in its final form, coming back down to earth with a bump. I might be worked up enough to feel the electricity on my skin, but I didn't get to where I am without putting rationality first, without putting *food* above even the kind of crazy thoughts she's pulling from me.

"It's…a burger," I say, blank, firm, and disappointed.

"No!" Willow says, a note of panic in her voice. She points at it as if to direct my critical look back toward it. "I mean…yes. Sort of. But it's a chorizo Kobe burger with garlic aioli, lime-zested mustard. It's Basque-influenced, only a short walk from the snobby French-oriented stuff you serve."

After a pause I take a deep breath and say, "Still, it's a burger. You think that's going to sit well on a menu next to beef bourguignon and bourride rapheloise?"

"You *need* something like this on the menu," Willow says, temper flaring a little now. "Every main we have is so rich and full, but the textures are all similar. It's all sauce-based. This has just as much richness of flavor with a somewhat drier texture. I can guarantee people would appreciate this." I glare at her, unconvinced. "I've made a variation of this with Roquefort cheese, too—if you really think it's not 'Michelin star' enough."

I let out a long sigh.

"Do I have to say it again?"

"What's wrong with it being a burger?" Willow snaps. "Everybody in this country eats burgers—from the poorest families to the overpaid actors you call your clientele. Even *vegans* make them."

"Precisely," I say calmly. "Everybody makes burgers. So why would we?"

"Oh I see," Willow says, folding arms, fully offended now. "It's not 'pretentious' enough for you, is it? Not 'extravagant' or 'upmarket' enough for your exalted customers?"

I glance at the burger again. It looks good, there's no doubt about it. Ingredients prepared so well my mouth is watering even with everything else going on, even though I've already eaten. I look back at her.

"It's upmarket," I say, "for sure. Looks great, smells great. But it's still a burger. Still just an elaborate version of something you can get for a dollar." I push myself off the counter and start to turn, shrugging a little apologetically as I turn to leave. "It's not for Knife. Sorry."

I haven't even taken a single step before Willow grabs my arm and yanks me back toward her, face twisted with outrage now.

"You're not even going to taste it?!"

"I just told you. It's not right—"

She picks the burger up and holds it in front of me, aiming it high like she's about to smear my face with it.

"Just taste it. One bite."

I laugh gently.

"Willow, we should—"

"*Taste it,*" she says, moving herself to squeeze me between the counter and her slim body, giving me no room to escape. So close I can see the glistening in her eyes, the way they're flickering between mine, the burger poised to push into my mouth.

For a few seconds I don't say anything, lost in the feel of her body lightly pressing against mine, lost in the hypnotizingly slight rise and fall of her cleavage. She's so close now I can almost see the trembling passion that lies just beneath that golden skin.

I release a little of the tension in my expression, put a hand over her wrist to hold it steady, and lean forward to take a bite of the burger, eyes never leaving hers. I release my grip and she heaves a breath before sighing a gentle, slightly victorious smile, taking a bite herself before laying it on the plate behind me.

It's good. *Really* good. The meat juicy enough to roll and push the flavors in my mouth like waves. The dull thud of the garlic mayonnaise setting up the spiky kicks of zest and chili. Arugula and onion relish fighting to set a bed of peppery, warm sensuality on the tongue. Even the buns—obviously rushed and a little less risen than they should be, but cooked with spelt, absorbing the juices of the meat and sausage, the run of the relish, are worthy of a pastry chef's respect. The balance and refinement of the textures, the revelation of broad, natural combinations, everything build up to something… exceptional. So good it ignites the passion within me, attunes me once again to raw sensuality, to the perfect form standing in front of me and the intense urges she's teasing from some primal depth.

"This is…better than I expected," I say, withholding further comment. Willow's face is hungry, awaiting more. I like this expression, and I take a few moments to savor it.

Food can do a lot of things. It can ease the pain of a hungry stomach, or it can slam you into the past, a memory you've long forgotten. It can be filler for the empty space in your body, your heart, or your mind. Maybe I've spent too long eating food that was better appreciated in photographs, food so meticulous and contrived in its conception that it made you feel the presence of the chef. Some food makes a critic of you, and other food reminds you that you're flesh and blood, beating heart and lusting tongue.

"Better than expected, yes," Willow urges, gesturing at the plate, "but what else do you think?"

I let the words disappear, feeling too animal to talk now, too physical to think.

"I think it's sensational," I say, slowly. "You're an incredible cook."

She lets out a sigh of relief, but my cock hears something different in her gasping exhale. I bring my thumb slowly to a speck at the side of her mouth, fingers resting on the round perfection of her jawline. She stills under my touch and catches my gaze, time slowing with the deliberateness of my movements.

I brush the speck, but don't pull away. Instead, I bring my thumb back across those ever-pouted lips, tracing their dip and fullness, letting her feel the texture of hands rough and scarred from a lifetime in kitchens, our eyes locked together in a moment of anticipation, emotions raging like an angry sea against the dam of the distance between us.

Her lips part slightly, I feel her shortening breath on my hand, and I push my thumb between those juicy, perfect lips, fingers pressing against the base of her ear. Her gentle gasp breaks the silence, before she closes those soft lips around my thumb, the sight of them pressing against my skin making my cock full against my pants. Her teeth gently squeezing my nail, tongue flickering as I push the finger inside the hot wetness of her mouth.

My other hand already on her waist, I pull her toward me, press her lithe body up against mine. Those magnificent hips swaying and rubbing against mine, her weight shifting onto me, breasts heaving, nipples so hard now I can feel them through that sweater dress.

"You're fucking incredible," I growl. Prelude to pulling her toward me, my finger in her mouth still, angling her head so I can taste the tenderness of her neck, run my sensitive tastebuds down the taut muscles, follow the path that leads me to the front of her chest. Quiet moans getting louder as I run my tongue down the softness of her cleavage, her dress my enemy now as I pull it down and bury my teeth in her breasts.

"Oh God..." she moans. "Cole..."

I pull away, pull my thumb from her mouth to leave it gasping, lips red and ripe. Wordlessly, I take her hand and lead her into the back office, before either of us can really think, and back up onto the desk, pulling her in front of me. I bury my hand into that hair and pull her face to mine, sucking down the succulence of her tongue with the hunger of a madman. Her tender throat stretched, swallowing gasps and purrs as I bite and pull on those soft lips, while her body undulates against mine. Her nipples still so hard I can feel them through our clothes, the tension of her ass under my smacking palm.

Willow pulls away for a second, breathlessly, then works my pants open with the same deft hands she used to work up the meal, and I grab the condom I always carry in my wallet.

She gasps when she sees my cock, hard and thick with the whole evening's worth of desire. She stares at it with almost fearful admiration, bringing those graceful fingers to trace its length softly and driving me so wild I almost howl.

"Should we be doing this?" she says, almost to herself, still stroking my cock with the gentleness of a lover.

"Shoulda thought about that when you decided to wear that dress," I say, holding out the condom. "What do you want to do?"

She smiles at me as she snaps the condom out of my hands, tears it open and slides it over my cock. I pull her lips to mine, taste them softly like a chardonnay, swirling tongues in each other's mouths. The gentlest of touches, plenty of time to taste, to appreciate, to let the ache for more really build up. I bring my hand under her dress, between her thighs, peeling the lace panties aside to tease the fruit of her pussy, squeeze the juices from her, make her ripe with desire as she turns my cock even harder with longing.

Her tight body turns to liquid, so that she melts against me. I'm leaning back on the desk now, the weight of her body against me. Our bodies acting as one, clambering and shuffling to find space, knocking things off the desk in our desperation for each other. I fall back onto the hard surface and pull her on top of me, her thighs straddling me, knees on the wood, her breasts exposed, the sweater dress just a thin strip of cloth around her waist now.

She stops for a second, a faint note of hesitation appearing in those eyes.

"You still think we're gonna regret this?" I ask.

"Only if we stop now," she says, voice slurred with desire.

I pull her body on top of mine, breasts against my chest.

"Then we'd better keep going," I growl into her ear.

We tumble together through the sensations of the evening. The smell of grilled peppers and soft bread, hard cock against soft pussy, garlic and lime aftertaste, rough hands against smooth breasts that press against the fine fabric of my shirt as our mouths feast on each other, her teasing pussy rolling over the head of my cock like an ecstatic torture, a perfect appetizer that can't satisfy.

I pull on her ass, smack it and draw nails up the arch of her back, urging her to let me in. She bites my lip and laughs, fighting me for pleasure, making me growl even harder with lust for the kind of woman who can do that. Until she can bear it no more herself, throwing her head back, taking all of me inside of her as she grinds her hips, riding me.

"Yes..." she purrs, eyes drowsy with sensation. "Oh my God, yes."

She's mine now, fixed upon my hardness, hips swaying, her breasts magnificently naked. She clutches at her hair as she rocks on top of me, eyes rolling back, mouth fixed open as she moans loudly, as if letting the surge of pleasure inside of her escape before it makes her explode. I watch her sway and throb above me, waves of electric pleasure flowing upward from our connected bodies, up through that tight stomach and those bouncing breasts, up through that pulsating throat and ecstatic face. A monument to beauty, one I worship with roving hands and panting grunts, until she's too full of bliss, too full for even the screams to temper it, full enough to burst.

She puts a hand over mine, the one I've been pinching and rolling her nipple with, pulls it to the center of her chest, clutches it as if for steadiness as she lets the desire overflow.

"That's it. Come for me, Willow. I wanna see you come, right here on top of this desk, right fucking now." I tighten my grip on her ass and thrust into her harder, deeper, my voice coming out harsh as I command her to let go.

A final, high-pitched wail gets tossed up at the ceiling, Willow moaning as she falls down the rollercoaster. The sight of her losing control makes it easy for me to join her, to slam myself inside her one last time, to push both of us out from madness and into light.

"Fuck," she says on desperate breath, as heat leaves her body and she slumps over me. "Cooking is a hell of an aphrodisiac."

I look down between her damp locks of hair splayed across my chest, her face sleepy now as she rests against it.

“Depends on who’s doing it. Now let me make you dessert.”

CHAPTER SIX

WILLOW

It's mid-morning in Los Angeles, and I'm sitting at the diner Tony suggested, stirring the foam at the bottom of my coffee cup lazily as I look out of the window. It's a nice place with a vintage 50's flair, kinda small, and with a great menu I'm more than ready to pick something from, but which I thought would be rude to do before Tony came.

For almost thirty minutes now I've been eyeing the attractive waiter (though he can't hold a candle to the flame of Cole's perfection) and watching the breakfast rush hour die down as I sip my coffee, trying not to think about last night, the lingering soreness I can still feel between my thighs.

"Spud!" I hear Tony call, turning to see him step inside the diner, open his arms, and make a beeline for me.

I step out of the booth and hug him—or more precisely, allow myself to be squeezed like a lemon.

"Relax, it's only been a week since I saw you," I mumble, even with my asphyxiated lungs.

Tony pulls back and laughs, taking a seat across from me. He pulls off his aviators to reveal emerald eyes that always made me kinda jealous.

"I'm just pleased to see you."

"Shut up," I smile. "I know you're just trying to make me forget how late you are."

It makes sense that Tony would end up in Los Angeles. Even though he's from Ohio, and I met him when we studied in the south of France, he's never looked quite so at home as he does with an L.A. sky behind him. His bronzed skin, meticulously arranged more-on-top brown hair, skintight T-shirt revealing a hint of his bare chest, immaculately sculpted pectorals—all of it fits in perfectly now that he's here.

"Oh, I've got a very good reason to be late, trust me," he says, conspiratorially. "Thanks for meeting me last minute." He looks up and gestures for the waiter to come over.

"What can I get started for you two?"

I grab the menu in front of me and say, "Are you still serving the carnitas hash?"

"We are."

"I'll have that then, please. And a lemonade."

"And for you?" the waiter asks Tony through a dazzling smile.

I look up to find Tony smiling back at him.

"What do you recommend?"

I watch the waiter lean a little toward Tony, his eyes almost alight with mischief.

"Something sweet?"

"No," Tony says, looking at me for a second and making me feel like a third wheel before turning back. "I'm trying to stay fit these days."

"You look like you're in amazing shape to me," the waiter says, and I almost drop my jaw at the way he doesn't hide the fact that he's looking Tony up and down like he's the one who's hungry. "I think you could have whatever you want."

Tony laughs and sits back.

"I'll have the same as her, then. But I'll definitely be back sometime for the sweet stuff."

I stare at Tony with a smirk as the waiter leaves and he finally peels his eyes away to look back at me.

"What?" he says.

"Nothing," I say, laughing. "Just wondering how long it'll take before he gives you his number."

"We'll just have to wait and see," Tony smiles. "You look great, by the way."

"Are you flirting with me now, too?"

"I mean it. You're looking good—especially for a girl who's been working her ass off in a Cole Chambers kitchen." He pauses a moment to study me like a connoisseur. "I don't know what it is... you've got some glow about you today...you look a little more relaxed..." His eyes narrow. "Wait—did you go out last night? Oh, you did. You definitely did. You hooked up with some mega hottie last night, didn't you?"

"What?" I say. "*No.*"

But the way I drop my head and the slight rush of heat to my cheeks isn't going to pass unnoticed.

"Yes you did!" Tony exclaims. "And you went all the way, I can tell. Good girl! Finally! Who was it?"

"Nobody. I mean...I can't say." I can't meet his eyes, knowing one look will betray everything. But my silence is incriminating enough to blow my cover anyway.

"*You fucked Cole Chambers?*" Tony hisses, in disbelief.

I sit upright and glare at him like a figure in a haunted house.

"How the fuck do you *do that?*"

"Oh please," Tony says, leaning back in his chair. "He's the one guy you would try to keep a secret. Not like you're gonna give me the 'I can't say' if you screwed the dish washer—not after I told you about that time I did. So how did it happen? You'd better tell me, or I'm gonna run through every scenario I'm imagining in my head in glorious detail until you crack."

"Ok, ok," I say, defeated. "Calm down, Sex-Columbo. To tell you the truth, it just kinda…happened. We had a drink together and then somehow—"

"Hold up: You went on a *date* with him?"

"No. It wasn't a date. We just hadn't talked yet, he wasn't there when they hired me."

Tony smirks, obviously skeptical of my explanation, which sounds weak even to me. "You said there was alcohol during this event, and was it at night, I'm guessing?"

"Is that some kind of L.A. thing nobody told me about? Look, it wasn't a date. Not exactly, anyway. We had a drink, some food, then went back to Knife so I could show him some recipe and…somehow we ended up screwing each other senseless."

Tony's eyes widen.

"In the *kitchen*? God, Willow. Isn't that a Department of Health situation? I don't know if I wanna eat there now that I know that."

"No! He pulled me into the back office, and then we got on the desk and—look, forget that, the point is that I just fucked my boss, and I'm a little bit concerned I might have fucked my job too."

Despite the exasperation in my voice, Tony smiles and shrugs nonchalantly.

"Well, good thing you won't be working there much longer."

For about the fifth time I stare at him in confusion.

"What do you mean?"

Tony pauses as the food is laid out in front of us, affording the waiter just a mischievous wink this time.

"Wanna know why I was late to meet you?" he asks, leaning forward. I nod. "I was on a call with a potential investor."

"Investor? For what?"

Now it's Tony's turn to look at me sideways.

"Have you seriously forgotten?" he says, sounding offended. "Our restaurant. Your rustic, Idaho'an…ingredients thing, and my astonishingly good taste and presentation coming together in a single place that'll blow this fucking town apart. It's the whole reason you moved down here, remember? To start over and take back your dreams?"

"Oh…oh yeah…" I say, still taken aback. "I remember, but I mean, I thought we were just talking. Fantasizing. Laying out what we would love to do, at some future point in time. I didn't think you—*we*—were actually going to go for it. Not right away, at least…"

"Spud," Tony says, using my Guillhaume-inspired pet name the way only an old friend could. "I might love L.A. but I'm not *from* L.A. When I say I'm going to do something, I do it. Now are you in or not?"

"Of course I'm in," I say. "It's still my dream. I'm just… anxious, you know? This is kinda quick. It's not that long since my last place failed. And I'm working now—"

"And fucking Cole Chambers now. Whatever. Anxious is fine. So long as you can still cook a mean beans, that's all we need. Now I'm arranging a meeting with these investors and you're gonna come too. I think they're the real deal and we need both of us there to show how serious we are. Are you with me?"

"Hell yes." I don't hesitate, feeling once again like a girl from Idaho in a city where nobody seems to stop for breath.

"Hell yes. That's exactly what I wanted to hear," Tony grins as we dig into our food.

I get to Knife at around two—hours before it'll open for the evening shift, but it's Tuesday, the one day each week the chefs sit down to eat together before work. It's a chance to talk shop and air any problems that might be brewing, though it's mostly a chance to share a meal with the people you're too busy working beside to spend any time with. This is only the second one I'm going to, but it already feels like I know the place better than my own.

At least I won't have to face Cole. I'm not quite sure how things are gonna go when we next bump into each other. I'm thinking I might go for a 'what we did in the office that one time was cool, but we should get back to reality' kind of vibe, though I'm worried it'll turn into a 'what the hell was that all about, and when are we doing it again?' sort of thing. Because the truth is that—even though it's complicated, and messy, and there are a dozen obvious reasons I shouldn't—I wouldn't mind a repeat performance.

I know Cole's a player, but maybe what I need, after all this time moping over my asshole ex and my failed restaurant, is to play around a little. Cole's definitely not going to get serious on me, and I'm too focused on work to get serious on him, so why not? Sure, there's a little voice in my head telling me it's a bad idea that could be dangerous—but I have to struggle to hear it over the loud tingles my body gets when I remember how good he was, the way he commanded me to come for him…

I snap back to the urgency of the present moment, step through the propped-open exit door and hurry through the kitchen, checking my watch to see how late I am.

"Hey! Willow!" someone calls from the kitchen.

I stop to find Aaron, a line cook from Brooklyn who makes everything sound like he's delivering a line at an open mic night. His round, bearded face sitting upon his round body giving him the appearance of a snowman, and his ever-present smile almost as big as his heart.

"Hey," I say, moving over to him as he plates some seared scallops. "Is everyone here?"

"They're sitting down," Aaron says, nodding toward the tables. "But if you help me carry the plates through they probably won't notice you're late."

"Sure," I say, taking the scallops from him and picking up a couple of other dishes.

I move through to the front of the restaurant, where the staff are already laughing and chatting with the easy energy of relieved tension, languishing in their chairs like soldiers waiting for action, already working their way through two bottles of the least-ordered reds, preempting the busy shift ahead of them. Two tables have been shoved close together to fit the dozen plus members of the kitchen staff and waiters, and as soon as I draw close they start picking food from the plates before I've even set them down.

A couple of them affectionately call out my nickname, 'Spud,' as I grab the bottle to fill a glass and take my seat.

The last time we did this, Cole wasn't here, and I'd figured that he wasn't interested in the kind of banal gossiping and trivial camaraderie that went on, so I freeze a little in surprise when he shows up at the door a few minutes in, flashing his diplomatic, assured smile. His hand is on Chloe's shoulder and she's grinning ear to ear. I flash her a little wave and she returns it happily before the raucousness of the other chefs takes over the moment.

"Hey, who's your new girlfriend?" Aaron laughs. "Little young, even for you."

"Quiet please, everyone," Cole says, ignoring the joke. "You remember I told you all about the Young Chefs mentoring program?

Well here she is, the most promising cook in Los Angeles County: Chloe Fernandez. Chloe? Welcome. This is my staff."

There are coos and greetings of 'hey Chloe' from the more interested members of the staff that Chloe returns happily, beaming uncontrollably as she waves back and takes in the group.

"So you wanna be a great chef one day?" Michelle asks between bites of scallop.

"Yeah. I really do."

"Better than Cole?"

Chloe grins. "I'm already better than him. He overthinks everything."

The table erupts into another wave of easy laughter.

"You got that right!" Michelle says.

"Ok wiseass," Cole says to Michelle, pulling out a chair for Chloe at the table. "Let's eat."

The number of people there, and the added interest of having Chloe at the table, means that seeing Cole again isn't half as awkward as I expected it to be. He spends most of his time at the other end of the table doing his best to entertain his young mentee, while I talk with Ryan beside me about his guitar collection. After a half hour, my full stomach and a glass of wine making it easy to smile as I listen to the stories around me, I almost forget that he's even there. Once the plates are empty, the volume starts to fade, and Cole seizes everyone's attention with that voice that makes it unmistakable he's the boss around here.

"Ok everyone," he says, clapping his hands together and putting his elbows on the table, a posture that leaves no doubt he's about to talk business. "Anyone have anything they wanna raise here? Any problems or issues? Kitchen? Waitstaff? Management? I'm all ears."

Cole looks around at a few of us, and I notice that his eyes don't meet mine. There are a few shrugs and shakes of the head around the table until Leo eventually says, "Did they get back to you about the abalone deliveries?"

"Nope. I'm calling them right after this."

"They've got to move them to Mondays."

"I know. Leave it to me. Anything else?"

"There's some rapper coming in on Thursday," Charlie says fretfully.

"Full entourage?" Cole asks.

"Possibly. Where should we put them?"

Cole tilts his head. "Let's rearrange the seating in the back of the dining room and keep some chairs available in case. Anyone else? No? Nothing? Ok, listen. I'm going to add something new to the specials menu—just for this week. See how it goes, see how the customers like it."

My pulse starts to pound.

"A new dessert?" the pastry chef asks hopefully.

"No. A main. Basque burgers *a l'ail et moutarde*. I've already shown Willow how to prepare it, so she can show the rest of you." My stomach drops. *He* showed *me* how to prepare it? Cole looks at the waiters as I feel my heart thump. "Maybe if you have some down time this shift. You guys can try it, get to know it, then suggest it to diners. And be sure you ask them what they think afterward—I wanna know what they think."

There are nods amongst the waiters, but I'm staring at Cole now, mouth open in astonishment.

"Why are you adding this?" Michelle says. "The menu's perfect as-is. And it's...a burger." I note the disdain in her voice but keep my mouth closed. As much as I want to defend the dish, I'm still too stunned that Cole is taking credit for my idea to be able to speak.

"I was thinking," Cole says, looking up a little like he's genuinely remembering, "our mains are good. Rich, full—but they're pretty similar in texture. I thought this might add something a little drier, something less sauce-based. Without losing that richness of flavor."

There are murmurs of understanding around the table, but it's all I can do to hide the swirling ocean of anger that's building inside of me. Leo frowns and leans forward, looking from me to Cole.

"Hold on," he says. "*Willow?* You taught the *new hire* how to cook it? When did you do that?"

Cole glares at Leo in a way that makes the bald-headed saucier almost shiver in front of us.

"We had a little catch-up yesterday, a progress report. I showed her then since I won't have time now. I take it that's not an issue?"

"Well," Leo says, glancing at me dismissively. "I mean she's only been here a few days, and she's already passing on your recipes?"

"If she couldn't handle it I wouldn't have hired her. Don't worry," Cole says, casting a look in my direction that seems loaded with mystery, "she can handle herself. Everybody get your asses in the kitchen. You've got an hour to do prep."

Cole claps his hands again and it's like a school bell, sending the crowd off in their separate directions, the sound of pushed chairs and stacking plates taking the place of the conversation and laughter. I hover around for a second, waiting for an opportune moment, and when Michelle strikes up a conversation with Chloe, I touch Cole on the arm to get his attention. He spins around, smiling a little when he sees that it's me.

"Hey." I try to keep the edge out of my voice, since my job is still in his hands, but I can barely contain my irritation.

"Hey," he says, his voice bassier than the one he used for the others.

"Can I have a word?"

"Sure," he says, taking my arm now and leading me off to the side of the restaurant. I catch a glimpse of Leo watching us, but ignore it as I try to hold my cool enough not to snap.

"What the hell was that?" I hiss angrily through gritted teeth.

"What?"

"My recipe."

Cole frowns, his confusion all over the furrows of his brow.

"Oh. Right. Like I said, it goes on the menu for a week, and then we see if you're as good as you think you are."

"*'I taught Willow how to prepare it'*?" I say, quoting him. "What was that all about?"

Cole's confusion turns into a flippant chuckle.

"What did you expect me to say?"

"I don't know. Maybe give me some credit for *my dish.*"

Cole chuckles again, even louder now, shaking his head as he does so.

"Wow. You know, maybe you *aren't* cut out for the restaurant business. You really don't see the problem there? Telling cooks who've worked for me for over five years that I'm letting the girl who's been here ten minutes put something on the menu? The last thing you need is to make enemies here. And it's not just petty jealousy or your life getting harder in the kitchen—there'd be other complications. Gossip about what's going on between us."

I take a breath, trying not to let Cole's firmness sway me.

"Still..." I say, searching for words to articulate the sense of injustice. "To just take it like that...let everyone think that you...you know, you should have given me something."

"Given you what?" Cole says, the chuckle gone now, replaced with the voice of a boss.

"I don't know," I say. "But you literally took the words out of my mouth and passed them off as your own. You don't have to tell them the dish is mine, but at least pass on some of that credit in my direction."

"Listen," Cole says, serious now, "credit goes both ways. What if your burgers are a disaster? What if the guy who orders it feels short-changed when he tries his wife's buckwheat galettes? Who takes the hit then? Me. It's my reputation attached to this restaurant, and to the food it serves—not yours."

I sigh and look down, struggling to maintain my frustration in the face of Cole's logic.

"Still," I say, shaking my head at his leather shoes. "I just didn't like the way you presented it."

After a second's pause, I look up and see Cole smiling at me, a little too much like the way he smiled last night…

"Look: Your dish is about to be served in one of the busiest restaurants in L.A., to some of the most discerning eaters, and in some of the best surroundings. Credit or not—most chefs would take that."

Michelle calls out to Cole, and he looks back to see Chloe waiting eagerly for him to come back. He raises a finger then looks back at me briefly to say, "Just hope that they like it," before walking away to lead the Young Chef outside, the two of them waving at the others like departing family members.

I think about what he said for a moment, standing in the corner of the restaurant as the others reset the tables and the sound of prep starts cranking up in the kitchen. The sense of something not quite right about what my boss did still stirring, unresolved, in my stomach.

Irritated and confused, I try not to consider that giving him the recipe isn't what I'm actually most bothered by—it's what we did afterward, and the fact that it seems he's completely forgotten about it.

CHAPTER SEVEN

COLE

I suppose I should be grateful to Chloe for keeping my mind off Willow. After leaving Knife I take the nine-year-old to a friend's seafood restaurant a few blocks away where we watch them handle the fish, descaling and gutting, marinating and fileting. I had regretted letting Martin talk me into the Young Chefs program the second after I had dismissively agreed to it; the last thing I needed was a babysitting job, especially with the opening of the second restaurant in Vegas. But after seeing how Willow handled the kid—and perhaps having her show me what *not* to do as well—I started to figure out how to get a conversation going.

Ice breaks between us as we watch the food prep, and soon, I start to realize that Chloe's nothing like the thumb-sucking brat I'd expected. She handles the sight of fish guts like it's nothing, and the smell only seems to intrigue her further. When she asks to try an oyster, and she slurps one down with a giant grin rather than squirming in disgust at the texture, I finally realize that we might just get along after all.

After a while, the shift dies down and the owner lends us a corner of the kitchen so I can work Chloe through different prep techniques. How to chop evenly and efficiently, how to slice and dice so that nothing on a vegetable is wasted. The different flavors from herbs and produce that can emerge even at the prep stage.

"This is boring," she sighs after I correct her handle on the knife for the fifth time. "Do I have to do it again? I know how to cut things."

"Sure. And most people know how to cook—but we still get paid for being the best at it," I reply.

Reluctantly, she draws the knife a couple more times across the onion, then pouts again.

"I don't know..." she says, musing with all the deepness of thought a philosopher might use. "I kinda like it better when it's all uneven. It looks less like a robot cut it."

I open my mouth, milliseconds away from delivering an expletive-ridden rant about the value of precision, about the need for perfection—the kind of rant that earned me a primetime slot on premium cable TV and millions of views online. Chloe's been a little too professional and mature, and I'm this close to forgetting she's just a nine year old kid and not a convict who's used to taking orders.

But then I remember Willow, the soft way she managed to bring Chloe to her way of thinking, how she would use humor and gentleness to teach Chloe about the ingredients we browsed at the market, and instead I suppress the hotness of my blood.

I take a clove of garlic and put it in front of her.

"Chop that just like I told you, as best as you can, and then we can leave."

Chloe stiffens and looks at the garlic with the determination of purpose.

"Do you want it crushed or sliced?" she says, and I can't resist smiling. Maybe some of my lecturing stuck.

"What if I said I wanted it as strong as possible, without any bite or tartness?"

Chloe nods.

"Crushed," she says, already squeezing it under the flat side of the blade.

Maybe the soft way *does* work sometimes.

Once our time is up and I've dropped Chloe back off with her supervisor, I start making a few moves around town, chasing down a few distributors, going to a meeting with my accountant that lasts way beyond the point at which it can be called torture, and then a sit-down with the new Vegas spot's interior designer to talk color schemes and textures for the fiftieth time.

Unfortunately, none of these activities are as compelling as Chloe's ideas about loving shellfish because she gets to keep the shells, so my mind ends up slipping back to Willow. Maybe I was a little harsh on her during that hurried conversation at Knife, but I had to put my foot down and reaffirm the boss-employee relationship again, rather than the girl-on-top one we'd established the night before. Not just for her sake, but for mine.

I could run wild with a girl like her. Spend an entire week in bed together and still feel like we're just getting our appetites wet. Her body like a map that I've only just set foot on, that still has so many places to explore, so many secrets to unfold. If she wasn't one of my chefs I'd already be planning the how, where, and when—but since she is, I still have to ask myself 'if.' It's clearly not a smart move. But then again, I'm not known for my smarts. I'm known for getting exactly what I want, and doing things my way.

Memories of her in that tight dress stick themselves into my mind throughout the day with the incessant force of a catchy song, so that even as I'm listening to my accountant reel off numbers, I close my eyes and try to relive the taste of her lips.

By the time I'm done for the day my suit feels like a straitjacket, muscles tensing and skin hot with the aggression of a caged bull. I make the car roar like a beast through the cool evening, yanking it through the winding roads that lead up to my place in the Hollywood hills. I bring the car to a slide-stop at the front door, too impatient to even park it properly, and step through the long building of glass and white walls as if there's something waiting for me. Tearing off clothes the way I'd like to do to hers, until I'm down to my boxer briefs, picking out a bottle of Pinot Blanc and opening it roughly. Wine in one hand, phone in the other, I go out to the deck and sit back on a lounger, letting the breeze off the swimming pool take the heat off my body. Slow sips from the bottle as I contemplate the L.A. skyline between my feet.

I'm barely below the neck on the bottle before I start thinking about Willow again, looking over to where Knife might be in the skyline and imagining what she's doing right now. Working a knife with focused delicacy, sipping soup through those lips, dancing between the other chefs on those long legs, skin alive with the warmth of the grills, eyes narrowed with the determination of purpose.

I'm prickling with lust before I even realize it, even the cooling air not enough to release the pent-up tension that all these thoughts of Willow are stirring in me.

There are a million reasons why this is not a good idea for either of us. I need to nip this in the bud. I pick up my phone and flick through the messages and work notifications to get to the contacts list I keep for times like this, sucking down wine as I scroll through the names and photos.

Models with bodies that don't need Photoshop, actresses who

talk dirty enough for an X rating. Leggy brunettes and manic redheads, nymphomaniacs with every kink in the book and shy types who let it all go at once. A list of perfect women who'd be here in a heartbeat, the push of a button.

But none of them is Willow, and tonight I'd rather have nothing than settle for something less.

I drop the phone to the side and replace it with the bottle, other hand already palming the hard cock in my briefs. This time the wine doesn't taste like wine, it tastes like her lips again, like that delicate, sensitive tongue against mine. A taste worth any price you'd put on it, worth searching half the world for.

I open my eyes to the shimmering sky blue of the pool, impossible not to imagine her being here, her long frame under that surface, flickering in the gentle lap of the water, gliding through it with the smoothness of that golden skin and the easy elegance of her movements. Difficult not to imagine those naked breasts as she emerges from the water, droplets catching the light as they trace that perfect shape, wet hair slicked back, that long neck.

Hand clutching my hard cock like a loaded weapon now, teasing appreciation of her turns to the uncontrollable desire to take her again. To lift that pool-drenched body in my imagination and lay her on the lounger, to spread her open and lick the wetness from her thighs, feeling them tremble from the cool breeze and my rough tongue. To taste her tender navel, the shiver of her stomach, the hardness of her nipples. Roll them under my tongue before sucking the full softness of her breasts. Eventually tracing a finger between her legs to reveal the path to her soul, the richest and most complex taste, the one that satisfies both of our hungers. A taste that has to be approached slowly, delicately, the tongue soft as a brushstroke, coaxing forth moans and sighs from her body. Soft, melting, and juicy, rolled and flicked, sucked and pushed, until it flowers in my mouth as her thighs shake, the sound of her helpless pleasure filling the air…

I come hard, orgasm slamming out of me, a coiled spring of tension that's been there for too long. But even in the aftermath, as I suck down another deep gulp of alcohol, tension seeping out of my body, there's only a little relief. Temporary and physical. The unresolved thoughts in my head still lingering—backed off into the shadows, but still there.

There's no doubt left in my mind.

This thing inside of me isn't going to rest until I've had her again.

I spend the next day in Vegas, letting everybody know how disappointed I am at the lack of progress in the new place. I have a lengthy meeting with the flooring contractor where we struggle to find a solution to the fact that she can't source the type of travertine I requested, all to the background music of construction workers drilling in the kitchen fittings.

Just when I think I'm getting somewhat close to achieving a sense of turning the chaos acceptable, Martin comes rushing through the doors of the place, almost running between the stacked-up furniture and half-painted walls, carrying a laptop under his arm.

"Cole!" he shouts desperately, as if I'm in danger of flying away. "Glad I caught you."

I nod to the contractor to show that we're done and look back at the hurried man.

"Something tells me I won't be glad, though."

"Well…" Martin says, pushing his spectacles up his sweaty nose, "probably not."

He might look a mess, this wiry man with black, side-parted hair that he keeps having to palm into place, but Martin's the only person

I trust to be my second-in-command. In another life, Martin would have been a fantastic chef himself, were it not for his constantly trembling hands and persistently flustered nature. It's his nervous disposition, however, that makes him perfect for keeping things running the way I like them—Martin basically does all my worrying for me.

"It's Holly," Michael says, with a look of dread.

I cross my arms, preparing for the worst. "Go on…"

"Now I don't know this for sure," Michael says, holding his palm up as if I'm a lion he needs to placate. "I just heard this. I'm trying to get through to her now, but…she might be pregnant."

"No. That can't be."

Martin gulps audibly.

"The rumor is that she went to Cancun with her ex-husband to get things working again about a month ago and…well, they worked. *Too well.* She's still there, and I'm having a hell of a time getting in touch with her, but she told Kyle that she might never come back—that she might just build a new life there."

I turn away from Martin to pace a little.

"And I'm only finding this out now? Less than three weeks before the opening?"

"Maybe she'll come back," Martin says, optimistically. "And we can start looking for replacements in the meantime."

"Replace my head chef? Just like that? You think chefs like Holly grow on trees? You don't 'replace' Kobe. Fuck!" I say, kicking a veiled chair into the wall. "Three years I worked with her. Three years! She knows my recipes as well as I do, and now she's ditching the greatest opportunity of her career for long walks on the beach with a guy she already dumped once?"

"Cole…" Martin says gently.

I march back toward him, finger jabbing at the air.

"*This* is what happens when you trust people. Time and time again. They leave you in the lurch."

"She might not really be stayi—"

"What is it about cooks?" I shout, the drilling stopped now, as the workers watch me pace the room in frustration, slamming my fist against a wall. "Am I the only one who respects loyalty anymore? Is everyone in this business just out for their fucking selves? Those criminals I worked with on the reality show had more integrity than most of the so-called professionals I've worked with."

"*Cole,*" Martin soothes once again. "*If* she's really not coming back, and *if* she can't work, maybe we can move Michelle here for a while. She knows the ropes."

I stop pacing to stare at Martin disdainfully.

"Michelle's serving eight hundred eaters a week in L.A. The place is killing it—why would I jeopardize that?"

"It's just a last resort. It would buy us time. Plus, the L.A. crew have worked together for years, they could survive without her for a little while."

I calm down just enough to take a few deep breaths and put a grateful hand on Martin's shoulder.

"Ok. You're right. I'm not happy. But ok," I say. "I'll try to think of who we could get to fill the spot—you do the same."

"Of course," Martin says. "And if you don't mind me saying so...maybe you should take the night off, go blow off some steam, you know? You staying in Vegas tonight?"

"No chance," I say, already pulling out my phone as I head toward the door. "Releasing this kind of tension is gonna take a hell of a lot more than some slot machines, my friend."

Luckily, I know just the thing.

CHAPTER EIGHT

WILLOW

It's Friday, and through some miracle of scheduling magic, I've got the night off. The idea of an evening with no responsibilities, nowhere to go, and utter freedom feels like a gift from God. A little time to think, to process things. To put my feet back down on the ground and see where I actually stand.

And it's not like I'm short of things I need to untangle. Fucking your boss when you were expecting him to fire you is something that you don't just set aside easily. Fucking your boss when he's an internationally-renowned celebrity chef is something that deserves a little reflection. Fucking your internationally-renowned celebrity chef boss, then having him take one of your recipes and put it on the menu of the hottest restaurant in L.A., without giving you any credit, is a hell of a lot to unpack.

And as if all of that wasn't enough, there's the sudden, unexpected potential for my dream of owning my own restaurant to come true once again. An upcoming investor meeting that I barely even remember agreeing to, let alone feel prepared for.

So on my day off I do the only thing that feels right with so much going on—I shut down. I sleep almost to midday, prepare a large batch of cheesy nachos and guacamole, then start binge watching the latest season of a TV show about supernatural detectives that's just about dumb enough to follow without my full attention, and just visually interesting enough to keep me above the level of comatose.

Bliss.

Until Asha comes home, full of the crackling energy she always has after her classes.

"Willow?" she calls from the hallway, slipping off her shoes before emerging into the living room.

"Hey?" I mumble around a mouthful of salsa, suddenly seeing myself through her eyes, horizontal on the couch, laptop on the coffee table, nacho bowl on my stomach, guacamole dip between my breasts, a sea of crumbs that makes it clear I haven't moved in hours. I hold the bowl out optimistically. "Guac?"

Asha's face is fixed into a horrified gaze for a few seconds before she marches into the center of the room and says, "Oh no. Uh-uh. I do not like this."

"What?" I say, wincing at the daylight she exposes by sweeping aside the curtains. "It's my day off."

"Exactly," Asha says, looking at me for a second and then turning away as if she can't bear more. "How long have you been lying there?"

I shrug and try not to let the cramps show as I sit upright.

"I dunno…couple of hours, maybe?"

"Mm-hm. And what episode of that show are you on?"

I shrug meekly.

"The seventh?"

Asha rolls her eyes with a new wave of disappointment.

"How long have you been out here in L.A.? A few months? It seems like you spend all your time either at work, or holed up in here hiding from real life. This city has so much to offer, and you never go out and soak it up."

"I'm…still getting comfortable. It's a lot to take in."

Asha pouts at me doubtfully.

"Los Angeles is not a place to get comfortable, it's a place to get adventurous! Is it any wonder you fucked your boss? He's the only guy you've met here."

"I'm just digesting. Recharging, you know?"

"'Recharging'? It looks a lot like moping to me. Look: You are too hot, too charismatic, and too fucking awesome to be sitting at home alone on a Friday night." A slow smile breaks on Asha's face. "Especially when there's a hot new club opening tonight, and your roommate just happens to have an exclusive invitation with a plus one."

"Oh no…" I groan, though I know the second I say it that there's no refusal when Asha starts talking this way.

"Oh *yes*," Asha says. "And I'm gonna find you a guy so hot he'll make you forget you ever laid eyes on Cole Chambers."

I let out a laugh as I get up to pull myself together—I doubt there's anyone out there who could make me forget Cole.

By the time our Uber is pulling up outside the club, I can't deny that Asha's right. It feels cathartic dressing fabulously and getting out into an electrically-charged night. I'm in a satin pencil skirt Asha lent me, a loose fitting blouse unbuttoned almost to my navel, and a delicate gold chain with a crystal pendant that hangs right between my breasts. She's in a pale pink dress that hugs her body tight enough to show off every toned muscle. A figure that could kick your ass as easily as it could stalk a catwalk.

The good feeling continues when we step out of the car in front of the building, an incredibly striking collection of curved walls and glass windows, more like a Gaudi-esque art gallery than something you'd expect to find in downtown L.A. The pink and blue neon lighting making it feel like some alien pleasure craft that crash landed on earth rather than some exclusive club for the city's thrill seekers.

Asha locks arms with me and marches me past the line of beautiful people, all glossy hair and slouching postures.

"Hey," I say, leaning toward Asha as much as I can while walking in heels, "I think that's actually the line to get in."

"Oh, honey," Asha says, smiling at me as if I said something cute, "You ain't gotta stand in line when you look as good as us."

I try to ignore the jealous stares and look as confident as Asha. We reach the door where two colossal bouncers stand beside a pert blonde woman with a Madonna mic and a tablet in her hand.

"Excuse me—" she starts, before Asha interrupts her.

"Asha Greene."

"Asha...Greene..." the woman repeats to herself as she scrolls down the list on her screen.

"You don't need to check the list," Asha says. "Connor would have mentioned me by name. We just spoke this afternoon."

"Oh! Asha! Right," the woman says, stepping aside as one of the colossi pulls up the rope. "But Mr. Anderson won't be able to make it tonight."

"I know," Asha says, stepping through and pulling me by the hand behind her, "who do you think is taking his spot?"

As soon as we get inside I lean toward Asha and ask, "Who's Connor?"

She lets out a flippant laugh before answering, "You've got a lot to learn."

Before I can say another word she pushes through the doors to the main room, and I'm suddenly assaulted by a combination of lights and sound that thumps through my body and shakes all my senses. Beautiful, ecstatic men and women jump and move as if dueling with the strobe lights that flicker over them, turning reality into a slow motion picture slideshow while bass shakes the air around us, pumps the blood in our bodies, ghostlike melodies floating through the violent, tribal drums with heavenly allure.

Asha pulls me deeper into the jostling throng and I see her laugh, head thrown back in the flashing lights, as the music shifts and slows, dulls itself as if it's underwater. A few songs later Asha puts a drink in my hand, but I'm already intoxicated, mind swirling, body alive with sensation. We agree on a protocol, to text if we need each other, otherwise we'll meet up on the second floor bar in about an hour, and then the music emerges clearer now, quickening somehow, an unresolved melody pushing back and forth, urging me further each time. When it reaches its climax, the whole places erupts, a sea of upraised arms, a tidal wave of euphoria passing from body to body.

Memories of the raves and parties I went wild at during college flood back into my body, a physical reminder of the exhilaration I felt when I wasn't concerned about work enough yet to turn down offers to go out. Except tonight I'm here, and I've already given up on tomorrow morning—so there's nothing to do but let myself go, just like old times.

I lose track of time, lose track of Asha, lose track of who I even am as I let myself unfold on the dance floor alongside men and women who share my energy and euphoria with every move. A million miles from even remembering what had me so wound up today, every minute I spend in this place a step further from the tension and stress of my life.

Then I see him. Up on the second floor, leaning over the railing that looks over the main dance floor. Even in the dark, in the crowd, amid the sensory overload of the lights and sounds and movement, those eyes are unmistakable—and they're staring back at me above an entertained smile. He notices me noticing him and raises his glass, but I don't do anything in return, just spin back and continue dancing.

Except his eyes are still on me, and I can feel them. Keenly studying every sway of my hips, every arch of my back. If he thinks he's just going to stand there and watch me all night long with that lusty gaze, I'll give him something fierce to look at. I glance every once in a while in his direction through narrowed eyes, giving him a glimpse of my half smile before turning away again. Cole's not the only one noticing me, and soon I find myself with a hot guy right in front of me, his eyes undressing me, his hands on my hips, mine on his shoulders, except it's not him I really want, and it's not his eyes that are making me move like this, because however hot he is, Cole is still the hottest guy in this club. I glance up at him every so often, over the guy's shoulder, wondering if he's getting jealous. Until eventually I look and he's not there anymore.

Exhausted, my mouth dry, and wondering if Cole is still around, I make for the steps leading up to the second floor bar, where I hope to get something cold to drink. Somehow, as I move up the stairs, the sound of the music seems to lessen, fading from the soul-shaking boom it was on the dance floor to a background rhythm that I can actually hear the people on the second floor talking over.

I move toward the bar, gliding on the exultation of physical activity, when the sound of my name draws my attention to the side.

"Willow." I look in the direction of the deep, commanding voice, and see Cole stalking toward me like he's finally cornered his prey. "Looks like you worked up quite a sweat down there," he says, eyes roving across my skin.

"I figured I deserved to let things go a little," I say, nonchalantly. Two can play this game.

He leans closer. "You drinking tonight?"

"No. I'm too thirsty for alcohol."

Cole lifts the bottle of water he's holding in his hand.

"I figured," he says, offering it.

I smile and take it, cracking open the sealed top and tipping my head back to gulp the coolness from the icy bottle, feeling his eyes upon me once again.

"Thanks," I say, gasping a little from the water's freshness. "What are you doing here, anyway?"

Cole laughs easily.

"Same thing as you, I presume."

I grin and shake my head. "Unless you were dragged here by your well-meaning roommate, I doubt it."

"Well…something like that. I know Jax Wilder."

He looks at me for a second until I realize he expects me to know who that is.

"He designed the place," Cole adds, when he notices my blank expression. "Wow, you really are new in town, aren't you?"

"People keep telling me that," I say. "This is a nice place, though."

"Yeah," Cole says, looking around appreciatively. "The acoustics are excellent."

I laugh.

"What's funny?" Cole asks.

"Nothing," I say, pushing a loose strand of hair behind my ear and feeling a new surge of heat through my body. This time it's not the music, but the way he smiles at me. It's so easy to remember why we did what we did on that desk when he smiles like that… "You like the acoustics, huh? Well, I haven't seen you dance tonight."

He steps a little closer, though I can hear him perfectly, and in a low voice, says, "All you gotta do is ask."

"Oh yeah?" I say, stepping closer to him now.

"Yeah," he says, voice low, but his mouth so close to my face I can hear the rumble in it. "How could I say no to you?"

I could blame a lot of things for what happens next. I could blame the darkness of the club, dark enough to feel like I can do whatever I want. I could blame the thump of the bass still moving through my blood, making my body come alive and bringing my urges to the surface. I could blame the sense of liberation I'm feeling, after dancing so many of my worries away. But when Cole is looking like that, his shirt tight enough to hint at the muscles beneath, his face as perfect and as mesmerizing as a gallery's main event and his eyes blazing into mine, who could blame me?

I put my hands on his chest and push him back through the crowd, against a wall, where only the faintest of moving lights traces the perfect lines of his jaw. Then I lean into him, pressing my breasts against his hard torso, and push my hungry lips onto his, our tongues thrashing as we devour each other's mouths. He pulls me closer, hands roving down the small of my back, searching for the gap under my blouse where he can put his rough hands against my skin.

"You look good enough to eat," he growls, kissing a line down the soft skin of my neck until I can't help but moan.

My fingers lacing into his hair, I pull his face up to mine again, urging us to fall deeper into each other, my body melting against his, our clothes an inconvenience now, an obstruction. His fingers rove lower, grabbing handfuls of my ass as his hardness grinds against my hip. I rub against him on purpose, eliciting a deep groan that gives me chills, widening my stance as his hand reaches up my skirt. His strong fingers glide up my inner thigh to stroke at the hot damp spot

I can feel soaking through my panties. The sound of the music and the crowd fall far away, irrelevant against the sound of our hurried gasps and desperate groans in this dark, private corner. My body pulsates and throbs, aching for more of him, yearning to tear off his shirt and put skin against skin, to feel the deep pounding of that powerful cock once again.

I break away from his lips to look around us, then push him further aside into a corner so dark even the roaming strobe lights can't find us, where I guide myself by the texture of his expensive clothes and sculpted body. My hands find his fly and zip it down while he growls into my neck. The moment I pull at the fabric his thick cock emerges, already engorged enough to fill my palms. Cole reacts to my touch by heaving that broad chest in a cut-off sigh, grabbing at my waist and pulling me to him impatiently, so that when I slide down he feels the curves of my body against the throbbing stiffness of his.

"Fuck," he murmurs between the thump of the drums, his hand caressing the top of my head as I take his cock in both hands. I can't believe I'm really doing this right now, right here in public, but more than that, I can't believe how much I want to. As dark as if I were blindfolded, I guide myself by touch, thick shaft between my fingertips, then palms, then lips. Tongue mapping its hot, veiny skin, rolling up and down that incredible length, his palm now fisting in my hair as he drives himself further into the back of my hungry mouth.

"Oh that's good," he growls, his voice dropping lower with pleasure.

I let him take control, let him pull my mouth over the head, let him tug me back and forth by my hair as he fucks my mouth, his thrusts getting more urgent as I suck deeper and harder. I roll my tongue over the texture of his skin, squeeze it between my lips until I can feel the blood throbbing. His cock fills my mouth, head grasping for the back of my throat, choking me slightly, so that even the release of breath is suspended in my body. I cup his balls and squeeze them, just firm enough to push him further into his growling, pumping mania.

The music thumps and wails, filling my ears as I suck and lick and choke on Cole, devouring him hungrily, so ready to swallow him down that I don't even care about catching my breath. I need this as much as he does.

When he comes I feel it as intimately as Cole, his desire and orgasm concentrated into a hot pulse that pushes across my tongue and into the back of my throat, a taste I suck down and lick clean as he slumps back against the wall and I rise up to face him. Then, as quickly as the urge took me, something snaps.

I pull back, and he looks concerned as I stand panting in front of him.

"Whoa, there. You okay?"

"Uh, yeah," I say, feeling like I've slammed into reality—or like reality slammed into me. "I guess I just got carried away."

"Guess I did too," he laughs. "Do you want to—"

I feel a touch on my shoulder and jump, turning to find Asha smiling too-wide, her gaze flicking between me and Cole.

"Hey," she says to me, before looking Cole up and down, and repeating in a voice much slower and more confrontational. "*Hey.*"

Cole acknowledges her with a nod. "Well-meaning roommate, I take it? I'm Cole. Pleasure to meet you." He extends a hand and Asha takes it, her mama bear stance gone now, fluttering her lashes in the dark.

"Asha," she purrs, "and the pleasure's all mine." She holds on a beat too long before letting go of his hand reluctantly. Then she glances at me. "Everything cool?"

"Yeah. We should get going," I say, tossing a wave at Cole before locking arms with Asha and dragging her away.

Once we've disappeared into the crowd, Asha leans over to me and through her broad grin says, "You were in a hurry to get out of there, little miss naughty. Hooking up with the boss again? No judgment from me, but..."

"I don't know what I was doing," I say with a groan. "I mean I *do* know, and I wanted to do it, but now...I guess I don't know if I really want to get involved with him if this is just gonna be some kind of bootycall situation. I thought I didn't care, but..."

Asha nods in understanding. "You think you two've got something going on, though? Something that could be more than a one night stand?"

"I think..." my voice trails off as I try to get a grasp on things. Then I shake my head. "No. I think I made a mistake. One I won't be making again."

CHAPTER NINE

COLE

I can still taste her the morning after. It's difficult to forget some things, especially when you don't quite understand them. And Willow's a mystery, even though it doesn't seem like she has any self-awareness about it. A girl beautiful enough to coast through life on a sea of attention and obliviousness, yet who somehow developed a raw talent the likes of which comes very rarely, who also happens to have the determination and principles of an old hand, yet who can manage to talk to a girl of nine like she's still a big kid herself. Speaking of which…

"I'm bored. You said you'd only be a minute. It's been *five*. I was counting."

I look up from my desk to see Chloe sitting on a wine crate, swinging her legs and pouting.

"Just one more second," I say, finishing off the signing of a few more papers. Then I put my pen down and look at her. "Ok then."

"Can we hang out with Willow?" Chloe says, after we regard each other silently for a moment.

Now I'm the one shaking my head.

"No. Her shift doesn't start for another five hours."

"Is she your girlfriend?"

I look at her, a little curious. Maybe it's true what they say about kids—they can sense things.

"What's with all the questions?"

Chloe smiles.

"I think you like her."

I clear my throat and shuffle the papers on the desk. "She's a good chef and she keeps my kitchen running smoothly. So yeah, I like her."

Chloe smiles even more broadly now, hopping down from the wine crate to come closer. Now I feel like she's the one playing games with me.

"You should ask her to be your girlfriend. She's funny. And pretty. And smart."

"You're gonna be a hell of a ballbreaker when you get older, aren't you?"

"What's a ballbreaker?"

I stand up and move to the door, gesturing for her to go through it.

"Come on. We're gonna get you in the kitchen today."

Chloe goes stock still. "Really? You really think I'm ready?"

"I really do. You nailed that prep work last week." I give her a high five and as she practically dances down the hall ahead of me, I start to feel like I might not be so bad at this kid stuff after all.

There's nobody in there now, it being so early in the morning, and once we're standing among the polished metal appliances and clean surfaces, I turn to Chloe—who stands wide-eyed with awe at all the gleaming tools and professional fixtures—and clap my hands, the closest I can get to creating a sense of excitement.

"So you've settled on a pasta dish for the competition, yes?" She nods. "Let's cook some pasta, then. Have you figured out what kind you'd like to use?"

Without missing a beat, she says, "Ravioli."

"Ravioli?"

"Yep," she says, assured. "I even know what I want to stuff it with. Something cheesy…hmm. And mushrooms, maybe. Like the ones we got at the farmers' market."

I nod, feeling a little swelling of pride at her growing confidence.

"You ever made your own ravioli before?" I ask.

Chloe looks at me a little uncertainly.

"Kinda? I usually just use lasagna sheets."

"Well then you're missing out on half the fun, and on top of that, pasta out of a box can't hold a candle to the kind you make from scratch. Quick: Pick a color," I say. "Green, red, black…"

"Red," Chloe says, responding quickly.

"Good choice," I say, moving to the vegetable stores to find beets.

Over the next hour or so we work up a dough, mixing in the puréed beets so that it turns a luxurious purple-red. Though I'm not as good as Willow when it comes to pulling silly faces, the magic of the pasta machine entrances Chloe—the same way it entranced me the first time I used one—and we bond over the careful process of flattening out the red dough until it resembles a thin velvet curtain. Chloe takes the task of keeping the counter well floured as seriously as a monk's prayers, and though I'm a little nervous those tiny hands are going to make a mess of the chore, Chloe exhibits a precision and skill that kinda shocks me.

"What are we going to do about the filling?" she asks. "It needs to be the best, so we can't afford to slack off."

I laugh, feeling in a good mood. This is the second time I've been compelled by somebody else, and just like the last time, I'm kinda enjoying it. "What do you want?"

"I have some ideas. What do you got to work with?"

I laugh again.

"Let's see," I say, moving toward the industrial fridge. "Time for a crash course in ingredient combination, I think."

For a while I work through a number of ingredients with Chloe—many of which she never seems to have tried before. Mascarpone, gorgonzola, chèvre; butternut squash, truffles; various fresh herbs and spices. I'm impressed both by her adventurous spirit in trying different mixtures, and her honesty in calling out the ones that don't work together. I can think of a dozen chefs I've worked with that had less persistence and invention than this nine-year-old.

"So?" I ask, standing up from the counter we've filled with bowls of various cheeses, ingredients and chopped vegetables. "What's it gonna be?"

Chloe peruses the selection with the severe seriousness of a critic one more time, then points at a bowl.

"That one."

"And what is that one?"

"Taglio—"

"Taleggio," I correct.

"Taleggio, rosemary, and I want to do roasted carrots with lemon."

"Changed your mind about the citrus, did you? I thought it wasn't your speed."

She blushes. "I worked with it some more and it turned out to be a good contrast for the herbs—it keeps them from tasting too heavy. But still..." she trails off, screwing up her face as she muses. "It needs something else."

I look down at the ingredients, thinking for a few seconds.

"You ever had a brown butter sauce?" I ask.

"Yes!" Chloe says, brightening up as she points a triumphant finger at me. "That's it!"

"Let's do it, then," I say, feeling like I'm getting into it as much as she is.

Once we're done separating the milk, mixing in a little chopped sage as well, we move back to the pasta and I show Chloe how to cut it into the frilled squares of ravioli, though immediately Chloe shakes her head.

"No," she says.

"What? These are perfect."

"No," Chloe repeats, a little more adamantly. "I want to cut it into different shapes."

"You can't cut it into different shapes," I say. "I mean sure, maybe that's good enough for a novelty restaurant, but if you want to be a serious cook then you cut ravioli the right way. You'll risk it bursting right open if you try anything too complicated, or you might end up with some pieces where there's too much dough and it cooks unevenly."

"I want to cut it into shapes," Chloe insists, looking at me as if I'm the dissident.

I pause for a second, once again asking myself what Willow would do.

"Ok," I say, giving in. "What shapes are you going to cut it into?"

"Lemon shapes, to match the lemon flavor on the carrots in the filling. But I'm going to need your help," Chloe says, with the lack of irony only a child can have. "So please try to do it well."

I nod, shrug, then say, "Sure. I guess you're the boss now."

Somehow, the elliptical shapes aren't too bad. Against all my suspicions, Chloe seems to have a good sense of correct proportions, covering just enough of the sheets with filling before we press the top layer of ravioli down. Forty minutes later, the pasta all boiled and drained, drizzled with just a little olive oil and fresh-cracked pepper for sampling purposes, we're eating away, and I'm genuinely impressed.

When Maggie comes to pick her up, even the teacher stays to eat a little, nodding in approval at the youngster's precocious talent. We package up the leftovers into a few to-go containers, say our goodbyes, and they start to leave.

"Hold up," I say, as they reach the door of the kitchen. I pick up one last container that they left behind and move toward them. "You forgot one."

Without missing a beat, Chloe says, "That one's for Willow. Tell her you made it for her. She likes food. So if you want her to be your girlfriend, you should do it."

Chloe looks at me with parental gravity, while Maggie shoots me an apologetic, slightly-embarrassed look.

"Yeah. Sure," I say, trying to make it sound sarcastic for Maggie's benefit, though when they turn to leave, I look down at the red lemon-shaped pasta, and feel a strange sense of contentment. Maybe the kid is right. Maybe Willow *will* appreciate it.

And judging by the way she ran off like Cinderella last night at the club, I feel like I could use all the help I can get.

CHAPTER TEN

WILLOW

Of *course* the investor meeting would be a last minute thing the morning after I've had a night out. What did I expect? A second to breathe? Time to prepare for a massive pitch? No chance. I never should have let Asha talk me into hitting up that second club and drinking those blueberry mojitos. But damn, we had fun—even with the Cole incident fresh in my mind. Then again, maybe all the fun I had was just a futile attempt to erase the memory of what I'd done with him against the wall of that first club.

What got me out of bed at the crack of dawn this morning was a call from Tony telling me he was already on his way to pick me up, and plenty of advice on how I should dress for the meeting. At least I'm too pumped full of anxious adrenaline to dwell on what I did with Cole last night, how badly I wanted him, how I almost lost control…

Half-asleep, the club's music still thumping painfully in my sinuses, I manage to get dressed and leave the house, where Tony is leaning up against his convertible with a broad smile.

"Finally! Sleeping Beauty awakes!"

He hugs me quickly, briefly scans my outfit with an approving nod—the way I'm getting used to people doing—then opens the car door for me to slump into the passenger seat.

"Is this really legit?" I ask as he hops in on the other side and turns on the engine. The second half of a Rihanna record fills the air. "I mean, who arranges meetings this sudden?"

"They're *rich*, sweetheart," Tony says as he revs the car recklessly out of the parking lot. "They jump on planes—Tokyo, Paris, New York—the way other people ride the metro. They're only in town for today, and we've got to grab the opportunity while we can."

I try to steady my nausea as Tony weaves in between the traffic, the thumping pain behind my eyes loosening a little as the air whips against my face and hair, pressing me back into the seat.

"Still," I say, straining to be heard over the roar of the engine, "we didn't have any time to prepare. Do we have a financial plan? Projections? Cost lists?"

Tony laughs, sending the fear of God into me as he tosses his head back, removing his eyes from the blurred road.

"Oh, honey. They're investors—not accountants. They don't want to have a bunch of numbers spluttered at them. They want an *idea*, a dream, a vision. People that they can believe in." Tony reaches out and turns my face toward him, my chin in his palm. "And who wouldn't believe in a face like yours?"

"You'd be surprised," I say, through squished cheeks.

Tony laughs easily again and only half-concentrates as he takes a corner at car-tilting speed.

"Look, these people are rich, and if they wanted more money they'd go to a stockbroker, or buy some real estate. But they don't. They want a place they can call their own, something to be proud of. Something fabulous and creative that they can feel they had some part in making."

"You make it sound so simple."

"When you have as much money as these guys do, it is."

Tony swings the wheel and guides the car up a small incline toward the front of a grand hotel. Tall and glass, the rails leading up to doors so polished they catch the sun like diamonds, the shrubbery around the building so perfectly manicured it's as if the hotel management put a hairdresser on staff to trim them.

"Sir?"

The red-suited valet steps toward us as soon as we exit the car, and Tony hands him the keys with a regal smile before we huddle up at the foot of the stairs.

"Tits and teeth, honey," Tony says. He puts a hand on the small of my back and one on my shoulder to fix my posture, then taps under my chin to get it a little higher.

"Why do I feel like I'm being entered into a beauty pageant?"

"Now," Tony says breezily, as we start up the stairs to the revolving glass doors, "the pretty boy is Andre, and the cute, chubby guy's named Lou."

"What are their last names? Shouldn't we use those?"

Tony stops for a moment to think.

"You know, I'm sure they told me, but the music was too loud. Anyway—"

"Wait—" I say, grabbing Tony's arm to stop him from carrying on. "*Music?* What do you mean? Where did you meet these guys?"

"Foam Night at The Male Room," Tony says nonchalantly.

I stop in mid-stride. "That gay bar you go to?! You're telling me you met these investors at a gay bar? And you're taking them seriously?"

It takes only a second for the mock-offense to spread over Tony's face as he crosses his arms dramatically.

"I'm sorry. I forgot that homosexuals weren't allowed to be incredibly wealthy."

"That's not what I'm saying, at all. It's just…I thought they were legitimate investors looking to conduct some professional business. Not a couple of random hot dudes you partied with."

"They are. I mean, they're both of those things. Trust me, Spud." Tony stands back and gestures up at the tall building in front of us. "Do you know how much the cheapest suite in this place costs? One night could pay your rent for a month. And it's not like I didn't do a background check on these guys. My friend—one of the bartenders—told me they splash cash around like they're filming a rap video."

I take a moment to consider, then shake my head and smile.

"You know what? I trust you, Tony. Let's do this."

"That's my girl."

We move up the steps, through the doors, past expensively dressed old couples, and into the gigantic, air conditioned lobby. So big it's as if somebody decorated an aircraft hangar with mahogany and velvet. I follow Tony as he heads off to the side, down some steps into the lavish bar.

"There they are," Tony says, flashing a wave at two men in nice suits sipping cocktails around a table.

We greet them with handshakes and air kisses, introduce ourselves briefly, and order green juices when they offer us something. After only a little small talk about the loveliness of the hotel, it's time for business.

"So," Andre says, his blue eyes twinkling beneath immaculate hair, "tell us all about yourselves."

"Well," Tony says, leaning forward as if he was waiting for the question, "as I said, we're two chefs who've been building up our culinary experience, working here and there in Los Angeles. We met while studying in France under Guillhaume de Lacompte several years ago." Lou and Andre glance at each other with raised eyebrows and appreciative nods when Tony mentions the Frenchman's name so casually. "So far we've been learning in the best kitchens, building up a wealth of proficiency and know-how, seeing what works—what doesn't work—and we've got a ton of ideas that we feel ready to implement now. Ideas that could really make a restaurant that is next level."

"Ideas, huh?" Lou says. "What kind of ideas?"

Tony looks at me, a cue for me to take over.

"Um...yeah. Ideas," I babble, nodding emphatically for a few seconds while I think of what to say. "Well...L.A. is a great place for food. I mean, everything grows in California pretty much, fruit, vegetables—and what doesn't grow here is only a short stop away. We're by the coast, obviously, so we get great fresh seafood. I mean, there's really no excuse for a restaurant in Los Angeles to not take advantage of all the local abundance with a menu that's fresh and seasonal and creates something genuinely unique, stylish, but still fundamentally what people want. Which is to feel good about what they're eating. Passionate, even."

"Right..." Lou says, screwing his eyes up skeptically. "But you want to build a restaurant, not just sell local fruits and vegetables. You can do that at a farmers' market."

"Yes," I say, still grasping at straws as my nerves go into overdrive. "But those are just the ingredients, the foundation for the menu. See, the problem is that most restaurants here don't celebrate what's great about this place. If you walk into any nice restaurant in the city you'll find caviar from Iran, imported stracchino, kobe beef from Japan—all prepared according to recipes the French and Italian invented."

"I don't know," Andre says, laughing. "Caviar and Italian cheese sounds pretty good to me!"

"Wait," Lou interrupts, even more concerned now, "is this going to be some kind of farm-to-table, organic food thing then? Because that doesn't sound very exciting. We've seen plenty of that around here."

"No," Tony says quickly. "This is nothing like those quasi-healthy fast food quinoa joints."

"Actually, the local organic thing isn't too far from it," I say, ignoring the look of panic now on Tony's face. "I only cook with ingredients I like. And that means stuff that's sustainable, fresh. Not frozen in the back of a truck for a two thousand mile trip."

Tony shakes his head at me, then quickly turns his attention back to the investors.

"The organic food thing is just a base-level thing. It's not the selling point! The selling point is the fact that we're the best chefs in the state. Our menu's gonna be…innovative."

Andre and Lou look at each other and laugh as if we're putting on entertainment.

"Really now?" Lou says.

"Yeah," I say, getting a little irritated and somehow gaining confidence in the process. "It is. And we are."

Seeing the sincerity in my face, and hearing the firm confidence in my voice, both of their smiles fade immediately.

"I've worked in the best places in the city," Tony says. "I'm not some naïve debutante—I know exactly what our competition is because I've cooked with most of them. And I'm telling you we can blow them out of the water. You've heard of Knife, yes?"

"Sure," Lou says. "Cole Chambers, right? We've been there a couple of times. The place is flawless."

"Then you've already tried Willow's food, probably," Tony says with a poker hand smile. "She's one of the best chefs there. Sure, Cole Chambers is the pretty face at the front, the guy who takes the credit, but who do you think is actually cooking the food in the back?" Tony points a sly finger in my direction. "And let me tell you, she's given him more than a few ideas, too."

Now I'm the one looking at Tony like he's crazy. What is he talking about? I didn't even tell him about the Basque burgers...

His bluff seems to work though, as Andre and Lou exchange a glance, uncertain of how to take us, no more entertained laughs now. Lou clears his throat, wringing his hands.

"I'm not really seeing it still. It's gonna be high-class like Knife, but it's gonna have organic, local food? It's gonna compete with Michelin starred restaurants but it's not gonna have things like caviar on the menu?"

"Fine," I say, smiling as if I care much less than I really do. "If you wanna do the whole 'bourgeois, faux-European dining experience' thing then there are a thousand chefs that could do that for you. You wanna make a restaurant that's just like Knife? Just like a dozen other places in the city? Go ahead. But don't be surprised if people still choose to eat at Knife."

"Right," Tony says, pointing at me, strength in his voice now as he finds his angle. "We're gonna do something totally unique, totally different. And we're gonna do it so well that you'll never want to eat caviar again."

"Imagine this," I cut in. "You go to dinner at Knife, where you stand in line for forty minutes before getting seated at a cramped corner table where you spend the next two hours in the dark just so you can have the 'privilege' of eating a teaspoon of overpriced imported caviar and a miniature steak drowning in heavy sauce, with —of all things—fried potatoes on the side. You go home, you feel heavy. You feel like you overpaid. And the worst thing is: You're still hungry."

Lou nods gravely and Andre rubs his chin thoughtfully. I feel like a total jerk throwing Cole's restaurant under the bus like this, but sometimes you have to exaggerate things to get your point across.

"Now imagine this. You walk into our restaurant—it's a bright space filled with natural light, exposed wood beams overhead and potted succulents on the walls. You're seated immediately, and the rotating menu tonight offers a carefully curated selection of west coast comfort food prepared with the freshest organic ingredients and cooked by some of the best chefs in the country."

"What exactly is west coast comfort food?" Andre asks, his face skeptical.

"How about golden fried free range chicken with local sage blossom honey and chili, coated with chopped peanuts and served alongside crisp asparagus and flash-fried sweet-potato croquettes in lemon and dill sauce," I say breathlessly, the menu items I've dreamed of serving for so long spilling out of me in a dreamy rush.

Andre lets out a quiet 'yum' across the table, and I know at least one of them is on board.

Tony leans forward, picking up where I left off. "Or maybe you opt for the slow-roasted red bell peppers stuffed with chili con carne cooked to perfection off a cinnamon base. Or the avocado and grapefruit salad with rosewater and herb dressing and pan-toasted almonds."

Then I cut in, "And for appetizers we have carnitas nachos with slivered pineapple, house-made kale chips with lemon tahini, and fresh baked rosemary focaccia or sourdough rolls for people to choose from. And these are just our preliminary ideas."

"I get it! California comfort food." Even Lou looks liable to drool now. "You're making me hungry, and I just ate," he says, and it doesn't sound like he's joking.

But despite the compliment, both of them are still looking us over critically, like they're not quite sure what to make of our pitch.

"So...?" Tony says, glancing back and forth between them.

"Well," Andre says, "this is the part where we tell you we'll think it over."

Something sinks in me. I know what that means. I've been through this before.

The deal is off.

"Wait!" I say, quickly pulling out my phone and scrolling through notes. "I did do a few mental calculations, looking at some possible locations online, thinking about what our initial outlay might be for the first six months in terms of operating budget. It was just some back-of-the-envelope numbers but if you'd like to get a general sense of—"

"That's fine," Andre says, holding up his palm. "We've seen everything we need to see here."

I swallow and lower my phone, body almost shaking with nerves and the agony of our failure, not even hearing the small talk Tony makes with them as we say our goodbyes and make our way through the lobby, back out through the revolving doors before Tony explodes into gasps of released energy.

"Holy shit," he says, almost panting.

"Oh God, I'm so sorry, Tony. I don't know what came over me. That was awful."

"What are you talking about?" Tony says, putting his arm around me.

"I don't know why I always go off like that when I'm talking about food, I just can't help myself when it comes to ingredients. I really apologize."

"Are you kidding?" Tony says, laughing. "That's why I brought you! That 'foodie passion' thing you do? It was awesome! They loved it."

"I doubt it. That sounded like a 'thanks but no thanks' to me.

They didn't even let me tell them about the plan, price ranges, what kind of location we wanted. You think they would have just dismissed all that if they were seriously considering giving us a chance?"

The valet brings the car to a stop in front of us and hands Tony the keys.

"Oh honey," he says as he tips the valet and we get inside. "We can draw up budgets and business plans all day long once they're ready to talk logistics. For now we just needed to give them something to whet their appetites, something to believe in—and *you* are somebody to believe in."

I nod, completely unconvinced, as he starts driving.

"Well *you* are somebody who can make people believe anything what was all that about me giving Cole a 'few ideas'?"

"Just a little creative embellishment. These investors expect a bit of that."

I nod and grip the door handle as Tony speeds up and starts passing other cars.

"Oh. That makes sense. At first I thought you'd heard a rumor or something," I say.

Tony looks at me, deadpan, and I experience the extreme fear that is becoming familiar as his passenger.

"What do you mean?" he says, all curious now at the prospect of gossip. "You really *did* give him ideas? You've been there what, two weeks? Damn, girl. Workin' it."

More for the sake of getting Tony's eyes back on the road, I say, "He maybe, sorta-kinda, might have put one of my dishes on his menu. Just as a trial run."

"No shit! That's incredible."

"I dunno. It just kinda happened after we got talking."

Tony shakes his head.

"The things a man will do to get a pretty young thing on his side..."

"It's not like that. I mean...we keep having our run-ins, I guess, but...I don't know. I don't want to get into anything with him. He's still my boss."

"Not for long," Tony says, gleefully. "Not if we get what we want."

Tony drops me off outside Knife, still buzzing with excitement as he tells me not to 'get too comfortable' there. Already a couple minutes late, I rush through the delivery entrance as I pull my whites from my duffel bag, heading straight for the women's bathroom to get changed and hoping nobody sees me scurrying in.

"Hey. Willow."

Fat chance at sneaking in undetected. The unmistakably commanding voice comes from the back office, and I rewind a few steps to peek inside. There he is, shirtsleeves pulled up to reveal those muscular forearms, shifting a crate of salt so that his muscles are pumped and squeezing, hair mussed perfectly like only a man who works with his hands can get it.

"Hey," I say meekly, putting mountains of effort into sounding as effortless as possible. "I know I'm a little late, but I'll make it up out of my break."

"Come on in. Let's have a word," Cole says, dumping the crate and sweeping another to the side with his foot.

I look back at the end of the hallway anxiously, as if I even have the option of saying no, then step inside the office.

Guilt isn't a feeling I enjoy—I guess that's why I always try to do the right thing. It's like a bad meal, sitting in your stomach heavily like an illness, impossible to digest, difficult to purge. Its aftertaste lasts a hell of a long time.

During the next few seconds, as Cole leans back on the table, scanning my outfit from the meeting earlier—cigarette pants with a crisp white blouse and tailored blazer—my mind works overtime coming up with excuses. For my lateness, for the fact that I'm hoping to start my own place, for the undeniable truth that the girl who slammed him up against the wall of a nightclub and wrapped her tongue around his cock last night was actually me, and that despite all my reservations there's nothing in the world I'd like more than to do it again.

"You look amazing," he says, once he's done taking in my outfit. "Special occasion this morning?"

"Uh…no," I mumble, effecting a feeling of coyness at the compliment. "I just did a little shopping. This is L.A., you know?"

Cole smiles at me.

"City finally getting its claws into you, huh?"

"Something like that."

"I like it," he says, leaving a silence afterward that feels like he's holding back.

"Look," I say, unable to bear the silence, the way he looks at me. "About last night…uh, I haven't had that much to drink in a while, and it's been so long since I went out. I guess I got kind of carried away…"

"I thought you said you weren't drinking last night?" he asks, his brow furrowed.

Shit. Caught in a lie by my hot-as-fuck boss, minutes before starting a shift I'm already late for because I was at an investor meeting for a restaurant I'm trying to open behind his back. Batting a thousand, Willow. "Right. Well. Anyway, I'm really sorry about everything. Do you mind if we just…like, forget about it? I didn't really think it all through, and I'd like things to remain professional between us. It'd be the best thing, I think."

Cole seems to consider it for a moment, though he keeps that enigmatic smile on his face, so I have no idea what he's actually thinking. Does he buy that I'm not interested?

"If that's what you'd prefer. Though I'd rather not forget about it," he says.

"What does that mean?"

"It means I wanna take you out. For real. You. Me. A date."

I laugh nervously, push hair behind my ear three times in a second.

"What about the last time we went out?"

"That wasn't a date. That was formal. Business," Cole says, waving it away.

"Well if that's how all your formal meetings end, I can only wonder how a date would." Now that I've said it, the array of images flashing through my mind are more than enough to send my pulse racing.

"Yeah," Cole says, stepping toward me, his voice lowering, "I wonder too."

I look up at him, half of me debating whether I should run out the door, while the other half of me fights the urge to tear off his shirt and pull him onto the crates on top of me. Instead, I settle for looking awkward and uncertain.

"I know it's a bit much to take in," he says, "me being your boss, you being new to L.A. You probably still think I'm like the guy on TV."

"And the magazines."

Cole squints a little. "What do you mean?"

"Well, you have a reputation. When it comes to women."

He laughs. "Even more reason to let me prove you wrong."

Suddenly Leo's voice comes through the door, shouting to Cole before he pops his bald head in the doorway.

"Boss! Boss! She's late again! This is getting—shit! There you are. The hell are you doing still undressed? We're fifteen minutes into a shift and you haven't prepped anything. We've already got an order of Basque and no garlic sauce!"

"Control yourself, Leo," Cole says, switching into boss mode easily. "You think anyone takes you seriously when you shout like that? Willow and I are in the middle of a meeting right now, so get back to work and leave my employees to me."

Leo glances from me to Cole, seeming to consider the bad idea of saying something else, before wisely shaking his head and disappearing.

"I'd better go," I say, pulling my duffel up on my shoulder and turning for the door. I look back before leaving though. "Um. I have Monday off—are you free then? We could do something, if you want."

Cole smiles, licking his lips like he just tasted something great.

"You like the beach?"

I grin. "It's one of the main reasons I came to L.A. But I haven't really had a chance to go yet."

"Perfect," he says. "It's a date."

CHAPTER ELEVEN

COLE

Time seems to slow until Monday. Every business meeting twice as long, every minute spent in cars and planes twice as boring. My problem used to be thinking about work when I should be having fun, now my problem is thinking about Willow when I should be working.

Her smell, her taste, her smile. The passionate way she talks about her ideas, her stubborn refusal to kiss my ass, the impression she gives of being an unlit firework of talent about to explode over L.A.

My impatience is all exacerbated by Martin running names by me of two dozen chefs he thinks could replace Holly, until they all blend into one. Now that I've seen what real talent looks like, now that I've watched it dance through a kitchen making work look like a performance, now that I've seen that headstrong dedication to perfect food, these other chefs pale in comparison, experience be damned. Memories pull me into a constant state of distraction and arousal, compelling me to check clocks and calendars until Monday comes around. It's been a long time since I had to wait to get what I want, and the waiting just makes the wanting even harder.

By the time Monday comes I feel like I've gone through a desert. I take my time picking out swim shorts and a t-shirt, take more time to stand in front of my cars and pick the right one. When you're an ex television celebrity and the most well-known restauranteur in Los Angeles, women start trying to impress you, rather than the other way around. You can wear pajamas and show up in a beat-up Civic and, if anything, it only makes you glow even more in their eyes. But Willow…something tells me she doesn't buy into all that shit. If I want to impress her, I'm going to have to work at it.

First off, there aren't many women who'd tell the owner of a successful restaurant their entire food philosophy is wrong. Not many who'd pin that owner against a counter and force him to try their food. Not only that, but Willow looks me in the eye, talks like she's not afraid of me, and doesn't hold back when it comes to her own principles or opinions. She's a challenge, and I like it. I won't even get into what she did to me with her mouth in that dark corner of the club, how hot it was when she made eye contact with me, how much of a turn on it was that we might get caught. That's a girl with some untapped talent right there.

I meet her at my favorite Santa Monica beachfront hotel. One with a private beach area that I know will give us some time alone. She's standing outside the front entrance when I valet my car, by the swaying palms that hide the footpath to the beach. A wide-brim straw hat, a wicker tote bag, and a chiffon kaftan over that tight body. Slightly see-through, so her bikini clad figure teases behind it like the haze of a dream.

I walk toward her slowly, taking my time to appreciate the view, and when we get close enough I make sure she knows how good she looks by kissing her on the cheek, a little too slow, a little too close.

"You look incredible," I murmur into her ear. "I'm not gonna be able to take my eyes off you."

"It's so beautiful here," she says, turning her blushing face away from me to gaze at the azure waves.

"You haven't seen it yet," I say, gesturing at the beach path.

I take her hand, leading her down the steep steps as we move toward the isolated cabana. A wood platform that juts out onto the pearlescent beach, a couple of loungers set out on it, folded towels neatly stacked on them, and a small table with a crystal vase of flowers and some bottles of expensive sparkling water. The scene surrounded by four posters holding up the thin white linen that acts as a shade, swaying in the breeze.

"Oh my God," Willow says excitedly when she sees it, hurrying her step to get there quicker. "It looks like actual heaven. This is amazing!"

"I'm glad you like it," I say. It's sincere. Willow's so different from the usual women I take out that I was worried about hitting the mark. "It's ours for the day. What would you like to drink?"

I glance over at the waiter emerging from the fauna, and Willow follows my gaze to see him.

"Something with fruit. Fresh," she says.

"Alcoholic or no?"

Willow shrugs easily, as if she's up for anything now that she's happy and relaxed.

"Sure," she says. "It is my day off."

The waiter nods graciously in her direction, much like Charles, as if he knows exactly what'll make the customer happy.

"We have a green tea mojito that is very popular," he says.

"Perfect," Willow smiles. "Cole?"

"I'll have a single malt whiskey," I tell the waiter. "Your choice."

"Very good, Mr. Chambers," he says, before turning primly and heading back.

Willow eyes me playfully.

"He knew your name."

"Don't believe what they tell you—TV still has reach."

Willow dumps her bag and pulls off her hat, swishing her hair in the wind to loosen it.

"Oh, I'm sure you come here often. I bet the ladies love it."

"Is that jealousy I'm hearing?"

"Nope," Willow says, laughing so that I know she's not lying. "Just figuring you out a little."

"You don't have to figure me out—I'll tell you exactly who I am."

"Is that so?" Willow says, pulling the knot at the back of her kaftan and sliding it away to reveal a body that stirs every masculine fiber inside of me. So lithe and beautiful it's almost torture to look and not touch. "Tell me then: Do you swim?"

I stand up and perform my own show, pulling off my T-shirt and standing proud, knowing the long hours I put in every week with my trainer at the gym have sculpted my physique to near-perfection.

"What does it look like?" I ask.

Willow looks me up and down, then shifts her weight to one side, sassily.

"It looks like you're probably too worried about your hair to be a good swimmer."

I laugh in disbelief.

"Imagine that, being judged as a swimmer by someone from Idaho. What coast is that on again?"

"Hey, I was the captain of my swim team in college."

"And I'm sure the swimming pools in Idaho are really something." I look out at the roaring ocean. "But I grew up by the ocean, it's another level."

Willow beams at me, bouncing a little with eager naughtiness. Then she winks, spins, and starts running down the short beach to the lapping waves. I watch her for a second, just admiring her, a little stunned at how this girl is bringing out a side of me I didn't even know I had. Then I take off after her, giving chase as she laughs back at me over her shoulder, until we're wading into the water, diving synchronously into a rolling wave.

We swim out a little, and I find out Willow wasn't lying. She's a good swimmer, good enough to tease me, to sweep away when I get close, submerge herself, long legs flicking into the air before they disappear. I let her go, enjoying the push and pull, satisfying myself with the sight of the water catching her wet hair, gentle laughter mixing with the rush of waves. Until she emerges right next to me, taking me by surprise. I whip around and grab her waist underwater, pull her toward me, a shrieked laugh emerging from that pearl white smile as she brings her sun-glowing face to mine.

"So," I ask, mock-seriously, "are you the kind of girl who kisses on a first date?"

"I don't know. Depends on the guy," she teases, leaning in.

We kiss slow and gentle, as if we've got all the time in the world, the Pacific stretching out beyond us making it feel somehow more private, more intimate. I can almost taste her happiness, taste her inhibitions fading in the beauty of these surroundings.

We pull back, and she grins again. Before I can say anything, she notices something beyond my shoulder, back at the beach.

"Drinks!" she says, pointing at the waiter putting them down at our loungers, and we break apart, swimming our way back to the cabana. Willow tosses me a towel and we dry off a little before sitting down, the table between us. We raise our glasses, clink them together, and drink.

"Oh," Willow sighs happily. "It's so nice out here. This is bliss."

She settles back on the lounger, and I drag mine closer to hers before doing the same.

After a while of staring at the Santa Monica pier on the horizon, I look at her, eyes closed as she faces the sun. Golden skin drying, her breasts moving imperceptibly with her peaceful breathing.

"You think you'll stay here?" I ask.

"In Los Angeles?"

"Yeah. Are you not feeling pull of the Idaho cornfields yet?"

"Not at the moment. But some day, sure, I'll probably move back. To be close to my family. Maybe when I'm older, retired. What about you?" She turns to look at me.

"Me? I'm not planning to go to Idaho at all, to be honest."

Willow reaches out to slap my arm playfully.

"You know what I mean. Are you going to stay in L.A. forever? Retire here?"

"I don't plan on retiring."

Willow eyes me for a few seconds, nodding, seeming to draw some kind of conclusion about me.

"You think I'm a workaholic," I say.

"Nope," she grins. "I know you are. You never know, though. Sometimes people mellow out in their old age." Then she winks, takes a slow sip of her drink, and closes her eyes as she tastes it.

I watch the muscles of her throat flex, my cock stirring in my shorts, and when she opens her eyes she notices my focus on her and tilts her head.

"So how did you get into cooking?" I ask her.

"Oh…I don't know. I've loved it as long as I can remember. I think it was my grandma who started it…" she says, looking dreamily into the distance. "She had this little herb garden, little pots around the kitchen. Basil and oregano, rosemary and thyme, mint and sage.

The smells were almost *magical*. I'd watch her cook, and I thought it was incredible how she would just pluck a couple of leaves, give them a little rinse, tear them into a pot, and make something that tasted wonderful. She gave me a couple of plants and I started making stuff with them. For a year I put mint on everything—even French fries."

We both laugh a little, though I don't take my eyes away from how alluring she looks when she's lost in thought.

"How about you?" she asks, looking genuinely curious.

I take a moment to think back, sipping my whiskey as I sift through old memories. "It was when I was about twelve or so, at a juvenile detention center—"

Her eyes go wide. "Are you fucking with me? You went to juvie? You *are* a bad boy."

I laugh and shrug. "I was there a couple of times actually. I was young enough that it didn't go on my record though. Anyway, they used to get these guys in—teach the kids a trade, get them onto a healthy path. Carpenters, welders, that kinda thing. One day this chef comes in. He gets us cooking these Spanish omelets. Of course, most of the kids fucked up, or didn't care enough to really try, but that was when I first learned I could do this."

"Wait a second," Willow says, leaning forward, intrigued now, "is that why Martin asked me to cook an omelet for the interview process?"

I smile at her.

"Yeah. See, most people—doesn't matter if they're a dad cooking breakfast or a seasoned chef who's been around the block—they think omelets are simple. You whip the eggs, throw them in a pan, add the filling and you're done. But there's so much more to it. You can just whip the eggs, or you can separate the yolks from the whites and whip them separately, and if you do that then do you use all the yolks or half? Do you add cottage cheese or a splash of pancake batter?"

She nods, following along as I go over every aspect.

"And then, do they wait for the eggs to warm up a little, or just whip them cold right out of the fridge? Do they use butter or olive oil in the pan? What kinda ratio? How melted is the butter? Don't melt it all and you're really gonna taste it. How do they manage the pan? Temperature, texture. When do they fold? When do they take it out? You know, the most common mistake is people taking it out too late because they—"

"Don't know that the eggs continue to cook on the plate," Willow interrupts, smiling satisfyingly.

I laugh a little.

"Right. And an omelet's so simple you can taste every mistake, every skill."

"Smart."

"That guy was the first one to compliment me on anything other than my left hook, so I realized I could actually do this, and do it well. I had some innate skill and the motivation to take it further. Once I got out I worked in kitchens any way I could, taking odd jobs at any restaurant that would take me until I finally rustled up enough money to go to France and study under Guillhaume. And that's where I met Jason."

Even saying the name feels like a jab to the ribs, and the waiter shows up just in time, bringing the whole whiskey bottle and a fresh pitcher of mojitos for Willow.

"Who's Jason?" Willow asks, once the man is gone.

"He was my best friend—pretty much my only friend at the time. We finished the course in Paris and then came back to L.A. together. Like everyone who makes it through the program, we wanted to start our own place right away, but we didn't have the money. Somehow,

Jason took care of that. He was smooth, good with people. He was on first name terms with everyone from the food truck vendors to the fancy chefs downtown. At the time I was still was too dark and brooding to take an interest in all that business stuff. Just a twenty-one year old with too many tattoos, an uncontrollable temper and an unhealthy obsession with making the best food I could."

Willow shifts uncomfortably, her eyes unable to meet mine, probably trying to give me space because I'm opening up.

"So we get the money, get the location, and before long we're in business. Or, I should say, *I* was in business. I was doing all the work, developing the menu, running the kitchen, managing a full staff, but I hardly saw Jason. He was too busy partying, getting into drugs, faking his way into every Hollywood party he could find. He took his share of the profits, of course—and then some. I found out later that he'd been skimming off our supplies and selling them to other restaurants. The real kicker came when someone told me he hadn't been paying the loan sharks back like he said he had. These weren't mom and pop investors, you know? They took their money whether you gave it willingly or not."

Her brows knit together in concern. "What happened?"

I pour out some more whiskey, and lift it as I consider the memory, sipping slowly.

"Jason comes in soon after I heard the news, gives me this long speech about how he knew he'd been fucking things up, and that he'd finally realized he needed to get his shit together. Full confession, heartfelt apology, the works. He told me I'd been working too hard, and to take the weekend off. After that, we'd figure out what to do and make it work." I take another slow sip. "And I trusted him."

Willow looks at me, a sympathetic expression on her face. "I'm guessing that didn't turn out well."

"I came back on Tuesday, drove straight to the restaurant first thing, and the place…it'd been burned to the fucking ground." I gesture with my hands at the scene, as vivid as the sea in front of me. "Just fucking blackened rubble and ash and dirt. Jason had put *his* name on the insurance policy, of course, and my name on the loans. He took the insurance money, and I never saw him again. I went to bed and woke up on Wednesday morning, twenty-four years old, with nothing but a pile of burnt bricks to my name, and nearly a million dollars in debt."

Willow shakes her head, her delicate features gone pale. "Holy shit…that's *awful.*"

"Not really, in the end," I say, taking a sip. "For the lessons I learned that day, it was worth it."

"What do you mean?" she asks, sitting upright now and leaning toward me intently. "How could anything be worth that?"

"You think I trusted anyone but myself after that day? You think I ever let a contractor quote me for something I didn't already know the price of? That I'd ever let my accountant put a tax bill or receipt through that I didn't spend as much time going over myself? I cleared that pile of bricks with my own two hands; laid half of them myself until I found a builder I trusted enough to help. Then I named what went in its place Knife, so I'd never forget the one Jason put in my back. I'll never have another business partner again."

Willow stares at me, her expression carefully blank, but her eyes wide with thought.

"Sheesh," she says eventually. "The lemon thyme thing makes a lot more sense now."

I let out a genuine laugh for the first time since I started telling the story.

"You know, you're something. You're the first person I let Martin hire for me. Usually I run candidates through all the hoops myself. But I've never in my life heard him rave about a new chef the way he raved about you. His instincts are excellent." I take a breath, watching Willow take a long drink from her glass, enjoying the way the muscles in her throat move. "It's not like it was the last time somebody stabbed me in the back. I've turned no-hopers into brilliant chefs, only to have them disappear without notice and pop up days later at some fancy place that promises them the world and ends up failing. I've had accountants that embezzled cash, waiters that stole food—and I've lost count of how many people have stolen recipes and suppliers once they've left. It's best to treat everybody like they'll eventually betray you in this business, because in my experience, they probably will."

Willow squirms a little, rubbing the side of her neck as if she can't get comfortable. I guess no one has ever given it to her this straight before. No wonder her restaurant collapsed. She's brilliant, talented, ambitious—but in some ways, still a little naïve about the world.

"I don't know," she says with a contemplative sigh. "That sounds like an unhealthy way to live. Doing everything yourself. Not trusting anybody. Always looking over your shoulder, still holding on to all of that no matter how many years go by."

I smile at her once more before lifting my legs back up on the lounger and lying back.

"It got me here, didn't it?"

I draw some more of the whiskey and close my eyes, listening to the waves and feeling almost as if they could carry me away. Maybe this is what therapy feels like. As if some knot deep inside of you that you didn't even know you were carrying is loosened. Then Willow's words break the trance.

"Does it ever get lonely at the top?" she says.

I open my eyes and turn to see her sitting on the edge of her lounger, looking at me anxiously now as if worried.

I let out an easy chuckle. "How could I be lonely? I own a restaurant."

"What does that have to do with it?"

I look at her, not quite understanding the question.

"How could I be lonely when I spend all my time around people, hundreds of people who turn up at the restaurant every week. And my staff. All the cooks I've worked with over the years. The parties, the events…I'm never alone. If anything I wish I had more time to myself—"

"That's not what I meant," Willow says, her tone more serious now. "That whole 'not trusting anyone but yourself' thing, it sounds kinda…sad. I don't know how you can live like that. I can't imagine living without any close friends, without someone you can open up to."

"Why does that sound like an offer?"

"Maybe it is." She laughs a little, almost nervously, then stands up.

Looking up at her, I say, "You need a break from my dark, painful past, I take it?"

She smiles. "I can handle it. But right now, it's just too gorgeous out. Let's swim."

Willow holds out her hand, and I take it.

CHAPTER TWELVE

WILLOW

It took a month of very tactful cajoling, but I eventually give in and attend one of Asha's gym-plus-boxing classes. As if my shifts at Knife weren't exhausting enough. Still, Asha's been right about pretty much everything she suggested up to this point, and the physical strains are the only thing keeping my mind off the emotional ones, so I give it my all.

I spend the first twenty minutes of her relentlessly high-energy class planning how to escape without anybody noticing, the next twenty minutes pitting mind against body as they both reach their limits, then the last twenty minutes on an adrenaline rush that's almost spiritual. By the time I arrive home (without Asha, she had a few more classes to go) I'm walking on air. My mind clear, my body gratifyingly drained, and with a craving for sugar that goes down to my toes.

Since Asha's not around to tell me why that's a bad idea, I decide to go for it and make cinnamon buns from scratch, picking up confectioner's sugar and cream cheese on the way home. Once I'm in the apartment, I take a quick shower and then get to work.

That's when my sister Ellie calls, when my hands are deep in the mixing bowl, working the dough together. I answer the call with my elbow and quickly tell her to call me back on the videochat program on her laptop.

Ellie's only older than me by five years, though in terms of figuring out what you want in life, she's pretty much at the end game. After marrying her high school sweetheart in her mid-twenties, an IT consultant named Greg, she had two beautiful girls with eiderdown-soft hair and stock photo smiles and settled down in an incredible three-bedroom on the outskirts of Boise, to focus on her dream job of selling her handmade wedding dresses online. One of her first clients ended up being the style editor at Vogue, and after the magazine ran a short feature on her vintage-inspired designs, my sister's business took off. Even her bathroom is perfect—it has an amazing view of the mountains.

Ellie's more than just my wonderfully successful and incredibly humble sister, however; she's my cheerleader, confidante, and—when times are particularly tough—therapist. She's been calling me regularly to check in since I moved to L.A., expecting a full rundown of everything I've been up to. Considering how quickly things have been happening lately, she'll probably have to start calling me daily.

"Hey," I say, as her beaming face fills the screen, her huge living room extending off into the background.

"Hey you!" she squeals happily. I move back to the bowl and start working the dough again. "Oh gosh! That looks yummy! I miss your cooking, Willow."

"It's nothing. Just cinnamon buns."

"Ughhh," Ellie groans, making a drooly expression. "I love your cinnabons. Comfort food?"

"Earned guilty pleasure, more like. I just got back from one of

Asha's boxing classes."

"Oh! How is she doing? And how was the class?"

"Great, and great."

Ellie sighs deeply, and I glance at the screen to see her smiling proudly. "It's all so awesome."

The comment makes me laugh, though I don't know why.

"What is?"

"You…there…doing all of that. Following your dreams."

I finish kneading the dough and cover it to rise a little, then start whisking the cinnamon.

"It probably sounds more exciting than it really is. How's Greg? And the girls?"

"They miss you. A lot. If you think *I* ask a lot of questions, you should talk to the girls. 'Is Aunt Willow going to be in a movie?' 'Has she met Selena Gomez?' Oh! And do you remember Carl, from the movie theater? He nearly had a heart attack when I told him you work with Cole Chambers. The poor boy almost asked me for *my* autograph."

"I don't know if you should be telling people that so quickly—especially since I was pretty close to *not* working for him just last week. Remember that?"

Ellie pauses before speaking, and when I glance at the screen again I can see she's grinning mischievously at me.

"Who could forget the lemon thyme incident? And the fairytale romance afterward? Speaking of…" she says in heavily insinuating tones.

I laugh a little uneasily.

"It's not a fairytale romance…"

"If you say so. How was the 'real date' with the big boss? Did you even go?"

"Yeah, I went…it was good."

After another moment, Ellie says, "Grr! Come on! Is that it? God, I hope you didn't tease him the way you're teasing me. Where did you end up going? What did you talk about? How did you…end up?"

I shake my head as I finish with the icing and clean my hands, wiping them with a towel as I lean back on the dining table so Ellie can see me properly.

"Well, the place he took me to was this, like, private beach type area at a fancy hotel in Santa Monica—"

"Oh God, seriously? That sounds fantastic."

"It was. I mean, it was beautiful. The ocean, the clean air, the ferris wheel at the pier in the distance. There was this little cabana we had all to ourselves, a waiter bringing us drinks—"

"I'm gonna leave Greg if you keep telling me things like this."

"We swam a little…hung out…talked. You know."

"What did you talk about?"

"I dunno…life. He told me about how he grew up, how he got interested in food."

Ellie tilts her head and looks like she's almost overwhelmed with happiness.

"That sounds so romantic."

"Actually…it was kinda sad. The stuff that's he's gone through. The guy did not have it easy, not by a long shot. He's way more intense than I thought—"

"Intense is sexy."

"—kinda lonely—"

Ellie claps her hands.

"Perfect!"

I laugh.

"You know," she says, wistfully, "I always saw you with a guy like Cole."

"What? A lonely millionaire with a dark past and a bad temper?"

"No! A broody, passionate type. A guy with a bit of attitude. And lots of ambition."

"You could have told me that when I was dating Nick."

"Ugh," Ellie says, rolling her eyes. "He's back living with his parents now, you know."

"That doesn't surprise me. Sometimes I think he was pinning all his hopes on my restaurant being a success—even though he couldn't leave fast enough when it wasn't."

"Forget him. Nick's the past. The future is Cole Chambers."

"Ellie! You haven't even met him!"

"Pfft. I've watched his show a dozen times. I can pretty much recite all his best lines at this point. And you know a man that fine is gonna make some super cute babies."

"Ellie! Enough!"

"Just saying!"

I shake my head and then check the dough, deciding to leave it a little longer.

"I'm not even sure he's into actual relationships, anyway. I mean, I searched for 'Cole Chambers girlfriend' online and it was a who's who of gorgeous Hollywood actresses and famous heiresses. He's probably just looking for a bit of fun, and to be honest, that's all I'm in it for, too."

"Willow," says Ellie, using the big sister tone she reserves for career and relationship advice, "you're *different* than those other girls. You're a great chef too, you have a connection. You literally just told me about how he told you how he grew up—that's not 'fun time' conversation, that's 'getting serious' conversation. Did you…"

"No. Well…we kissed a little but that was it."

Ellie waves her fists in coiled excitement.

"It's happening!"

"No! Ellie, come on! It's just a little fun, don't get any ideas about it being—"

I'm interrupted by the sound of my phone buzzing against the counter.

"What's that?" Ellie says, peering into the camera as if she can look beyond the computer. "Is that him? Well? Is it?"

"Um…" I say, picking up the ringing phone. "I'm gonna call you back in just a second."

"No! Willow!" Ellie says, reaching toward the camera as if she wants to climb out of the screen and stop me. "Let me listen! Please!"

I click off the chat window and answer the phone.

"Willow?" Cole says.

"Speaking," I reply, almost surprising myself with how hearing him compels me to smile.

"How are you?"

"Little tired," I say, checking the dough again, "cooking up a storm. Same as always."

"You should take a break sometime."

"I should. I'll have to check with my boss," I tease.

Cole chuckles warmly.

"Actually, I think he might have something in mind."

His deep voice, even over the phone, feels like music, striking at some deep, primitive urge in me. My skin tingling, an emerging tension that makes me stroke my own neck.

"Oh yeah?"

"Come with me to Vegas for a couple days. I've got most of the distributors lined up but I want to really nail down any problems in the menu; see if there are any gaps, run the cooks through their paces. I'd like a second opinion, a second pair of eyes, and since Martin is busy finding new chef candidates, I'd like that second opinion to be yours."

"Two consecutive days off work?"

"You'll still be working, make no mistake. We'll cut a few tables at Knife, the crew will manage. And I'll pay you overtime, of course."

I take a moment to think of what to say, mentally performing acrobatics to read between the lines and figure out if it's as professional as he makes it sound.

"I've got to ask…why me? I mean, I've only worked at Knife for a few weeks. Wouldn't one of the other chefs know your style better than I do?"

"You've got good taste," Cole says, without missing a beat. "Plus, you're one of the few people with the balls to tell me when you don't like something. You disagree with me about food, and that's what I want in a second opinion: Criticism. I might not act on it, but it's what I want to hear."

I let another moment drift by, feeling the inevitability of this trip encircle me.

"Can I just ask...is this all business, or…"

Cole laughs again.

"It's absolutely business," he says nonchalantly. Then, in a voice that seems to come from some unresolved urge, from that broad, hard-muscled body, "Until the business is done. After that…well, it's up to you. Though I did only book one suite for us to share…unless you'd prefer your own room. The trip still stands, regardless. I need you there."

"The suite works great," I blurt, understanding the implication, and figuring that I can always book myself a separate room later, if need be—although I can't imagine wanting to…

"Great. We'll leave tomorrow morning."

"So soon? Um…ok. Sure. Should I book a flight, or are we

driving, or—?"

"I've taken care of all the details. Pick you up first thing, say around nine?"

"That's perfect. Looking forward to it."

Cole hangs up, and I stand in the kitchen feeling dazed for a few seconds before remembering that Ellie is probably still waiting in front of her computer. I call her up again and dump the dough onto the counter, ready to roll it out.

Ellie appears on-screen pouting disappointedly. It doesn't last long, though.

"Sorry about that," I say, as I start forming the buns.

"Was it him?" Ellie asks, her pout disappearing in the face of immense curiosity.

I nod.

"Ha! I knew it." Now she's all smiles again. "And what did he say?"

"Uh, not much…just wanted to discuss some business stuff…"

"*Willow…*"

"Fine! He wants to take me to Vegas for a few days to help him with the new restaurant."

Ellie squeals so loud I have to reach over and turn the volume down with flour on my fingers.

"Greg!" she calls off-screen. "Willow's in a relationship with Cole Chambers!"

"I'm not in a relationship!" I plead.

Ellie laughs and looks back at me through the screen.

"Sorry," she says, warmly. "I'm just happy for you. And I just want to see you happy. Not just this Cole thing, but everything else. The job, the Vegas trip. It's great to see you moving on, getting over things not working out in Idaho. You deserve better, and you're capable of so much more. I'm just glad you're finally on the right path."

"Yeah," I say, looking back at her affectionately. "I know."

"And listen, whatever happens with Cole, just enjoy it. Although, I mean…it wouldn't be the worst thing in the world if you fell madly in love with each other and could invite us down to eat at his restaurants for free…but so long as you're enjoying life then who cares what you call it? You do you."

"Thanks, Ellie."

"Look," she says, suddenly hurried. "I'd better get going to pick the girls up from dance class. Greg's cooking his ragu tonight."

"Does he still use parsnip instead of carrot in it?"

Ellie shrugs lovingly.

"You know Greg—he likes what he likes."

"And that's why we like him."

"Ok, call me when you get back from Vegas."

"I will. Say hello to Greg and the girls for me."

We sign off and I finish baking the cinnamon buns, taking a few hot ones piled high with icing straight to my room, still wearing the big smile my sister always leaves me with.

I lay back on the bed, my muscles sinking gratifyingly at finally being able to rest, and let the sugar hit of the cinnamon buns send a gentle buzz through my blood. Then the phone rings again.

I tense up, half-expecting it to be Cole again, but instead see that it's Tony. I drop the bun, put the plate aside, wipe my fingers on a napkin and pick up the phone.

"Hey—"

"They said yes," Tony interrupts.

"What?"

"They said *yes.*"

I sit upright in the bed.

"The investors?"

"The investors. They said yes."

I lick my teeth with my tongue, staring into space as I struggle to process the sudden information.

"What…how…we didn't even—"

"They said they loved us!" Tony crows, and I can hear that he's as stunned as I am still. "And that they think we're onto something. The local food thing, the L.A. twist on classic comfort cuisine, the unique approach—they loved all of it. Most of all, though, they believe in the two of us."

"You're sure?"

"I just got off the phone with them right now. Get this: They said they want to do everything they can to get the restaurant up and running in *ten months*."

"Ten months? That's impossible."

"Nothing's impossible."

"It would take that long just to find a location and lease it."

Tony laughs in amazement.

"Not when one of your investors made his money in real estate."

"Who?"

"Andre. He owns a bunch of locations around L.A. already, and said he could sweep through a lease if we had something in mind. Isn't it *incredible?* Spud! We're gonna open our own restaurant in less than a year!"

He laughs again, and I get up to pace the room, rubbing my brow.

"Tony, hold on. Did they say anything about the actual budget? Finances? Are we talking a taco stand or a two-story eatery here? I mean, what's the catch?"

"There's no catch," Tony says, sounding a little offended now that I'm bringing down his high. "I told you, these guys have so much money they don't even need to think about it."

“Did they actually show us any money? Apart from some rumor you heard from a bartender, they could be con men.”

Tony takes a second to speak again, but I can almost hear his frustration with me in the silence.

“Am I crazy? Or do I get the impression that you aren’t absolutely ecstatic with the prospect of having your own place in Los Angeles? Am I an idiot for thinking you’d actually be happy at this news? This is your dream! Our dream. And it’s finally coming true!”

“I know,” I say, trying hard to sound as enthusiastic as Tony and only making it more obvious I’m not. “I guess it’s just…a lot to take in.”

“Is this about your last restaurant? That’s in the past, Willow. You made some mistakes, yes—but that just means there’s less chance you’ll make them again. Look, I get that it was demoralizing, and traumatic, and humiliating, and probably left you feeling like you were jilted at the altar, or like—”

“Alright, alright,” I interrupt.

“—but this is your chance to rise from the ashes like a phoenix in a chef’s apron! You should be happy you’re getting this second bite of the cherry!”

“I *am* happy—or, I *will* be happy if it actually turns out that way. I just want something more to go on than a promise and a time frame. I’ve only spoken to these guys for twenty minutes. Am I supposed to quit my job and start getting my hopes up based on that? One of us needs to keep our head on straight.”

Tony sighs. “Ok, you want something more concrete? We’re going to check out some locations the day after tomorrow. Let’s see if you’re li’l miss cynical then.”

I let out an apologetic huff as I slump back onto the bed.

“I can’t—not the day after tomorrow, anyway.”

“Why not? Don’t tell me you can’t throw a sick day at work.”

“I’m going to Vegas with Cole. He wants me to help him with his new place.”

This time I can sense Tony’s brain working hard in the silence.

“So that’s it, huh? You’re ditching me for the handsome celebrity. Giving up your lifelong dreams for a hunk with good credit. Straight men are right: You women are awful.”

I laugh and pick my cinnamon bun back up.

“You would do exactly the same thing—and be twice as resolute about it.”

“I know. It’s just the jealousy talking. How long are you gone for?”

“Just a few days. In the meantime, text me pictures if you end up going to look at the locations. When I get back we should all sit together and talk it through. If these guys are for real—and I repeat: *If*—then I’ll be just as excited as you are.”

“Ok, Spud. I’ll see you when you get back from your romantic getaway. Just don’t get married at some drive-thru chapel while you’re there—not if he wants a prenup, anyway.”

“And that’s my cue to say goodbye…”

“Ok, honey. I’ll send you the pictures. *Then* you’ve got some groveling to do, missy.”

CHAPTER THIRTEEN

COLE

Willow's kinda quiet when I pick her up and drive to the airport, as if she's trying to restrain the natural spark that usually makes her blush and bluster in the same sentence. That mixture of self-assured but genuinely warm that I'm starting to think I'm addicted to, replaced by a more formal, clipped kind of tone. I wonder if she's afraid of flying, if I should have just driven us all the way to Vegas instead.

"You nervous?" I say, as the airport looms at the end of the highway.

"No. Not at all," she says, smiling quickly before looking back at the road.

I can tell something's on her mind. Something she doesn't want to talk about. I wonder if it's apprehension over where things are going with us, or simple work/life stress. For now, I'll give her some space to think. I've got something I'm holding back myself.

I park the car and we wheel our bags into the airport, Willow a little taken aback by the fact that I bought us first-class tickets. Over the course of the hour or so flight she opens up a little, relaxes a little, and the shy smiles and sharp comebacks make me start to relish her proximity. Her skinny black jeans brushing against my leg and the elegant chasm of her cleavage that it takes all my willpower not to be caught looking at starts to twist at my groin, as if she's got a hand there, gripping me with the tight magnetism of her beauty.

While my mind starts running wild with enough ideas to fill an entire erotica section, I keep the talk as focused on the business at hand as possible. There will be time for play later, I tell myself.

Once we land in Vegas one of the staff members that Martin's just hired meets us outside baggage claim to take us to the new place.

In the back of the car Willow asks, "Do you have a name for this new restaurant?"

"Not yet," I say. "Though Martin suggested 'Fork,' and it was such a terrible idea that I haven't been able to shake it."

She laughs and turns back to look out the window, as if rewarding me for making her laugh by exposing the perfect line of her neck.

'Fork' is coming along nicely, and when we arrive I take Willow on a little tour.

"The place is incredible," she coos, as we pass by the kitchen, where the chefs are cursing and cooking up a storm. "It might even turn out better than Knife."

"The fittings are all in," I say, sweeping a hand across the kitchen. "Pretty much all that's left is cosmetic. Painting, decorating. Colors, materials—that kind of thing." I gesture for her to return to the main seating area. "I actually wanted to get your opinion about some of that too."

Willow turns to me, the look on her face that same one she gets when she's about to offer an opinion, but instead she stops herself, settling for a simple, functional smile instead.

"Sure," she says.

"First though, let's eat. If you're up for a tour of the menu now?"

"Oh hell yes. A man after my own heart," she teases.

We move back to the main area to sit side-by-side at the large round table in the center—the only table that isn't stacked up against the wall or covered in linen. I pop open a bottle of sparkling water and pour a full glass for each of us.

"So…" Willow says, looking around her as the raucous sound of the chefs' shouting increases, "how is this going to work, exactly?"

"The kitchen will prepare every single item on the menu for us," I say, pulling out my leather-bound notebook and Montblanc pen. "Just the way it would be served to a customer. Course by course. You'll try a bite of each and then tell me what you think. Whatever it is. Don't hold back."

Willow nods confidently.

"Ok. I can do that."

When the plates start coming, Willow transforms. Whatever was on her mind all morning is gone now as that burning passion and wisdom about food starts to show itself. If there's one thing I've learned about her in the short time I've known her, it's that the path to her heart is through her stomach—only it's more like a bullet train than a path.

"Can I see a menu?" she says, after taking a bite of an appetizer salad.

"Sure, I've got a printout right here," I say, pulling the sheets from my briefcase and handing them to her.

She flicks a sheet, sees what she needs to see, then shakes her head.

"Yeah, ok," she says, pointing at the salad. "Maybe this is just me, but I would not use this dressing. The orange zest is overpowering. It's amazing, but if someone orders it and then orders the fish with the mint-roasted potatoes the flavors are going to clash horribly."

It takes only a half second for me to understand what she's getting at, insight so clear I almost kick myself at letting it pass. I scribble down a note as Willow pushes aside the salad to try something else.

"Oh," she says, eyes lidding over with pleasure. "This salmon mousse…"

"You like?" I say, enjoying her expression.

"I *love.*"

"So do I."

She looks at me for a beat, a slight moment of wild, inarticulate tension passing between us, before the presence of the watching waiter and the obligation of the job at hand pull us back to reality.

"You know, maybe a dash of something red to make the color pop. Paprika? Saffron?"

"Slow down," I say, scribbling in my notebook. "You're critiquing faster than I can write. And we've got a long way to go."

Willow doesn't slow down, though, and for the next three hours she runs through ideas, impressions, and opinions that would put a dozen food critics out of business. We argue over the Escoffier sauce, agree completely on the wild game dish, and both teach the other something when it comes time for the eclairs. I go through about seventeen different emotions with her during each course, swinging from offended and contemptuous of her American-style ideas, to marveling at the utter brilliance with which she seems to cut through to the heart of what makes great food.

Tongues alive with the onslaught of flavors and textures, bodies humming with the satisfaction of a thousand different ingredients, minds almost working as one by the time we reach the final dessert, I find myself realizing something very singular: This woman is absolutely incredible.

She slouches back in her chair, hands on her stomach as if it were potbellied and not as perfectly toned as the rest of her, and sighs happily.

"Is that it?" she says.

"That's it," I say, slapping my notebook shut.

"That's a hell of a menu."

"You just made it a hell of a lot better."

She looks at me with a curious smile.

"I doubt you're going to take any of my advice anyway."

"Is that because of a lack of confidence in yourself? Or in me?"

Willow tilts her head slightly.

"In you, of course."

I laugh along with her and check the time.

"We should get going," I say, standing up.

"Aren't we going to talk interior design?" she asks.

"Soon. For now I've got something more important I wanted to show you."

Willow squints at me, trying to decipher my half-smile—and then my phone rings. It's my second in command, so I need to take the call.

"Give me a moment," I say with an apologetic expression, taking out my phone and walking out of earshot. "Hey, Martin."

"Hi, boss. Just wanted to give you an update on the guy I mentioned—the one working at the Italian spot down on Mateo. Now he's pretty happy there, and I'm still not sure he'd move to Vegas, but I honestly think if we make an offer that—"

"Martin, stop," I say firmly. "I've changed my mind."

He doesn't talk for a second, and when he does he sounds completely perplexed.

"What about? I don't understand."

I look back at Willow, sitting and chatting with one of the chefs, making him laugh, the guy looking like he's already as besotted with her as I am.

"I'm gonna do what you suggested; move Michelle up here to Vegas."

"Really? Ok...well...yeah. That's good. But we'll still need to find a replacement for her at Knife."

"We'll need a replacement—but not for the head chef."

"I don't follow."

"I think I'm gonna offer the position to Willow."

There's a pause. "*Willow?* The one I just hired as a line cook?"

"Yeah."

Martin's disbelief sounds like a cough, spluttering for words.

"Cole," he says, his voice taking on a soothing tone as if he's talking me off a ledge, "she's worked there for a couple of weeks. Plus she had hardly any experience before that."

"She's a phenomenal cook," I say, looking back at her again and winking when I catch her eye. "Why would I hire somebody else when one of the best chefs I've ever seen is already working for me? She's got the skills, the training—and she's got instinct. You can't learn that."

"Yes. But…well…she's never been a head chef before. It's one thing to be a great cook, another to lead a whole kitchen. It's a big step. Most people spend years and years—"

"Give her one week and I guarantee you she'll make that kitchen her bitch."

"I don't know," Martin says, and I can almost hear him rubbing his brow. "The crew won't like it. The new girl suddenly being their boss after a couple of weeks, getting a job that any one of them probably feels more qualified to do. Will they take orders from her?"

"I didn't hire them to be advisors."

Martin sighs, and I can tell he's mulling it over. "Leo will probably quit on the spot, you know—I don't think he likes her."

"Good. It'll save me the trouble of firing him."

"Cole…"

"Like I said, I'm only just now thinking about it. I haven't actually made a move yet. We still need to talk to Michelle about Vegas, anyway. So why don't you go ahead and carry on with the shortlist, and we'll talk more when I get back."

"Yeah. Ok."

"Great. See you then."

"Wait!" Martin says, a split second before I hang up. I wait, but all I hear are throat-clearing sounds as Martin struggles to get his thoughts out. "Is this…never mind. Forget it."

"You want to know if this is because I'm fucking her." Martin coughs as if the very idea offends him, but I save him the trouble of protesting. "The answer's no. You should understand where I'm coming from, Martin. Hell, you're the one who hired her. You've seen what she can do in a kitchen."

He lets out a nervous laugh.

"Sure, sure. I know she's good. It's just a question of whether she's good *enough.* I mean, I know you have faith and all, that's obvious, but do you really trust her that much?"

I look back at her again. She's at the bar now, leaning over on it and sipping martinis with the cooks.

"Yeah. I trust her."

I finish up the call with Martin and go over to peel Willow away from the chefs, with whom she's already in so tight you would never guess she'd just met them. We go outside and get into the car, Willow bemused by my eagerness.

"Where are we going now?" she asks.

"It's a surprise."

Twenty minutes later we're pulling up beside a dusty airstrip, the Nevada sun beating down on us. Willow shields her eyes and scans the shimmering horizon.

"What are we doing out here?"

I nod in the other direction, and she suddenly notices the helicopter starting to spin its blades. She looks back at me, grinning like a kid on Christmas, and I put a hand on the small of her back to hurry her toward the chopper.

"You ever see the Grand Canyon?"

"Not in person," Willow says, almost laughing with surprise.

"It's one of the most majestic places on earth—spiritual. Especially when you see it from the sky."

We duck under the hard pressure of the whipping blades and I open the door for Willow to climb in, getting in after her. The pilot has us buckle up and then lifts us up, spinning away dramatically and making Willow squeal through her overwhelmed smile.

Before long we're swooping through those sunset-gold cliffs, the grandeur around us making us feel insignificant, even at this height. The horizon all around us filled with that ancient landscape, etched and scarred and formed by time, a history written by nature itself.

But even that can't compel me as much as the woman beside me, can't tempt me to peel my eyes from her, can't diminish the magnificence in her face. Unconsciously, our hands find each other's, fingers interlocking, as if they were meant to go together.

The chopper veers and dips, pressing our bodies closer. Willow lets out a sudden laugh and we find ourselves staring at each other, our faces inches apart.

"How did you know?" she asks, the roar of the blades stealing her whisper, but her lips easy to read.

I take a second to think about it, to wonder what it was that made me understand she'd like this. But the answer doesn't come, the feeling something I couldn't put into words. An answer, a meaning, a thought, that I can only give by moving my lips across that unbearable distance to hers and kissing her with everything I have.

CHAPTER FOURTEEN

WILLOW

I wake up to the sound of running shower water, light and echoey in the massive suite. A gentle aroma of tea tree oil shower gel tickling my nose and making me roll between the soft, rustling sheets onto my side. I open my eyes to the large, open plan hotel room, the clear window letting in a cool morning light, the messy king bed, and the hazy memory of all the things Cole and I did to each other last night, the scenes flooding back to me in vivid detail.

More than anything else, though, it's the tender sensitivity of my naked body, my insides still humming, vibrating on some satisfying frequency, as if still bearing the impression of his cock, that reminds me.

We'd stumbled back up to the room from the hotel bar, where we spent the last few hours of the evening eye-fucking each other while talking about the perfect way a chocolate gateau needs to crumble, the most sensuous texture for its filling to be. Using words like 'melt' and 'tight' and 'full' until the words seemed to lose all their original meaning, and the truth of our thoughts were only thinly veiled. Then, half-arguing over whether the garlic in puttanesca should be sliced or crushed, we left the bar. A mixture of alcohol, lust, the musical rhythm with which we talked, the liberation of being in this new place, this luxurious hotel, all finally coming to an inevitable conclusion.

He kissed me in the elevator, and I danced out of his grip when the doors opened on our floor, the low rumble of his teased pride music to my ears. It must have taken us twenty minutes to make the thirty paces to our room, Cole's hands finding my body again and again, pulling me into kisses so good I almost achieved vertigo, until he pulled away breathlessly and said we'd better get somewhere we wouldn't be caught by security cameras or gawked at by other guests.

Inside the massive suite he slammed the door behind him, leaving all his restraint on the other side, turning into a sex-god beast. And I let go of modesty, gave myself to the hunger of his hot mouth on my neck, the insatiable grip of his hands spreading my thighs wide open, the relentless stroking of his rock-hard cock pounding deep inside me, never having been so aware of my own body as when he made me the object of his ravenous appetite. Clawing at the rug in dizzying rapture, pressed against the window as if Cole wanted the world to see him taking me, bent over the bed gasping for breath, watching his torso in the mirror as he thrust back and forth, faster and faster, groaning as his fingers dug into my hips and he slammed into me from behind like a force of nature.

"Fuck me, fuck me, fuck me," I panted, out of my mind with the need to feel every inch of him inside me.

"Say please," he commanded, tugging my ponytail so hard that my head tilted back to stare up at the ceiling.

"Please."

He smacked my ass and I yelped at the sting.

"Louder," he growled.

"Please, Cole. Please fuck me." I couldn't believe the words that were coming out of my mouth. I had never been like that with a guy before. And I loved it.

Just when I thought I couldn't take any more, he rolled me over onto my back and pushed my knees up over my head with one hand, driving himself so deep into me I yelled out loud. He didn't let up, not for a second.

I came moments later, and then he did, so intense it was like an out of body experience, our moans sounding like they were coming from someplace far away as the earth-shattering shockwaves radiated through us.

The memories have me so hot all over again that I don't think I can stay in this bed by myself a minute longer.

As I get up and stretch, I look over at the chair by the chest of drawers to find my clothes folded neatly. I smile. *So Cole.* I can imagine him picking up the clothes carefully from the floor, where they'd been discarded with all the glee of Christmas wrapping paper the night before, and carefully folding them away in that precise way of his.

The intense, lush memories of carnality give way to something else now, something warmer, more intimate than even sex. The articulate and determined way he talks about food to me, as if I were an equal rather than his employee, the way he respects my opinion, even if we disagree, arguing as if it genuinely matters to him what I think. I remember the way he opened up to me at the beach, exposing his wounds and trusting me to treat them carefully.

In this hotel room, listening to the sound of hot water against his body, I realize that he's not just my hot boss anymore. No longer just a beautiful man with whom I share some physical connection. Irresistible lust, uncontrollable hungers, and alluring seductions might have led us so far, but now there's more to it. Something meaningful. And I know from experience that sex isn't that good unless there's something deeper going on.

I pad over to the window, still naked, and admire the view, the cool blue light picking out the edges of a few clouds. The sparkling city of Las Vegas empty and asleep still, dormant and recuperating until the neon will be ignited and lead thousands of people to its lavish enchantments once again.

The nagging thought that I managed to ignore throughout yesterday and last night emerges again in the clarity of the moment. *Maybe I should tell Cole about Tony and our restaurant?* Maybe he'll actually be happy for me. Maybe he'll understand that I've got too many ideas of my own to cook for anybody else—except no. Every time I try to visualize the moment I tell him, I can't imagine him smiling with happiness. His story about being betrayed by his closest friend, the way he confessed he doesn't trust anybody, the fact that I was the first chef he allowed Martin to hire for him…I can only imagine that face going as hard and as cold as it did when he pulled me out of the kitchen the first time we met.

Besides, I'm sure the new place isn't going anywhere anytime soon, no matter how enthusiastic and optimistic Tony is about it. Nobody gets to just start their own restaurant based on a single investor's meeting with some random guys they know nothing about. There's no reason to stir things up just yet. I have a little more time to enjoy this thing with Cole, whatever *this* is.

I move through the suite to the bathroom, find the door ajar, and push it aside. Cole's shadow plays behind the frosted glass like a kabuki show. Even in the hazy shadow the broadness of his arms as he scrubs his hair can be seen, the sculpted 'V' of his torso impossibly mouthwatering.

Now that I'm this close I can hear him hum, out of tune, some Rolling Stones song that I can't quite remember, but he does it with such conviction I can't help finding it funny. I lean up against the doorway and enjoy the show a little, until he pulls off what I think is meant to be a dance move and my quick giggle gives me away.

"Hey!" he says in surprise, sliding the shower door aside and looking at me through the steam. "How long you been standing there?"

"Long enough to know never to go to karaoke with you."

"Is that so?" Cole flicks water from his eyes and reaches out, pulling me by the hand under the hot stream. I shriek playfully and find myself pressed up against him, the water rolling down our faces as I look up at him.

"Maybe we could duet," I grin.

"I'm counting on it."

"I'll bet you are."

Our wet lips crash together, as fluid as the water. His body hot and pumped against my sleep-cooled blood. We press our skin together, like two slow dancers in the hot rain, until I feel his desire rise, pressing between my thighs.

"Waiting for you to wake up has been the hardest part of my day so far," he murmurs into my ear.

"Well this has been the hardest part of mine," I whisper back, wrapping my hand around his cock, my insides turning hot and liquid as he groans in my ear.

"Turn around and put your hands on the wall," he commands. "It's about to get a lot harder."

When I arrive back in front of my apartment in L.A., in the middle of the night, even the small carry-on bag I took with me feels like it's full of bricks. I don't know whether it was the workload, the late flight (we missed the early one, in a post-coital slumber so deep we slept through both of our alarms), or the fact that we must have worked through half the kama sutra, but I'm shattered when I mount the steps and push open the door to my apartment.

I hear Asha's thumping feet before I've even shut the door.

"Oooh!" she says, emerging from her room in a bathrobe to hug me tightly before pulling back. "Girl, I missed you!"

"I've only been gone for two days."

"Sure, but I had a craving for pecan pie last night that drove me crazy."

I stop while Asha steps back and studies me carefully from head to toe, meeting my gaze again with a raised eyebrow.

"Mm-hm," she says as if confirming something.

"What?" I say, looking down at my jeans and T-shirt.

"Girl, you look like you've been fucked, fed, and flexed."

I laugh a little tiredly.

"What?"

"I was gonna ask if it was a good time—but I can see by your face that it was. That little rosy color in your cheeks, that little sass you have now when you stand. You look about five years younger and I *know* that's not what a work trip is supposed to do."

"Um…yeah," I say, shrugging with a little embarrassment, a little blush at being reminded of the 'work trip.' "I guess you're right."

Asha laughs eagerly and takes my bag while I move into the living room and let my tired body fall onto a seat.

"Thanks," I say, as Asha returns from the kitchen and hands me a bottle of water, almost licking her lips with anticipation before sitting on the couch, directing her entire body in my direction, unwilling to miss a word.

"So?" she says. "Go on. How was it?"

I take a deep sip of water and look up at the wall as I try to find the words, a decent point to start at.

"It was…*fantastic.*"

"Oooh!" Asha squeals, tucking her feet up under her and leaning toward me even more eagerly.

"I mean, it's hard to believe that it was only two days. It feels like we've just spent a month together. I…it was just…really great."

"Wow…" Asha says, smiling warmly.

"I mean the restaurant is amazing, the food he's planning is incredible, and it was really awesome helping him decide on—"

"Pffft! I don't wanna hear about the work! I wanna hear about you two! Did you…"

"Yeah, we did," I say after a little pause. "In the hotel suite, on the floor, in the shower." Asha's eyes widen. "In the back of the new space, the public bathroom of this classy bar…"

"Whoa," Asha says, fanning herself a little. "Did you even get a chance to *talk?"*

"Oh yeah. We talked about everything. Food, ourselves, what we want out of life…"

Well, I mostly told Cole what I wanted out of life—leaving out a few key details when I mentioned my 'future' dream restaurant. I trail off into silence and start chewing my lower lip as the nagging reminder of Tony's recent hustling and our maybe-possibly-but-probably-*not*-about-to-happen restaurant comes flashing into my brain. There's no way it's going to happen. Not this soon. But if it did, and I kept it from Cole this whole time…no. I can't afford to think that way. The chances of it all coming together so fast are basically nil.

Asha shakes her head and smiles as she throws herself back on the couch.

"What a whirlwind. That sounds so romantic."

"It was. Kinda," I say, staring into the distance as I recall all those conversations again, tapping into what I actually feel as if I'm in confession. "He's different than what I thought. I mean he's exactly like you'd suspect: Confident, meticulous, kinda stubborn, but…there's more to him. He can be really sweet. Like at lunch today, he switched our desserts because I tried his and liked it more. And I noticed that whenever I would talk about food his eyes would linger on me for a second before he spoke—as if he was really, genuinely thinking about what I'd said. Most guys just glaze over when I start talking about food. I mean I know Cole's a chef too, but it's really nice to have someone just…get it."

When I finish talking I turn to Asha and see that she's got a knowing grin on her face.

"What?" I say.

"You're falling for him. Hard."

"No!"

"You are, Willow. I'm not blind. You sound a high-schooler talking about the MVP of the basketball team."

I look down, unable to really deny it.

"Is it that obvious?"

"Pretty much," Asha smiles.

After a little silence I take a long drink of water and sigh deeply.

"I'm just on a high from the trip, it'll probably pass as soon as I'm back at work—*real* work."

Asha frowns and sits up. "Why are you so intent on not having fun?"

"What do you mean?"

"I mean that you're seeing a guy who's incredibly hot, rich, and—according to you—pretty charismatic, not to mention fantastic in bed, but you act like you wish you were single again."

"It's not that…I just don't want to delude myself. I've been burned before—not just by men, but by being optimistic, expecting things to work out, hoping for the best. I don't want to let my emotions out and suddenly find them being trampled on. This could be nothing, you know? Just fooling around. I don't want to go thinking that it means something when I don't know if it actually does."

Asha sighs, and I can't tell if she's feeling pitiful or unconvinced.

"The guy just took you on a two day trip to a fancy hotel in Vegas so that you could help him with his new business and screw you silly. And before that he took you to a private beach spot and opened up about his deep, dark past. He's giving you everything he's got. What more of a sign do you want, girl? Are you still gonna be calling it 'nothing' when he proposes?"

I laugh nervously, half imagining Cole on one knee before quickly pushing the image away. "Everybody and their grandma knows Cole Chambers likes sex—and like I said, he spent a hell of a time getting it while we were away. Maybe that's all he wanted? Maybe that's all I am to him? A business trip where he can get a decent second opinion while getting his rocks off at the same time."

Asha's expression is dismissive now, and I can tell she's losing patience, though she's sweet enough to keep trying.

"Quit asking what *you* are to him and ask yourself what *he* is to you. Didn't you ask him at any point how he felt? About what exactly you two had between you?"

I shrug, feeling naïve as I do so.

"It seems kind of quick to be asking. Do people really do that?"

"*I* do," Asha says, swinging her head as she says it, and emphasizing the words in an almost musical way. "See: Men love it when you don't know where you stand. *Especially* men like Cole Chambers. They're like predators. It's all good when they're hunting you down, got you in their sights, doing everything they damned well can to get your panties off, but once they finally do, they don't know when to stop playing and decide to commit."

Asha gets up and nods for me to follow as she moves to her bedroom.

"I don't think it's that simple," I say, as she starts moving around the room. I notice the dress laid out nicely on the bed, the handbag emptied on the dresser.

"Of course it's that simple," Asha says as she peels off the bathrobe to reveal her underwear, and checks her body in the mirror before pulling her braids back to clip them. "You know, Cole might be waiting for some sign from *you* that this is more than just sex."

"I doubt it," I say, as I sit on the edge of her bed. "Cole doesn't wait for anything, pretty much."

"Well you need to ask him outright what's going on, what he wants, and make damned sure he's on the same page as you."

"You make it sound so easy…hey, where are you going?"

Asha smiles as she peels her dress from the bed and holds it out in front of her.

"I don't just talk a good game," she says, winking. "I've got a date with a heart surgeon who's been turning up to my classes for a couple of months now, chatting me up after class—although he's already got the body of a middle-weight." Asha pauses to delicately zip up her dress and check herself in the mirror again. "I've spent the whole week driving him crazy with sexy pictures, and I figured it's about time both of us got what we wanted."

"Lucky guy."

"*If* he plays his cards right. What do you think of this perfume?"

I watch (and occasionally help) Asha get herself ready, enjoying the sight of her confident, well-practiced routine. In a funny kind of way, nothing has felt more 'L.A.' than what Asha's getting herself into; two confident people who know what they want, going for it no holds barred, and no doubt getting it. It's a long way from my teenage experiences, wearing my lucky pair of faded jeans to go out with guys in shirts that were crisp from underuse. Sipping sodas at a diner where the truck drivers and farmers would grab quick lunches. Maybe parking at that spot in the woods to fool around clumsily. Maybe she's got the right idea. Maybe it is that easy to just put yourself out there.

"Listen, honey," Asha says when she's finished dressing, putting her hands on my shoulders so that she can look me in the eye sincerely.

"I know it's cheesy but you've got to follow your heart. Your head will stop you from doing anything, and your body will make you do things you regret—but your heart will always lead you to happiness—even if the path there is a little bumpy."

I smile, suddenly feeling a warmth in my chest and a little flicker in my eyes.

"I'm a chef. I know how good a little cheese can be. Thanks, Asha."

She pats my cheek gently, grabs her bag from the bed, then walks out of the apartment with an elegance and speed that's incredible for the height of her heels.

I go to my room to get ready for bed, head still spinning from everything.

Maybe Asha's right, maybe I should forget the things that keep walling off my feelings. Maybe I should forget Cole's reputation, the fact that he's my boss, the unlikely possibility that I may have to tell him I might be leaving soon to start my own restaurant. Maybe I should quit telling myself that the sex between us is just too good to pass up, that it's only his body making me go weak, that it's just lust and desire drawing me back to him again and again.

Maybe I should let go of the way Nick used and hurt me, release the restricting chains of the past that keep me from dipping more than a toe in the future.

Maybe I should just admit it: I'm falling in love with Cole.

CHAPTER FIFTEEN

COLE

I'd never heard of puppy chow before Willow mentioned it while talking about comfort food, her hand going to her chest and her eyes closing over that half-smile the way she does when she talks about something she really loves. The satisfied look imprinting the words on my memory, a detail I knew it would be smart to remember. One of the many details I learned on our trip to Vegas, along with the almost-imperceptible freckles across her nose, the birthmark behind her left thigh, the ever-so-slightly odd way she pronounced the word 'aromatic.'

I had to look up what the dessert even was: Chex cereal mixed with melted chocolate and peanut butter, powdered with a layer of confectioner's sugar. It made me smile, thinking of the chef for whom no béarnaise sauce was quite good enough, having an affection for sugar-coated cereal. It felt like both another page revealed in that complex character, and another mystery to unfold.

I wondered who had made it for her during her childhood that she loved it so, whether it was the mom she missed, or some beloved grandparent or aunt she had stayed with on weekends. I wondered if that simple snack reminded her of something, of late nights watching movies with her sister, perhaps, or of being treated after doing her chores. Maybe it had been comfort food for the sake of emotional comfort, an easily made sugar hit that dulled the pain of some sad event, a comforting sweetness when she wanted to wallow in self-doubt. A food like that had to have some emotion behind it, some memory, and I wanted to know, to understand, so that I might get even closer to her.

That's why I decided to make it for her as a surprise—if only to see that half-smile again.

It's late when I get home, around nine, carrying a grocery bag of cereal and the other ingredients. Willow would be at her shift now, so I leave her a text asking her to come over when she's done. It wouldn't surprise me if she said no—nobody understands better than I do the need to rest after a hard shift in a place like Knife, plus it's only been a couple of days since we spent every waking second within grabbing distance of each. But she texts me back just a short while later.

Sure. But I'll smell like the kitchen.

I feel a rush inside of me, lust already stirring at the answer, then quickly type back.

You can shower here.

Her reply is quick.

I'll bet I can.

I spend the next few hours tidying up—not that the place is messy, but more for something to do with the sense of unfulfilled action tingling in my muscles. I rush order a few flowers to soften the man-cave look of the vast apartment, put some chairs out by the pool, in the perfect spot to look over the city, and spend way too long trying to figure out what kind of drink might go with puppy chow.

Then, I poor myself a glass of whiskey and try to relax.

Around midnight I open the door to a surprised-looking Willow and try to hold back the smile that seeing her brings out of me.

"Hey," I say, pulling her toward me for a kiss. When she pulls away her eyes are still wide and shocked. "You ok?"

"Yeah..." she says, looking around. "I just...I thought I had the wrong house. I thought maybe this was a modern art museum or something. This place is *huge."*

I laugh gently as I close the door behind her.

"You should see the one in Spain. Come on," I say, putting a hand on the small of her back, a little closer to her ass than it needs to be, "I'll give you the tour."

For the next fifteen minutes I lead her around the house, giving her the backstory to the artworks that adorn the walls, the different reasons I love each of my sports cars, talking her through the custom designs of each handmade piece of furniture. Willow coos and smiles throughout like a kid in a candy factory. Usually I take a little pride in showing things like this, the things I've worked for all my life. It satisfies my ego. But this might be the first time I'm showing these things simply to make Willow smile, simply because that face she makes where her lips part and her eyebrows go up to show she's impressed is impossibly cute.

"Why are those shutters curved like that?" she asks when we're in the dining room.

"Oh, well see, this is the western side of the building. The thing about California evening light is that it has this really precise, clear quality, coming from over the Pacific. So when you have straight shutters it kinda cuts through in a really direct, harsh way, and I was concerned the house would be too angular as it is, so I had these shutters custom-made with a slight bend and rough edges to make it more—why are you looking at me like that?"

Willow laughs a little and shakes her head.

"I know how you are in a kitchen, but I didn't realize you were that particular about *everything*."

I laugh as I move my hands around her waist, pulling her toward me a little to look right into the brown swirls of her eyes.

"I just know exactly what I want," I say, staring as deeply into her as I can.

She blushes a little before glancing down.

"Well, I kinda feel like a mess, standing here in my dirty work clothes surrounded by all this engineered perfection."

"If you're a mess, you're a beautiful mess. The kind of beautiful mess a guy like me needs," I say, before taking a long, slow kiss from those rose petal lips. When we break apart her expression is soft, tender, and I can tell her mind is working overtime to try and read between the lines of what I just said. I decide not to let her dwell on it. "Come on," I say, taking her hand, "I've got a surprise for you."

I lead her back through the house, her curious pleas only making my playful expression more gratified, until we're out at the pool. Willow scans the skyline, the glowing blue of the water against the darkness of the night, until eventually she sees it and half-gasps.

"You cooked for me?" she says, as I lead her to the small table at the edge of the railing, beyond which the drop of the Hollywood Hills merges with the twinkling city lights.

"Not sure you would call it cooking," I say, flaming her curiosity even more.

I pull out a chair and she sits down, eyes focusing on the silver dish cover as if she might see through it if she concentrates hard enough. I light the candles I set out and then make an elaborate gesture of putting my hand on the bell, enjoying her eager anticipation one last time before pulling it away dramatically.

"Oh!" she squeals, mouth opening wide with delighted disbelief. "*Puppy chow!* Are you kidding me? This is the best!"

I shrug nonchalantly and sit on the chair beside her, facing the skyline.

"How did you know?" she asks, surprise turning to bemusement. "I mean…I never told you…"

"You mentioned it while we were in Vegas—offhand, but you mentioned it," I say, still enjoying the wonder in her face.

She pulls the bowl near, taking in the smell a little like it's a gourmet broth, then delicately takes one and puts in her mouth, finally showing me what I wanted to see all the while I was making it. That semi-orgasmic, almost spiritually satisfied look she gets when she's tasting food she likes.

"Oh my God…" she says, chewing slowly. "You have no idea how good this is; how many feelings this brings back. Did you try it yourself?"

She picks another up and holds it out for me. As I take it from her fingers and pop it into my mouth I nod, unconvincingly.

"It's…um…yeah."

Willow laughs.

"God…I can't believe the Michelin-starred chef Cole Chambers just made me puppy chow."

I laugh along with her and put my arm on the back of her chair, hand on the soft curve of her shoulder. "I wasn't sure what we should drink with it," I say, drawing the cooler beside the table closer to us. "Is beer ok?"

"Beer's great," Willow says, as I twist the top off a bottle and hand her one.

I grab another bite of the food and open a bottle for myself, turning my gaze out to the cityscape and feeling my soul fill at having Willow beside me.

"So how was your shift?"

Willow finishes swallowing and tilts her head.

"It was good. Hell of a crowd tonight, and apparently the highest tip count this month. Although we did get somebody sending back the gazpacho soup because it was cold."

I laugh and say, "Been a while since that happened."

"I think Leo still hates me, the Basque burgers are selling great, and the success of escargots continues to confuse the hell out of me even though..." Willow trails off, then turns to me, her face a little anxious now. "Listen, Cole...I know this is probably awkward, and sudden, and maybe kinda...soon. And maybe your head isn't in the same place as mine, or you feel like it's not the right time, or...I don't know. But I just...can I ask you something?"

For a moment my stomach lurches, like my body is already expecting the worst. Is she quitting Knife? Did she get offered a job at another restaurant, or something back home in Idaho where her family is? Or did Leo say something awful to her at work today? If he did, I'll fire his ass so fast it'll make his head spin. My fist involuntarily clenches and I have to work to relax my hand, clearing my throat and forcing my expression to remain calm.

"Of course," I say, keeping my voice neutral despite the turmoil I'm feeling inside. "What's up?"

Willow drops her eyes for a moment, then looks back up and focuses her gaze on mine. "I just...I'd like to know...what *are* we? I mean, maybe it's crazy of me to say that considering how long we've been seeing each other, or whatever it is we're doing. But, the puppy chow, Vegas, all the time you seem to want to spend together...I don't know. Am I reading too much into this? I'm a little bad at interpreting the signals when it comes to men."

I watch her a moment, then angle myself a little more toward her, lifting a palm to press against her cheek.

"Remember that first night we went out together?" I say. "Our 'business meeting'?"

Willow looks aside, a little embarrassed.

"Every time I prep a Basque burger."

I laugh gently.

"I mean when we were still at the concept bar, talking. Remember what I told you the secrets of great food were?"

"Sure," Willow says, looking up a little as she tries to recall. "Make it look good, make people pay a lot for it, and make people want more."

"Well, I missed something. I didn't tell you that those secrets can also be applied to great sex, too."

Willow stares at me as if I'm crazy for a second. "Pardon?"

"Think about it," I continue, "Looking good, making someone chase a little, leaving them with just enough that they don't regret it...except you disagreed with me. You said that it had to mean something, that there was more to it than superficial pleasures, that for it to be truly great it had to satisfy. I mean, I know you weren't talking about sex, about relationships, but to me there's always been a thin line between food and love. And you've convinced me. On both counts."

"I..." Willow says, breathing deeply as she's overwhelmed. "I don't even know what to make of that."

I take her hands in mine.

"I've spent my life eating fine foods—even this past week I must have had a dozen meals that cost a fortune and tasted like heaven. But ever since then, what I've craved more than anything are those burgers you cooked. I mean, they're good, don't get me wrong, but it's the fact that *you* made them for me, and with such passion. What just thinking about them makes me feel. Same as this puppy chow right here does for you," I say, grabbing one and popping it in my mouth, Willow's lips turning up at my words. "It's this simple: What I really want is you."

We look at each other in the night, the turquoise glow of the swimming pool casting lines of light across her face, accentuating the soft curve of her cheek until it almost aches for me to see how beautiful she is. Her eyes lock onto mine, as if seeing something new for the first time, and her smile answers me before her voice does.

"I really want you too."

Our faces move closer, so slowly it's almost imperceptible, close enough for me to see those freckles in the dark—as if kept secret just for me—close enough to smell the sweet cocoa on her breath, close enough to feel the air crackle with the electricity between us…

Then a piercing xylophone tune breaks the magic. Willow pulls her head back, startled and frustrated as she pulls her phone from her pocket.

"Sorry," she says, shaking her head as she checks her phone. "Just a friend."

I shrug easily and grab my beer again while Willow mutes her phone and puts it aside. She smiles apologetically, brushes a strand of hair over her ear, then takes more puppy chow. That electric moment has dissipated, but the tension between is now replaced by something calm and relaxed, something that feels solidly connected in the best way possible.

"How are things going in Vegas?" she asks. "Did you—"

She cuts herself off when the phone vibrates loudly on the metal table.

"I'm so sorry, I thought I put this on silent," she says, flicking through her phone a little more, then setting it down again.

"It's going well. I took your advice about the indoor herb garden —though I still don't know if it's really the right choice."

Willow shakes her head with a grin. "It's the only choice—that's the problem when you have a restaurant in the middle of a desert. It's either the indoor garden or coordinating bi-weekly delivery of fresh herbs from around the country along with the rest of the—"

She stops again, noticing my eyes going to the bright light of her phone.

"Maybe you should take that," I say. "Seems like it might be important."

Willow anxiously looks at the phone, then back at me.

"Do you mind? I'm sorry. This timing sucks."

"Please. Go ahead."

She takes the phone and disappears into the house, and I turn toward the city lights. When Willow returns about fifteen minutes later, she almost clatters the chair over as she tries to pull it out.

"Whoa," I say, helping her steady the chair and watching her sit, stiff and straight on it. "Everything ok? You look a little…"

"I'm great! Everything's great…absolutely," she says quickly, tucking her hair behind her ear rapidly. Her smile looks a little forced now, disappearing as she grabs at her beer like it's a life raft. She drains it quickly, and then pulls the bottle away from her mouth, gasping for breath.

I watch her for a second, her cheeks flushing a little. "Another?" I suggest.

She nods eagerly and I pop another open for her.

"You sure everything's ok?" I ask.

"Of course!" Willow says, before taking a long drink of her beer. She waves at the air. "It was nobody. Just a friend. Tony. He's gay."

I smile at the notion she might think I'm jealous of a male friend.

"Cool," I say, nodding at the puppy chow. "How's he doing? Long time no talk?"

Willow takes one quickly and starts talking, as if uncomfortable with the silence now.

"Um. It's just…it was nothing. He's just worried about…something," she says, rubbing her cheek as she speaks. "He wants me to meet up with him tomorrow morning, to talk. I guess."

I put a hand on her leg.

"Well I'll make sure I wake you up early enough, then."

Willow lets out a short, awkward laugh, and struggles to meet my eye.

"Actually, I should be getting home now. I have some things I need to take care of." She stands up. "Nothing to do with you, with *this.* I mean this was amazing, really. The house, the puppy chow… everything. Thank you so much. Sorry I have to run."

"No, it's fine," I say, standing up with her. She still seems skittish, and I put a reassuring hand on her shoulder. "You sure you don't want to talk about it? You look kinda spooked. Maybe it's something I can help with?"

Her forced smile is a little more sincere now.

"Thanks, but no. It's just…a Tony thing. Anyway, I'll be fine. Let's do something again soon, okay? And I promise I'll have this all sorted out by then."

"Hey," I say, lifting her chin to me. "Stuff happens. You think I don't know that? And you don't have to take a burden all on yourself. I'm here."

Willow looks at me, less jittery now, melting a bit in the honesty of what I'm saying.

She nods at me and says, "I know. I know you are. It's just that this is about—"

"Tony—yeah, I got that."

She laughs a little, and so do I, the awkwardness melting away.

"I'm sorry," she says. "It's just a me and Tony thing, I guess."

"Stop apologizing," I soothe, bringing her face to mine for a soft kiss. "I've waited long enough to find you. I can wait another day."

CHAPTER SIXTEEN

WILLOW

If comedy is all timing, then life has a hell of a sense of humor. There must have been all of two seconds between Cole telling me that he wants me, and Tony beginning his phone assault to tell me his big news. News that even now, in the back of this cab, after confirming it with him multiple times, I still can't quite believe.

The money is in the bank.

Not 'on its way.' Not 'they'll get it when we need it.' Not 'available in asset form.' But there, in cash, sitting in the business bank account that Tony set up and gave me access to while I was still laughing off the whole thing as a pipe dream. And it's not small change, either. It's a six figure number I'd be happy to retire with.

I still can't get my head around it, despite Tony sending me multiple screenshots of the account balance, as well as a video of him screaming 'we're rich, baby!' with the screen of his computer in the background.

I take a deep breath, watching the streetlights pass by, and try to grasp onto at least one of the exploding thoughts in my mind, until I give in and just call Tony.

"Hey!" he answers instantly, his voice almost accusing. "Are you done satisfying every need your celebrity boyfriend has?"

"He's—" I stop myself before saying that he isn't my boyfriend, and instead say, "he's not here now. Tell me again: What exactly did Andre and Lou say?"

"They said: Here's enough money to start a drug cartel, now go build the most fabulous eatery in America and make all of our dreams come true."

"*Tony.*"

"Ok," he says, his voice lowering a semi-octave as he gets serious. "It's an equity deal. And I negotiated us some pretty fucking good terms if I say so myself. We get full control."

"Full control?"

"*Everything.* The menu, the interior design, the location. It's all up to us. All they want are free meals and to see us sustainable after the first year. Then they start taking their money back along with a percentage off the back end once we're all paid up."

"Did you sign anything?" I say, fumbling the tip to the cab driver and getting out.

"Yes, I did. And you need to sign your part still. I feel like it's just my ass on the line so far, and I have to tell you, Willow, it's getting a little scary how reluctant you are about this."

"I'm sorry," I say, slamming the cab door shut and hanging out on the corner to finish the call. "I'll sign. It's just…I don't know. It's a lot happening all at once."

"I get it," Tony says, sympathetically. "Business isn't your thing, but soon you'll be in your element, picking staff, building a menu, cooking up a storm."

Even those simple, insinuating words send streaks of excitement through me. To be in charge of my own menu again, my own kitchen. To have carte blanche to put everything I know to be true into practice again—only this time it won't be at the end of a dirt road in the middle of nowhere, it'll be in Los Angeles.

"Believe me when I say that I don't want anything more than that."

Tony lets out a soft chuckle. "I know. Anyway, did you look at the pictures of the locations I sent you?"

"Yeah..."

"And?"

I sigh a little before saying, "Well, I think I know why they don't get Ansel Adams to do rental ads."

"What are you talking about? The pics were beautiful."

"Right, *too* beautiful. I need more than close-ups of wall skirting with wonderful bokeh, or artful pictures of ceiling beams emerging from shadows. I mean, don't get me wrong, I'd hang those pictures on my wall, but I still have no idea what the places you visited are actually like, Tony."

"Hmph," Tony grunts, sassily. "Well, you'll come with us tomorrow and see for yourself, right?"

"Sure," I say, suppressing the guilt and worry that keep trying to rise in my voice. "I'm all in."

"Perfect. We'll see you first thing."

After we hang up, I find myself practically running into my apartment, making a beeline for the kitchen where I get to work whipping up a few dozen fruit tarts to distract myself from the stress of keeping this all a secret from Cole and anxiety over whether or not this is all actually happening. But even giving in to my sweet tooth and tiring myself out over a hot oven aren't enough to help me fall asleep.

Andre and Tony come to pick me up at six-thirty in the morning, meaning I should have had about five hours of sleep. Unfortunately, I spent all night staring at the ceiling and trying to make sense of the jumbled puzzle that has become my life this past week.

I twisted and turned in bed all night, criticizing myself for thinking this would never happen so soon and getting myself caught in this position. Though to be fair, when you take your chances with both hooking up with your ridiculously good looking celebrity chef boss, and the best friend who promises you a financing miracle to start your dream business, you don't expect both of those long shots to come to fruition. Especially not at the same time.

So at dawn, while the streets are still relatively quiet with the sound of the city sleeping, I descend the stairs of my apartment toward the two well-dressed men standing in front of the Mercedes AMG, and find I'm completely wired and nervous from a lack of sleep and way too much pre-bedtime sugar that's probably still circulating in my system.

I smile at Tony, who bows his head as he plucks his sunglasses from his collar and puts them on. Then I shake hands with Andre, impressed by the excellent cut of his suit. The kind of suit that makes you wonder why any guy would ever wear something else.

"Morning," I say, my voice a little sluggish even though my body's tingling.

"Morning," Andre says, smiling with positivity. "It's good to see you again."

"And you."

"I don't usually enter into business with people I've met only once," he says.

"Well, I guess Tony talks enough for both of us anyway."

Tony jabs me gently in the arm.

"He's certainly filled me in a lot about you," Andre says warmly. "All good things, of course."

I look at Tony and blush a little.

"Well…I love him too. Where's Lou?"

"Oh, he's back in Dallas doing some work. He left me with the fun stuff—speaking of which…"

Andre turns back to the car and reaches in to the open passenger side window, pulling out a leather-bound folder.

"I've got the contract right here," he says, searching within his blazer pocket for a pen, "for you to sign."

"Um, actually," I say, holding up a palm, "maybe we should look at the locations first."

I glance from Andre to Tony, who's glaring at me stonily. Andre keeps the smile, but raises an inquisitive eyebrow.

"I mean, I'm sure the contract is great," I explain quickly, "and I'm sure Tony has done a great job of making it fair and everything but…it's just that if I do sign that contract and we end up struggling to find a location, I'm not sure that….well…"

"*Willow!*" Tony hisses under his breath, as if Andre can't hear him.

"You know, location is just really important," I go on, to both of them now, "and it can be really tough finding the right place. My last restaurant struggled because—"

"*Willow!*" Tony interrupts. "Are you seriously doing this *now?* Do you think that—"

"It's alright," Andre says in a calm, breezy voice, putting a hand on my shoulder. He tosses the contract back into the car. "Look, we want you because of your principles and your knowledge. You're a creative type, and I'll be damned if I become 'the man' forcing you to toe the line."

Tony sighs, his face relaxing as if he just evaded certain death.

"Besides," Andre says, "I'm sure you're gonna love at least one of the places I'm gonna show you today."

"I hope so," I say. "But I'm gonna need some coffee before I can love anything this early in the morning."

After a quick pit stop for the darkest, strongest roast I can find, we get back in the car where Tony's enthusiasm almost feels like a fourth passenger.

"You're gonna love this place," Tony says as we pull up at an address downtown, outside what looks like an abandoned warehouse.

We follow Andre as he wiggles the key into the lock, Tony so excited he's almost skipping around me, then enter the vast space.

Inside, huge pillars support a ceiling of exposed pipes, red brick-work textures the walls, and three floor-to-ceiling windows allow the morning light to cast itself through the dust onto the rubbled floor.

"Isn't this incredible?" Tony says, stepping in front of me. "Doesn't this just scream 'style' to you? It's like Warhol's factory, a place for real creativity to explode. Jesus…" Tony shakes his head in marvel, slapping his palm against one of the pillars. "The things I could do with a canvas like this."

"It's amazing," I say, taking it all in. "But it's too big."

Tony looks at me doubtfully, and Andre raises that eyebrow.

"What do you mean?" Tony says, sounding a little like a child being told Santa doesn't exist. "You could seat three hundred people in here!"

I shake my head.

"How would we be able to serve quality, well-prepared food in those numbers right off the bat when we're still struggling to make a name for ourselves? We'd have to serve Big Macs, and even then we'd probably struggle. And can you imagine what a place this big would feel like during the quiet weekday hours? It would feel like an empty theater."

"So we'll make this part a bar," Tony says, moving toward one corner and gesturing.

He looks at me hopefully, and I look back with a frown.

"It wouldn't work. This place is big enough to house three businesses—and running it would be about as difficult. This could work after a few years, but not right now."

Andre checks the defeat in our faces one more time, then smacks his thigh and begins walking back out the door.

"Bye bye baby," Tony says to the vast, empty space, before I helpfully take his arm and console him away.

After a twenty minute drive to the outskirts of Hollywood, Andre brings us to a busier street, one with plenty of foot traffic. We get out of the car and follow him toward a quaint building between a high-end salon and a shoe store.

"This place was actually a restaurant before it shut down and we picked it up," Andre explains as he searches the ring for the right key. "Some British themed, pub-type place. They actually had the building made for it."

He pushes open the door and we step inside. Andre follows and quickly steps in front of us to carry on the tour.

"Now because this place was a restaurant, it's still got all the connections for the kitchens and stuff—plumbing, electricity, cold storage. We'd have to equip it with our own appliances, of course, but technically there are no big structural changes needed here. You could have this place serving dinners in just a couple of months if you like it."

Andre stops and I feel both of the men's eyes bore into me expectantly. I can almost sense their held breath.

I let out a sigh. "No."

Tony leans toward me, as if he didn't hear me.

"What was that? No?"

"No."

They glance at each other for a second, then look back at me, the silence heavy.

"Is that it?" Tony says. "Just 'no'?"

I shake my head and step forward into the dark space.

"It's…it's awful."

"What's wrong with it?" Tony asks.

"It's…faux European."

Tony frowns and throws up his hands. "Ugh! You always say that and I never know what you mean!"

"I mean that it's another one of those places that just seems ashamed of existing in America. Why is it so dark in here? This is California, for God's sake! I feel like I'm in a basement. And so much dark oak paneling, as if it's scared of being snowed in, and the ceilings are so low…a hobbit would feel claustrophobic walking around! And these *windows!* When was the last time you saw windows like this that weren't in a period drama?"

"Who *cares* about the windows!" Tony says. "What does serving great food have to do with Gothic windows?"

"Everything. The place has to work as a whole, a complete experience. I want to serve food that makes the customers feel energetic and alive—this place will make them feel like they're falling asleep in a Jane Austen novel."

Tony is about to reply but Andre puts a calming hand on his shoulder.

"The lady hath spoken," he says in his good-natured way, and we turn around to trudge back to the car, Tony shooting me the stink eye the entire time.

The third place is a beautiful building in Culver City that I reject before I've even entered as soon as I smell the burning rubber and hear the screeching drill of the garage next door. The fourth is an okay-but-small location in Midtown that I dismiss when I notice that the windows look out upon an eyesore of a government building across the street. Each time the words between me and Tony get more and more terse, while Andre's interventions and peacekeeping become more and more necessary.

When we turn up at the fifth place, a low-ceilinged location tucked behind wildly-unkempt bushes, Tony's beyond caring about decorum.

"So what about this then, Goldilocks?" he says, melodramatically. Opening his arms wide and looking at me as he backs into the center. "What's wrong with this one?"

"The ceilings are too low in this one too," I say, deadpan in the face of his derision. "And the walls seem to be made of paper, you can hear the traffic from the street on all three sides."

Tony snorts derisively, looking at Andre for a second as if for support.

"And the feng shui is wrong," Tony adds sarcastically, "and the air doesn't smell like roses, and you've got a feeling the place is haunted too, I'll bet."

I glare at him and fold my arms.

"You don't have to be a jerk about this, Tony."

"*Me?!* You're the one who's been making us drive all over Los Angeles since—"

"Tony," Andre says, almost habitual now, "let's ease up and—"

"No," Tony interrupts him back. "Andre, can I have a word with Willow? In private?"

Andre stops and glances at me to check if it's ok. I nod that it is, and he shrugs as he steps past us.

"I'll go wait in the car then. Take all the time you need."

Tony waits for him to go, then looks at me, his anger faded now, leaving a deep disappointment in its place.

"Willow..." he says slowly, as if carefully searching for the words. "What's going on? Why don't you want this to happen?"

"Of course I want this to happen."

"I don't think you do," Tony says ruefully. "Ever since I negotiated this investment you've been pulling back. First you don't believe in it enough to commit, then Andre brings the papers and you don't want to sign them, now we're looking at place after place and all you keep saying is no. People would kill for some of the places we've seen."

"Tony," I say softly, moving closer to him, "I just want to do this right. I don't want to do a half-assed job of this. Like you said, this is a one-in-a-million opportunity we've got."

Tony sighs, wringing his hands with exasperation.

"Windows? I mean we're rejecting places because you don't like the windows? We can always put in new windows, at some point."

I shake my head. "If you settle for windows you hate then you'll end up settling for second-rate ingredients from distributors, then you settle for chefs who turn up on time but can't cook for shit, and before you know it you're just another restaurant that people like because it's close and the food is just about edible."

Tony turns away from me and takes a few steps, as if contemplating. After a few seconds he turns back and I can almost see pity in his eyes.

"Cut the crap, Willow. I know exactly what this is about."

"What?"

"It's about *Cole Chambers*," Tony says, shaking his head a little in contempt. "You're in love with him. And now that you're happily banging your celebrity millionaire boss you're afraid to ruin it, so you're jeopardizing our whole venture."

"What?!" I yell so loud that Andre can probably hear me. "That's *insane,* Tony! I mean…maybe that's part of it, but…it's complicated. There's more to it than that."

Tony looks up and smiles sadly again, shaking his head as if my fumbled words are all the evidence he needs to know he's right.

"Look, you're a little bit right," I say, striding toward him to show I'm being direct. "I *am* in love with him."

"I *knew* it!"

"But this is my *dream*," I say, the force of a lifelong wish behind my words now, a direct honesty that even Tony can't look away and deny now. "And even love isn't going to stop me from making it a reality."

Tony and I stare at each other for what feels like both an eternity and a split second, our eyes telling each other far more than any words. Finally, he nods.

"But that also means," I say, once I see that he understands now, "that this place has to be worth it. If I'm gonna betray him…lose him…if I'm gonna get hurt…then this can't just be some restaurant I happen to own—it has to be the place I always wanted it to be, the place *we* always dreamt it would be. Anything less than that, and I'm losing more than I gain."

We stare at each other again, and this time he pulls me toward him for a hug.

"Ugh," he says, and I can hear the feelings blocking in his throat, "I hate it when you get all emotional on me."

"I hate it when you get me emotional."

We break apart and Tony rubs his face, sniffing a little.

"Ok," he says, taking deep breaths. "Let's get back to Andre and try to convince him he didn't invest in a couple of bickering schmucks who can't even find their own assholes."

We leave the building all smiles and walk toward Andre, who's leaning against his car, swiping at his phone. He looks up at us when we draw near, eyebrow raised.

"Everything ok?" he asks.

"Yep," I say. "We're good."

Andre checks both of our expressions, then nods.

"So maybe we should show her the one," Tony says.

"The two-floor?" Andre says.

Tony nods.

"What's 'the one'?" I ask.

"The one that I know you'll love," Tony says, confidently.

I check my watch quickly and shoot him back a pained look.

"Is it far, though? I have to start a shift in, like, thirty minutes."

Tony smiles a little knowingly.

"Oh, that's not a problem. See, the reason I thought you wouldn't want to visit this place is that it's pretty close to Knife. A couple of blocks away."

"Ah…"

"Is that going to be a problem?" Andre asks, looking between us like a third wheel who's out of the loop.

I take a moment to purse my lips, then answer. "No. That's not a problem at all."

We bundle into the car and after another quick ride pull up outside of the property, a two-story corner building set in a larger complex of boutique shops. It's boarded up with plywood currently, torn gig posters hastily stuck to them, and the junction it points to is busy with people, cafes and bookshops and antique stores sharing the other corners and giving the surroundings a local color and vibrancy that was absent at all the other locations.

"This would all be glass, of course," Andre says as we step out of the car toward the skeleton of a building. "All the way up."

"Uh-huh," I nod. I can see it already.

He unlocks the place and we step inside to a decently sized area, the second floor a loft space that runs around the edge, a wide, spiral staircase with ornate railings twisting up to the platform.

"Let me tell you," Andre says again, as he goes into real estate mode, "this place is *hot.* And by hot I mean that I've already had nearly a dozen offers for it. An art curator from NYC wants to make this a gallery, a bunch of brands want to make this a retail clothing store, and you're not the only restauranteurs who've been here either. Do you know Sylvain Thibault?"

"Of course. Sure," Tony and I chorus.

"Well this was going to be his American flagship—but I guess he got sidetracked. Once the windows go in there's gonna be a lot of natural light. Great place to people watch—especially on the second floor—if you like that kinda vibe. And all the Indian laurels on this street make for a decent amount of privacy out front, which will likely appeal to any celebrity clientele. Anyway," Andre says, pointing at a large window that separates the back of the building, "this could be easily converted into an open window to the kitchen area—or just knocked down altogether if you really want to meld the spaces."

"Mm-hmm," I say, lost in thought, imagining what we could do here.

"I'm not gonna lie," Andre says. "This place is expensive. If you guys wanna use this place it's gonna have to be a hell of a business."

"Of course. Show her the back," Tony says keenly. "The outside."

"This way," Andre says, striding away. He unlocks double doors set at the end of a small passage, and pushes them open for us to walk through. The studio-sized space a tangle of overgrown weeds, car junk, a moss-clogged fountain and dumped, weathered furniture.

"It's a mess right now," he says, as we step out onto the rocky space, an ivy-covered brick wall on one side and a window to the kitchen on the other. "Looks smaller than it actually is, due to all this trash, but you could use this for storage or…I don't know. Use your imagination a little and you could even make this a little outside dining area—with a *lot* of work, of course."

I stand there, frozen for a moment, taking it all in as the two men cast their gazes on me again, waiting tensely for a verdict. I'm overwhelmed. The morning sun is shining through some tree branches overhead, casting soft, dappled light all around me. I can smell the ocean not too far away, the air is cool, and birds are chirping nearby.

"Well?" Tony says. "Willow, what do you think? It's great, right? ...Willow? ... Are you *crying?*"

I cover my mouth with my hand, but it can't stop the built-up emotion that threatens to explode in wet tears from my eyes.

"This is it..." I say, voice shaking and slow from overpowering sensations. "This is my restaurant...I'm here...I'm really here."

Tony looks quickly at Andre, then back at me before shouting out and grasping me in a tight bear hug. Andre laughs and comes to join us, until the two men are smothering me in a sandwich of fine fabrics and cologne. Squeezing me so hard I can barely breathe, though I don't care anymore—because I'm already in heaven.

The shift I put in after I sign the contract for Andre is probably the most difficult one I've ever done. I cut my finger chopping shallots, almost ruin a filet, and take twice as long to plate the dishes as I usually do. For the next few days I can't think of anything but color schemes, kitchen layouts, renovating that back garden—all the things I said I would do if I ever owned a place, the mental recipes I've spent my life concocting.

The excitement and nerves swirl inside of me like a perpetual hurricane, keeping me awake at night and daydreaming all day, every fiber, every pore of my body entirely taken over by the task of making this fantasy become a reality. The future stretching out ahead of me now like some magical, winding path that I want to run down.

It's almost enough to make me feel better about Cole. *Almost.*

At first I avoid him, citing a lack of sleep, feeling overwhelmed at work, a few personal tasks I have to take care of. Hoping that maybe, given enough time, I'll somehow figure out what to do about us. It helps that Cole spends the next couple of days handling business in Vegas, which is a relief for me, though I still feel waves of guilt slam into me every time we exchange flirty texts late at night.

Eventually, however, sordid text messages aren't enough to keep that kind of appetite satiated, and I arrive home one day to find Cole standing by his Maserati outside my apartment. He grins when he sees me, opening his arms wide, and I feel a different emotion flooding me when I fall into his embrace. It's so much harder to ignore what I feel for him when his body's pressed up against mine. I almost feel like throwing all my dreams away just so I can spend a little longer in those arms, so I can spend an entire month wallowing in bed being engulfed by that physical charisma.

"Hey! What are you doing here?" I say, finally pulling back.

Cole pulls my chin toward him and steals a kiss that I can feel he's been thinking about since we last parted. It steals the unsettled tension from my body, the stress of my work shift, the twist of reconciling my dilemma, and softens me until I feel like I could fall into him forever.

"I missed you," he says softly, once we part.

"I've been working hard," I say, playfully. "So have you."

"You work too much," Cole says, his hands still squeezing my midriff against him, fingers gently clenching and unclenching against my skin until my whole body is humming.

Something turns in me at the comment, as if seeing a glint of light at the end of a tunnel. I smile and press a finger into the chest exposed above the second button of his shirt.

"Well…maybe I should quit," I say, trying to keep the hope out of my eyes, trying to make it sound like nothing more than an innocent joke.

Cole laughs softly, and I feel the rumble of his ab muscles against me.

"As if I'd let you go anywhere," he says, and I have to struggle to keep my smile. He kisses my forehead and then steps away to open the car door for me. "Come on."

"Where are we going?" I say, getting in.

"Let's call it a surprise," Cole replies.

"Hmph. I'm getting used to those."

It's only when we park outside the Hollywood Bowl that I notice the picnic basket Cole pulls out from the back seat. He slams the door shut, takes my hand, and leads me through the lot until I can hear the sound of classical music.

"What's that?" I ask him.

"The L.A. Phil. They rehearse here in the summer, and anyone can just come through and listen."

"Oh," I say, enjoying the sweeping strings for a second before turning to him. "So you're cheaping out on me, huh? Am I not worth the real thing?"

Cole laughs and stops to look at me.

"I'd fly you first class to Tuscany in a heartbeat if you told me you liked the anchovies there."

I smile as if I find it funny, but there's no hint of a lie in his eyes. Just pure, devoted resolve. A restrained but wild passion for me that almost scares me with its power. But beneath the rush of love and desire I feel in that moment is a dark shadow, a lurking reminder that I'm going to betray him. I look away, hoping he interprets it as simple shyness.

We reach the box seats and settle down, Cole setting the basket between us and opening it to reveal still-warm bread, a spread of cold cuts, effervescent jams, and a number of dips and salads.

"Did you make all this?" I say, as Cole expertly cuts the bread with a serrated knife.

He chuckles warmly.

"Did I never mention that I like to cook?"

"Actually," I say, taking a slice of bread from him and fishing around in the basket until I discover a salmon mousse, "I figured you were sick of it, and that's why you went into the business side of things."

"It wasn't the cooking I got bored of—it was the people I cooked for," Cole says, punctuating it by offering me a tub of mixed olives.

I grab one and chew slowly, if only to hold back the escalating nerves.

We eat and talk, until our bellies get full and the words start to run out, allowing the orchestra to take over the mood. Until the basket is closed and put away, and we're sitting next to each other, his arm around me, my head on his shoulder, his fingers stroking my hair as we allow ourselves to be carried by the music, by the diminishing fire of the sunset in the hills beyond.

The realization comes slowly, as slow as the sweeping movements of the music, as the veiling of the night sky: I'm happy. Happier than I've been in a long time. Maybe ever. Here, against him, in a love so real and present I can smell it in his scent, feel it in the tenderness of his fingers in my hair, hear it in the soft thump of his heart and the deep swell of his breathing, and everything else seems irrelevant, pointless. My sister's advice, Asha's, it all starts to make sense. Why would I need anything more than this?

And why am I about to throw it all away?

I remember Asha's advice to 'follow your heart,' but which way do you go when your heart is split in two?

CHAPTER SEVENTEEN

COLE

She's turned my world upside down, inside out. And the thing is, I love it. If you had told me before I met her that there would come a time when I would delete the numbers of the models in my phone, when I'd be carefully preparing a picnic and agonizing over each thing I put in the basket, then I'd have said you were crazy, and probably had security escort you off the premises. But here I am.

I've never run from a challenge, never stopped at an obstacle. It's just that, until now, the challenges I've faced have been the ones best tackled with brute force, with determined strength, focused decisiveness. Challenges that have made my body ache, my emotions spike, my talents stretch to their limits. Problems solved with animal strength and stubbornness.

But Willow…she's a different kind of goal, and now the challenge is different. Now I need to open up old wounds and finally let them heal, unfurl the barriers I've erected between me and the world, allow myself to trust, to express, to love. It might be the hardest thing I've done yet, but the payoff is incredible.

I'm in such a good mood that I almost forget I have a mentoring date scheduled with Chloe when I turn up at Knife early one morning. She's standing out front with Maggie waiting for me, and after exchanging a few pleasantries with Chloe's supervisor I lead the girl into the restaurant to spend some time in the kitchen.

It's not exactly what I had in mind for today, but if anything Willow has had me losing my temper a lot less, and going with the flow a lot more. We make for the industrial fridge to see what we can play with and then spend almost an hour cutting fresh produce into fancy shapes and building colorful mason jar salads, all while I give Chloe a lengthy discourse on where vinegar, salt, and different varieties of olive oil come from.

Maybe I'm starting to warm to the kid, or maybe it's just this new perspective, but the time flies, and I'm about to show Chloe how to make Knife's secret recipe house pesto when Maggie arrives to pick her back up. We thumbtack the pesto idea for next time, and once they're gone I clean up and perform checks across the whole restaurant.

Michelle arrives first, as always, and I grab her attention as she's putting on her whites in the hallway and tell her to stop by the office for a chat.

She looks calm but a little surprised as she sits in front of the desk, still tightening her dark, unruly curls into a ponytail.

"What's up?" she says anxiously.

I don't blame her for feeling a little bemused; Michelle's good enough that we barely need to say anything to each other anymore. As a head chef she's basically a machine, efficient, unyielding, and if she were to cash in all the days off that she's owed we wouldn't see her for months. Over the years she's worked with me she's also learned exactly how I operate, and can pretty much pre-empt what I'm gonna do before I actually do it—so the surprise in her deep brown eyes isn't entirely unwarranted.

"How are things?" I ask, leaning forward in my office chair.

Michelle laughs, a short and easy one, ever relaxed and resourceful.

"Is this a performance review or something?"

Now I laugh. "No, nothing like that. Just been a while since we touched base."

Michelle eyes me keenly. "You know you can be direct with me, Cole."

I nod and laugh again. "Right. Ok. Tell me, what do you think about Willow?"

"Willow?"

"Yeah."

Michelle pauses a second before speaking.

"As a chef or…"

"As a chef," I say, smiling. Michelle's as observant out of the kitchen as she is in it.

"Well she's pretty great, honestly. Works fast, good communication, stays calm. She's been a little off her game the past few days, but we've been a bit busier than usual and I'm sure it's nothing worth worrying about. All in all I can't fault her."

I nod. Figures she'd be slipping a little here and there since we got together—I'd be slipping too with the way my mind's been flying.

"You think she'd make a good head chef?"

"For the Vegas place?" Michelle asks, pausing again to pout and think. "Yeah. Probably. I know she's young but she's no amateur—she's definitely 'got it.' It's hard to say for sure, but I could definitely see her as head of a kitchen—later if not sooner. She thinks fast on her feet, is always on top of what's going on in the kitchen, and there's nothing she can't cook…she doesn't take any shit, either, despite Leo doing his whole 'hazing' thing."

"Good. That's what I wanted to hear," I say, leaning back a little at her confidence-affirming words. "It's not for Las Vegas though—it's for here."

Michelle frowns, looks at me, then shakes her head. "I don't understand. Are you letting me go?"

"Never. Nothing like that. But how about this: How would you feel about taking on the Vegas place?" I ask. "I'd rather have an experienced head like yours in charge of a new team than Willow."

Michelle sits back as if winded by the news. "Hmm," is all she says.

She stares stonily at some spot on the wall behind me, face blank, though I don't need to be a mind reader to know she's thinking at a million miles an hour.

"Of course, I'd do everything I can to support you out there. Find you a nice place—or put you up in a nice hotel suite until we find something you like. Relocation costs all covered in full, pay raise, and I'll throw in a healthy bonus. New car. Whatever you want. I don't want you thinking I'd put you out there 'cause you're not doing a good job here—if anything, you're the only person who I know will have that place running like Knife inside a month. You're the best I've got."

"Yeah," Michelle says, "I get it."

She stares a little longer.

"Do you want to take some time to think about it?"

"No," Michelle says, looking back at me finally with a smile. "I'll do it."

"You sure? I know it's a big move, and you've been in L.A. half your life."

"Yeah," she says, with a little more conviction now, smile a little broader. "To be honest, I could do with a new challenge. I'll miss the crew here, for sure. But this is just what I need right now. I've been feeling lately like, 'what's next?' and I think this is it. The next step."

"Congratulations. You're gonna do a hell of a job."

I offer my hand across the table and Michelle shakes it firmly.

"Little drink to celebrate?" I add, standing up and moving toward the wine crates.

"No thanks," she says, standing up and tightening her ponytail again. "We're low on béchamel and I'm expecting quite a few orders of the tuna mornay today."

"Well don't think you're going to Las Vegas without having a drink on me first."

Michelle laughs as she makes for the door, stopping once she has her hand on it to turn back. "Cole…"

"Yeah?"

"Did you speak to Willow already?"

"No. I was waiting for your answer first. I'm going to ask her today."

Michelle nods.

"Well, she should be in for her shift soon. You want me to send her in?"

"That's the idea."

Michelle leaves and I take a moment to relax now that the hard part is done. I had no idea what she would say—Michelle's life is a closed book—and if she'd said no to the Vegas job, I would have really had to rethink things.

Now, though, it's just plain sailing. All I've gotta do is wait for my girl to walk through those doors, and then offer her the job of a lifetime. I take the flowers I picked up for her and the delicately-wrapped gift out from under the desk and place them in front of me. I select the perfect wine from the crate and pull it close, ready to open and celebrate.

I'm about to make both our dreams come true.

CHAPTER EIGHTEEN

WILLOW

I dash into the rear entrance of Knife feeling like the forces of excitement and euphoria are carrying me, a hurricane of glee that pushes me onward. The windows I picked out are going into the new location today—Andre assures me that his guys are the best—and it'll be done by the time I get off work if I want to see. It's a small thing, but it sets a smile on my face that I haven't been able to remove all morning, and though my body is going through the motions of putting on my whites and starting my shift, my consciousness is flying about thirty-thousand feet in the air.

"Hey Michelle. Hey Warren. Hey Carrie," I say, chirpily. Then, even though—no, *because*— he hates it, "Hey Leo, how you doing?"

Before Leo can grunt and shake his head at me like an old man seeing a young couple kiss in public, Michelle comes over.

"Willow?" she says, and I look to see a rare kind of smile in those strong, dark features. "Cole's in his office. He wanted to have a word with you."

"Oh, sure," I say, nodding, my heart racing now for different reasons.

I finish washing my hands and take my time drying them as slowly as possible on the journey to the back office. Once again it feels like things are moving way too fast for my Idaho-cultivated pace. I've signed the contract, the windows are going in, and Tony's sending me interior decorating inspiration pictures throughout the day—it's all really happening, and that means it's really time for me to come clean with Cole. The longer I keep it a secret the worse it's gonna be when he finds out, the deeper we'll have embedded ourselves within each other, and the higher the chance of him discovering it himself, which would be a disaster (the location is only a few streets away, after all).

I need to tell him.

Now.

Except I can't. I've managed to put it off this long by telling myself I'm just 'waiting for the right opportunity,' but I'm starting to wonder if there's ever a 'right' time to tell your boss and lover that you're betraying them. That you're repaying their faith in you as a chef by leaving to start your own restaurant, and perhaps even worse than that, responding to the trust they've put into you as their lover by doing the one thing that emotionally scarred them permanently. Plus, every time I'm with Cole it's like nothing else exists. I fall for him deeper each time we talk, with every intimate touch, every look from those eyes another knot that bonds us together. How can you do the right thing when it means hurting someone you love? How do you follow your dreams when it means giving up what you've worked so hard to build? I've spent nights sighing myself to sleep over it, praying for some intervention that'll somehow make it better, some other way for this to go that might make everybody happy.

But maybe I'm wrong. Maybe he might not be upset, maybe he'll appreciate that this is my dream, and that I couldn't say no.

Maybe being with him and working on my own place is absolutely fine. Except every time I think those things I remember the pain in his eyes when he told me about Jason betraying him, the vulnerability in them when he said he trusted me. That resolute defiance to never trust anybody ever again, to never open up to anybody—a defiance he gave up starting on our first night out, when he told me all his secrets.

I stand outside the closed office door, take a deep breath, and knock quickly.

"Come in," Cole says through the door.

Here goes nothing.

"Hey," I say, as I step into the office and Cole walks toward me, shoulders rolling, his body seeming even larger in the small room.

"Hey, babe," he replies, shutting the door behind me and taking me in for a slow kiss, the kind he usually gives me first thing in the morning, as if thirsty for my lips. A kiss that makes time slow, turns my insides to warm honey. A drug that makes me lose my sense of place, struggle to catch my thoughts, as if they were passing birds.

He pulls back and smiles at me for a second, gazing at me as if I'm the most incredible thing on earth, so sincere I can almost believe it myself. Then he moves toward his desk.

I laugh nervously.

"We probably shouldn't do that at work," I say, just trying to shift the mood somewhere more pragmatic.

"Who cares? I'm the boss," Cole says, leaning back to pull a bouquet from behind him. "I don't like keeping secrets anyway."

My stomach drops. I move closer to take the flowers from him and smell them.

"Flowers? Why…what are these for?"

"For being talented…smart…fascinating…and," his hands wind around my hips, pulling me to him so that he almost crushes the flowers between us, "so incredibly sexy."

I laugh and try not to make it obvious I'm pulling back, making as if I'm adjusting my whites.

"Also," he continues, pulling a bottle of wine from nearby, wielding it the way he does when the wine is particularly good, "to celebrate."

"Celebrate?"

Cole smiles even more broadly, and I can see the deep joy within him, the buildup of enthusiasm that led up to this moment. He doesn't answer right away, as if savoring it, and instead scoots a chair beside me with his foot and leans back once again on the desk.

"You're gonna wanna sit down for this," he says, happily.

"Okay..." I say slowly, easing back into the chair, still clutching the flowers on my lap.

"You know Fork is on track to open in about five weeks, right?"

"Sure," I nod.

"And that we were still looking for a head chef," he goes on.

"Yeah. You found someone?"

"Better than that. I decided to move Michelle there. I just offered her the position about five minutes ago and she said yes. That *does* leave a spot open here, however..."

I experience the same kind of slow motion terror that I imagine car crash observers do. The rush of adrenaline, the prickle of fight-or-flight responses, the sensation of sheer, unavoidable helplessness that only exists in that moment after something has been set in irreversible motion, and the inevitable fate it's going toward.

"Uh huh," I mumble.

Cole pauses, drawing the moment out once again, his enjoyment of it—and his obliviousness to my discomfort—evident in the sparkle of those eyes.

"Willow. I want you to take the position. I want you to be the head chef here at Knife."

After a long pause, I manage to unstick my vocal cords.

"Oh. Um. Wow."

A crack in Cole's smile appears when he sees my reaction, but it quickly repairs itself. He chuckles warmly.

"It's a lot to take in, I get it. I didn't really want to tell you at the start of a shift and give you no time to absorb it, but I couldn't wait any longer."

I drop my head in my hands, unable to look at him. "Cole…I just…"

"You deserve it though. You've been fantastic here since you started, you've got the raw talent and the drive, and to be honest, I should have thought of this ages ago. Would have saved myself a lot of trouble. Better late than never though."

"Cole…wait…"

He kneels in front of me, and I look up into those darkly narrowed eyes, still sexy, as if he's so unused to being happy he can't quite smile without it seeming somewhat dark.

"You know, this could be the start of something incredible," he says, his voice lower now that his face is so close to mine. "We could take this place to the next level. You were so right about those burgers—they brought the rest of the menu to life, balanced out all the serious dishes with something simple and low key. And your ideas about Fork… We work so well together. The way we challenge each other—"

"Cole, please…"

He takes my hands in his, too lost in the momentum of his own ideas to recognize the panicked look on my face for what it is.

"We could collaborate," he says, eyes up now as if watching his dreams play out above my head. "I mean, Knife would still be a restaurant focused on French cuisine, but together we could put a twist on it, a stamp. Just think of what we could come up with together. My experience and your creativity."

"No," I manage to say, though I don't say it forcefully.

Cole's eyes look back at me, his smile dropping a little.

"Ok," he says, standing up again and leaning back on the desk, "we don't have to collaborate. Just an idea. You could just take the head chef position and carry it on as normal if you're not comfortable doing more just yet. We can revisit—"

"*No*," I say, this time with the heaviness it requires. "I mean, no to the job. I can't be your head chef."

Cole freezes, the glint in his eye dulling as he looks at me. "You can't be serious. You really want to stay a line cook? You're better than that and you know it. If you're anxious we can take it one day at a time, have you move forward at your own pace—"

"No," I say, my stomach dropping as I realize that this is it, that there's no turning back. "I can't be your line cook anymore either. I have to hand in my notice. You see I'm…well, I'm starting my own restaurant."

Cole's face hardens, his eyes squinting at me as if trying to read between the lines of what I just said. "You can't be serious. You're starting…your own restaurant?"

"Yes."

I see his jaw shift a little as he grinds his teeth. "Why didn't you say anything? How the hell did this come about? When did you even have time to—?"

I squirm on the chair a little, until I'm so uncomfortable I just stand up.

"Well…when I came to L.A. I…it's complicated. I have this friend, right, and…look, forget the 'how,' the thing is—it's happening. I didn't think it would, but now it is, and it's all been so crazy. We have investors and a location and we—"

"*We?*" Cole snorts, everything about him taut and angry now. "Who's 'we'?"

I take a deep breath, struggling to find the best route through this explanation.

"A friend. Tony, I think I mentioned him to you," I say. The words come out sounding pathetic, too common and familial to reflect just how bad I feel, just how much I recognize the tragedy of what I'm doing to him.

Cole shakes his head and looks up, laughing darkly before he turns away, moving behind his desk as if he can't stand not to have a barrier between us.

"Oh, this is too good," he says, sarcasm and anger mixing in his voice.

"I didn't want things to turn out like this," I say, moving close to the desk now as if to keep him close. "It just happened so fast, it all got way out of—"

"Hold on," Cole says, his smile grim and heavy now, as if clinging to his shred of irony in order to comprehend this. "So the night you came to my apartment, the night I made you that snack you liked, and you came back from a phone call with Tony all confused, leaving in a hurry…" Cole leans over the desk. "You knew then?"

"I…that wasn't…"

Words fail me, every explanation I come up with sounding even more incriminating in my head. All I can do, finally, is nod.

Cole's head drops, and for the first time I see the small, book-sized gift on the desk beside him, wrapped in pink paper and tied with a red ribbon. He raises his head again, eyes even darker now, even more distant.

"And when I took you to the beach," he says, voice slow and thudding, as if he knows the answer already, "and I told you about how Jason betrayed me, scarred me so deep I couldn't trust anybody else until I met you—" He stops himself to take a breath and find his words again. "And you sat there, all sympathetic and concerned, telling me it was a 'lonely way to live' and 'so sad' that I didn't trust anyone. Did you know then?"

"Look, Cole, it's not like that—"

"Did you *know*?"

He doesn't shout, but the words are as powerful as bullets, impossible to ignore.

"Not really…I mean, kind of. It wasn't really…" I wince and get frustrated with myself for not being able to express this. "It was just an idea…I didn't think it would really happen. I mean, maybe in a few years or something, but never this soon. This is what I came out here for, though. It's my dream. Aren't you even…a little bit excited for me?"

I know even as the words come out that they're the wrong thing to say. Cole drops himself back into his chair, muscles slumped, his fingers drumming on the table, as if impatient to see the back of me now. After a few tense moments where I mentally toss and turn to find the right words, the right angle on this whole situation, Cole lifts his hand and makes a tight fist, professional and guarded.

"You have a location already?"

"Yes." I take a deep breath again, pausing before I have to deliver another hit, like a reluctant boxer. "It's…a couple of streets away. On the way to Santa Monica from here."

Cole closes his eyes.

"The corner building? The one that used to be a gallery?"

"Yeah," I say quietly.

"So…" he says, looking at me again, "not only are you leaving me—you're about to become my competitor."

"No!" I say, unpersuasively. "Of course not. The food we're going to make is completely different. And the whole vibe—"

"Knife is the best restaurant in L.A.," he interrupts. "Anyone anywhere close to us wouldn't bother with any other restaurant. Other places exist in our shadow. Except now you're going to give them a choice to make. Because even though I feel like I don't know really know you anymore, the one thing I do know is that you're a killer chef."

"Oh come on, Cole," I say, starting to feel desperate, "it's not like Knife is going to go out of business."

Cole smiles, his expression like ice.

"Alright," he says, drawing himself upright in his chair and pulling himself toward his desk. He picks up the wrapped gift and drops it in a drawer, sliding it shut forcefully. "I'll have Martin reach out to go over your final paycheck with you—"

"Cole…"

"—and I'll have someone come in to cover your shift today." He pulls his phone from his pocket and gestures at the door, avoiding my eyes. "So if you wouldn't mind."

Suddenly, with all his walls back up, Cole becomes a stranger, somehow even more shut off from me than the first time I met him. "I'm sorry," I whisper.

"Don't apologize. You're just following your dreams. I get it. I've trampled over people to get to where I am."

I shake my head. "It's not like that."

"In this business, it's always like that." He stands. "You know your way out."

I start to say something else, but the understanding that anything I say beyond this point is just another stab, another punch in the gut for both of us, stops me. Damage done, wounds raw, even being this close starts to hurt.

I turn my eyes away, and make for the door.

We're over.

CHAPTER NINETEEN

COLE

"Are you kidding me?" Martin says, nervously pushing back his hair like a man quitting cigarettes.

"You think I like jokes where I'm the punchline?"

It's after midnight and we're sitting at a table in the dining room of Knife, the sound of the dishwashers singing Spanish songs lifting the silence just above unbearable. Between us are a few leftover gougères, though Martin only managed a bite of one before I told him the news and he dropped it on the table.

"So we're back to square one," he says, exasperated. "Square *zero*, since the ship has sailed on the candidate I was chasing."

"Looks that way," I say, before sipping long and slow on my wine.

Martin shifts in his seat uncomfortably. He picks up the pastry, brings it to his mouth, then decides he can't eat again and drops it.

"So with Michelle going to Vegas and no replacement, we're down a head chef *and* a line cook at Knife now. Meanwhile Fork is opening in less than a month so you can't be here to supervise."

"I know," I say, pouring the last drops of the wine into my glass.

One of the dishwashers comes into view, poking his head beyond the kitchen doors.

"Uh, boss? We're done."

I raise a hand.

"Sure."

"Should we leave the door open out back?"

"No. Lock it up. We'll leave out front. Oh…wait. Could you bring a bottle of wine from the office?"

"Sure. Which one?"

I pause for a second, try to think, then realize it doesn't matter anymore.

"Whatever. I don't care."

This makes Martin glare at me, almost fearfully. He watches with a kind of macabre pity as the bottle comes and I pour it lazily into the glass, down it, then pour again. For a moment, I can tell he wants to question it, but then he lets it pass, present problems still occupying the forefront of his thoughts.

"I suppose you'll want to keep Michelle here, then?" he says, eventually.

"No. She's still going. She raised her hopes—she likes the idea. Least I can do for her."

Martin nods. "Maybe that's smart. She'll get Fork to hit the ground running—and by the way, we still need to come up with a name. At this rate we're gonna be stuck with 'Fork'—which I don't mind—but you did say you hated it."

I watch the red liquid swirl in my glass a little, allow the viscous way it clings to the glass to hypnotize me a little, then raise it to my lips.

"I'm gonna call it 'Vérité.'"

Martin studies my face for signs I'm joking.

"*Truth?* You want to call the place Truth?"

"Mm-hmm," I hum into my glass. "We need a little more of that in this world."

Once again Martin stares at me like a concerned teacher, likely considering whether he should make an intervention. Eventually he decides against it, stiffening up in his chair instead and putting his palms on the table, the way he always does when he's galvanizing himself to deal with a problem.

"Ok," he says, his voice a little sturdier now. "So then the first thing we need to solve is the head chef for Knife. I'd narrowed my list down to two when I was looking for Fork—I mean, Vérité—but one of them is in Europe now, and the other is not going anywhere. There was a third chef up in Oregon that—"

"I'll do it," I say, putting my glass down and topping it up.

Martin looks at me for a second.

"You want to take over the search?"

"No. I said I'll *do* it," I repeat. "If you want something done properly, you've got to do it yourself. You and Michelle can handle Vérité. I'll take over here."

Martin takes another considered pause before speaking.

"You want to get back into cooking again?"

I nod. "I wanna revamp the menu too," I say, taking my glass and standing up to pace around the table a little, looking around at the place as if with new eyes. "It's too accessible, too simple. Too many potatoes. People could make our cassoulet at home. It needs to be more sophisticated."

Martin gives out an incredulous sigh.

"What do you mean? You won your Michelin stars on this menu. We already have a hard enough time finding chefs capable of doing even the most basic dishes on it."

"You don't get anywhere by resting on your laurels," I say, still ambling around the place, listening to the way my voice reverberates around the room. "I'm getting sick of this décor, as well. It's so... California. Have somebody come by my place. I have a Lautrec that would work better. Maybe put a couple of the Cartier-Bresson prints up, too. And another thing: We'll do a taster menu. A dozen small plates, charge a few hundred bucks a head."

Martin's incredulity reaches intense levels now, and when he speaks I can hear how dry his throat is.

"A taster menu? You said that they were too pretentious—even for you."

"Yeah, well, things are different now," I say, ruminating on the woodgrain of the maître'd counter. "We're gonna raise prices, roll out a new menu, and start producing food sophisticated enough to win literary awards."

I drop myself back into the seat opposite Martin and allow his astonished gaze to take in my sincerity.

"The food *is* sophisticated," he says, shaking his head. "And we already charge some of the highest prices in the city."

I open my arms wide.

"*I'm* cooking here now. People would pay a hundred bucks for a glass of water if they thought I poured it. They'd probably say it's the best they've ever had, too."

He's silent for a minute, and I pour myself another glass of wine and start thinking more in depth about the new menu, where I can source the most difficult-to-find ingredients, how soon I can schedule a nice long research trip to Paris.

"Cole...I know we don't usually talk personal stuff," Martin finally says, tentatively. "You and I have never really...you know... opened up, or anything. It's not really my place. But I have to ask you, 'cause this is...well, these changes you're talking are pretty dramatic. Are you sure your head is in the right place for this right now? I know that you and, uh, Willow had…well…something going on, and..."

"You're right, Martin," I say, staring at him humorlessly. "It's not your place. Yours is the 'how,' not the 'why.' So don't ask me anything like that again. Oh, and I want you to fire Leo. Tell him he might be the best saucier in America, but his bouillabaisse still tastes like fresh sewage. He's welcome to drop by and taste mine if he wants to learn how it's done."

It takes Martin a few seconds to digest what I'm saying, but when he does he pulls out his notepad officiously and starts writing.

"Yes, boss."

For the next few months I work harder than I've done since I built the place. I turn up to the restaurant before sunrise and leave by moonlight, a flurry of swearing and high standards as I whip the kitchen into better shape than it's ever been. I kill items from the menu like traitors to a dictatorship—the Basque burgers go first, of course—and replace them with items evermore complicated. Truffled chicken quenelles over cured seabass, hand dived scallops with shiso and dried Japanese mushrooms, clay-baked young ginger, fennel, and candied beetroot, smoked bone marrow, pork, and blanched quince.

The plates become works of post-modern art, food pornography that instills hunger at first glance. Mandarin, pear, and pinenut napoleons so delicate and towered so high that they defy gravity. Coq au vin that commits the transgression of using white wine—and gets away with it. Hazelnut and ginger macarons so perfectly concocted they have to be eaten within minutes of being cooked.

I take as much time over the presentation as over the cooking, raging at chefs who put down a line of cherry preserve on the thyme-roasted veal that's a quarter inch too long, losing my shit when I see a leaf of arugula on the feta and lemon puree olive salad that isn't glistening with the exact shade of green it needs to be. I reject several sample menus for being printed paper that doesn't evoke quality. Two new line cooks quit within days of this baptism of fire, before the third one, a woman who relishes the battle-like atmosphere I've created, finally sticks. Broccoli and cheese soup becomes 'charred calabrese broccolini and stilton soup with walnut-encrusted croutons,' is served in a bowl the size of an egg-cup, and has fifty dollars added to the price.

I do all this with Willow's words echoing in the back of my mind. 'Food should look like food… It should be made with love… It should satisfy…' I do all this to defy her, to go further in the opposite direction, as if this difference in philosophy might increase the distance between us, between what I feel for her. *Felt* for her. I do it all to prove her wrong, to somehow numb the betrayal of what she did, what she's about to do.

I work til my muscles ache, til the skin on my hands goes tough with the heat of pan handles again, until I'm spending so little time at home that my place starts to feel unfamiliar. I don't have time for days off, or eating out myself—or even Chloe's lessons, anymore.

It works, for a while. Word spreads that I'm back in the kitchen, and almost immediately Knife has lines that stretch beyond the famous seafood place down the street. The food critics start pouring in with the masses, each of them looking for a reason to stand out by giving our new menu a critical reception, and none of them leaving with it.

Each night, as I agonize over the chicken and pistachio galantine's imperfections, I have to delete several voicemails from my phone. Offers to return to television and guest star on cooking shows, invitations to exclusive clubs and parties, requests to give interviews on the 'return of Cole Chambers.' Knife's success already reaching sensation levels that almost rival its opening.

Except…

Here I am, alone in the back office, unaware of the time but for the fact that the dish washers have gone, feeling empty and unfulfilled. A gaping hunger inside of me that no food or wine can fill; no glowing, verbose review with a prestigious name on top of it, no celebrity customer's compliments, not even the cell number of a voluptuous Italian actress, which she scrawled on a cocktail napkin tonight and had Charles promise to make sure I received.

I look at the napkin on the desk, pushing it around a little, with tired, blistered fingers. The number ends with a heart—an insinuation of what lies at the other end of the line if I call. I pick the napkin up and hold it in my hand, as if trying to divine what would happen if I called. The coy flirting, the insinuating chatter, the meeting, the move, the morning after. She'll play hard to get a little, verbally spar with me as a kind of test, then give in beautifully, as if being typecast as the bombshell in every movie had compelled her to do the same in life. Except all I want to do is fall into bed arguing about the right way to make seafood risotto.

I scrunch the napkin up and toss it into a wastepaper basket, then get up from behind the desk, every sound I make loud in the heavy silence of the empty restaurant. My muscles ache as I move through the place, turning off lights and setting the alarm system. I clench and unclench stiff fingers, callouses re-hardened on hot pan handles, my back cracking when I pull my shoulders back after hours spent hunched over counters.

Locked up, I walk slowly across the lot to my parked Porsche, breathing deeply, the night-released jasmine cleansing senses that have been overwhelmed by flavors and smells throughout the shift. I don't know why I do it, but I don't turn right out of the parking space. Right toward the road that'll lead me to my empty house, where I'll turn on the TV, pour a glass of whiskey, and fall asleep before I've even taken a sip or changed the channel. Instead, I go straight. Straight toward Santa Monica, just a couple of streets…

I pull up across the street. Close enough to see the giant, etched wood sign hanging above the entrance, close enough to make out the familiar sight of a half-furnished restaurant inside, but not too close, because there's a single light on, and a single figure moving around inside. I check the time. One-thirty-three am—and it's a weekday. Even here in the middle of the city, the streets are so dead that even the streetlights feel like a waste of electricity.

And yet there she is. The figure could be anyone at this distance, but those movements are unmistakable, that poise too well-remembered for it to be anybody else. And besides, it's not like anybody else would be up at one-thirty in the morning working in a restaurant that isn't supposed to open for another couple of weeks.

Chow. That's the word on the sign. The name of the place. Something about the name makes my gut tighten, forcing me to remember that night out by my pool, the look of joy on her face when I pulled away the cloche and showed her the dessert I'd made her. A memory now tinged with bitterness, where recalling it feels like swallowing a jagged pill.

I watch her a while until I figure out what she's doing: sanding wood. I see the panels leaning up against the wall, broad and circular, like table tops. She's working the edges so they'll curve softly, I realize, and I can't help smiling. Who else would think about such details? Me, maybe.

For about an hour I sit there, observing her, feeling the knife she stuck in my back twisting a little more with each passing minute. The distance across the street feeling like miles, rather than yards, impossible to traverse. The cold, hard determination that gave me everything in life making me almost hope that the restaurant crumbles, so she'll come running back full of regret and apologies.

For a moment I imagine what it would be like to go to her now, just talk, see how she's doing. Maybe help with the sanding. See if she wants to get a coffee sometime.

But no.

I learn my lessons, and I learn them well—even if I have to learn them the hard way.

I start the engine and drive away.

CHAPTER TWENTY

WILLOW

"Where do you see yourself in five years?"

"Um…working here?"

"Right…ok…and finally: Do you have any questions that you'd like to ask us?"

The teenager squirms in his ill-fitting shirt, so starched it sounds like rustling leaves.

"Uh…when would this job start? Like, 'cause I'd have to give a two weeks' notice to my manager at McDonald's if I get it."

Tony clears his throat. "Well, we'll get back to you about—"

"Tell them first thing you can," I interrupt. "You're hired."

My partner turns to me, stepping a little to the side to block the kid from seeing the alarmed expression he shoots me. Then he spins around quickly, all professional smiles, and tells the interviewee, "Would you mind giving us a minute?"

The kid shrugs, confused and daunted, then turns to walk out of the almost-finished kitchen and into the behind-schedule seating area. As soon as he pushes through the nylon curtain we're using for a door, Tony shoots me that alarmed expression again.

"Willow, what are you doing?" he hisses.

"I like him."

"Are you serious? He's a high school drop-out who's been working the fryer at McDonald's for a year."

"That shows he's got dedication and a great work ethic! Besides, we've only got two weeks til the opening. And he can *cook*," I say calmly, pushing the exquisitely fluffed, perfectly prepared omelet toward Tony, as a reminder.

He sighs and looks to the heavens.

"So he can cook an omelet. Who cares? My sister can make omelets—but those and Hot Pockets are about the extent of her culinary ability."

"She can't make one like this," I say, chewing on a piece and savoring the perfect texture. "Trust me. You hire a kid like that, pay him a decent wage, cultivate his skills, and he'll break his back for you. Have a little faith."

Tony's answer is drowned out by the loud sound of clattering coming from the front. He settles for giving a shake of the head and going to see what the commotion is. Struggling through the door is a tiny Asian girl with turquoise blue streaks in her hair carrying half a dozen flat packages more than half her height in length, their weight and size too much for her to navigate through the mass of furniture parts and boxes.

"Tacoma?" Tony says, rushing to her aid.

"Yep, that's me," she beams happily.

"Ok great, welcome, let's get these things unwrapped so I can check them—then we'll put them in the back until they're ready to go up. You," Tony says, pointing to the nervous teenager still standing like a frightened rabbit in all the chaos, "what's your name again?"

"Shane."

"Shane—give me a hand with these paintings, will you?"

"Did I get the job?"

Tony sighs a little, glancing at me, then waves his hand in an exasperated manner.

"Sure, but only after you help with these packages."

It was Tony's idea to use the restaurant as a kind of art space, putting a different local artist's work up on the walls each month. He sold the idea to the artists by telling them restaurant customers were a 'captive audience,' not the kind of exhibition-goers who walk straight to the most colorful piece in the gallery and ignore the rest. The local artists would get to showcase their available-for-sale work to the hundreds (Tony's estimate) of diners a month, while we would get free, always of-the-minute art for our restaurant. It was a win-win, as Tony loves to say.

We spend about an hour sorting through the paintings, beautiful mixed media portraits of women textured with 3D materials like metal and fabric, then hash out some of the details of the job with Shane, telling him to turn up on Sunday to start running through the recipes with the other hires. Once that's done, Tony consults the to-do list on his phone as we sit up on the only finished table and take a brief, rare break to work through some fresh iced teas.

"Oh," he says, noticing something, "I forgot to tell you. We have three critics—potentially—coming to the opening. Two are maybes, one definite—but the definite is from the *Los Angeles Times*."

I cough down my soda to look at Tony as if he's insane—which he patently is.

"The *Times* is gonna be here? On *opening night?*"

Tony nods happily.

"Shouldn't we wait until the restaurant finds its, you know, 'groove,' before we start asking for the big guns to come in and criticize us?"

"Come on! It's going to be an *event!* We're going to *explode* on this city with our opening! God…I feel like I've been engaging in foreplay for months and I just wanna…" Tony shakes and grunts in a way that I'm pretty sure is similar to his sex face, "already."

"Sure…" I say, brushing plaster from my paint-specked boyfriend jeans, "and it *will* be an event. For family, friends, people who are interested. But it's not like we have to prove ourselves completely in one night."

"Oh, honey," Tony says, with a convincing sense of pity, "I'm sorry. I keep forgetting you're from Idaho. See, you don't get second chances here—and you sure as shit don't get to prove yourself over the long run. The opening night is box office time. That's when you make your money, *and* your reputation."

"You're thinking of the movies."

"This is L.A. Everything is the movies."

A truck pulling up and honking its horn outside signals the end of our break. I hop off the table while Tony glances at his phone again.

"Can you handle this?" he says. "I've got to go file that form for the Department of Public Health."

"Sure. I'll catch you later."

When I go outside, two men have already descended from the truck, one of them slamming open the rear door and unloading boxes while the other plucks a pen from behind his ear and starts studying a folded bunch of papers in his hand. He's a short guy in his forties, skin leathery from working in the truck, his eyes small and dark. He barely looks up as I approach.

"One box sea bream, one box red snapper, one squid, one mussels, one crab," he says.

"These should have come earlier this morning," I say, confused.

"I was told before nine-thirty—the latest."

The guy looks up at me for the first time. He checks his watch.

"What is it? Ten twenty…eight? Less than an hour out. I'm sorry."

I frown at him but he's already turned his attention back to his order list.

"An hour late is an hour late," I say. "You ever wait an hour to eat at a restaurant?"

He looks up again, and upon seeing that I won't let it go he softens a little, smiling.

"I'm sorry. Fishing season's full swing right now, you know? We had a hell of a lot of deliveries to make, and a little trouble with the boxing. I figured since," he waves his pencil at the covered glass behind me, "you guys weren't even open yet that you could take the hit. Won't happen again, I promise."

"You know, the next couple of deliveries I have from you guys are the ones we need for the opening. If those are even five minutes after nine-thirty then it's going to—"

"Relax," the guy says, chuckling with a fatherly ease. "I understand. What do you think I'm gonna do? Screw over a relationship with a new customer? If I did that I wouldn't be in business as long as I have been."

I relax a little, realizing that my shoulders have been hunched with tension all this time.

"Ok," I say, making it sound like a sigh. "I'm just making sure everything goes right."

"Trust me. This is my job," the guy says, still smiling. He looks back at the restaurant behind me again. "Place looks good, and this location is great. You guys are gonna make a killing."

I smile, the offhand compliment in his comment somehow feeling way more meaningful than it should.

"That's the idea," I say.

"Where do you want these?" the guy unloading says, kicking up the hand cart.

"Oh, just put them in the kitchen. I'll sort them out." I hold the door open for him and then turn back to the other guy. "Hey, actually, I wanted to ask something."

"Hm?"

"Since it's our opening, and we're expecting some pretty important people, do you think you could, you know, just make doubly sure that we get good, fresh stuff? Especially the squid—we cook it in this marinade, see, and when it…anyway, we just need really, really excellent stuff—we'd be willing to pay a premium, even."

"Uh-huh," the guy says, looking at me as if deep in thought.

"Say…ten percent?"

He thinks about it a little longer, then smiles easily.

"Say no more. I'll get you the freshest seafood we have. Sign here," he says, handing me the paper. "You know, usually we charge twenty percent for that kind of…offer. But for an attractive lady like you I'm willing to make an exception."

I hand the paper back and smile, pretending to be flattered. There aren't many things that would suppress the feminist in me, but line-caught salmon that can take a yuzu and chive marinade well is one of them.

"Thanks a lot," I say quickly, spinning on my heels to get back into the restaurant.

I start working through the boxes, refrigerating and freezing some of the seafood for the chef training and run-throughs, then begin to prep the rest for the start of training tomorrow, scaling, gutting, fileting, and marinating to have good examples ready to show.

It feels good, being in a kitchen again, working with my hands.

Even if the kitchen is empty, and this food isn't for a customer. For a month now I've been a nonstop negotiating, interior designing, event planning machine—but I haven't actually been able to cook much, beyond trying out some stuff for the menu. Even the slippery, smelly, cold texture of fish feels great in my hands now, like coming home.

With each thing falling into place, the artists' work, the discussion with the distributor, the prep for the chefs, I feel my dream get closer and closer to coming true, the line dissolving between my mental vision of what this moment would be, and the reality in all its fish-smelling glory. Like finally adding paint to the elements of a sketch I'd been working on since I first tasted oysters and realized I wanted to be a chef.

But then there's Cole. Never far from my thoughts. His distinctive outline still standing in the depths of my emotions, so powerful, so suppressed, so ever-present that sometimes I almost feel like he's standing beside me when I work late at night.

I miss him. As stupid and pathetic as it sounds, I miss him. In the brief moments I have a second to think about anything other than the restaurant, it's always about him, our time together. Unresolved and ended in that abrupt, unjust way. Only the sheer amount of work that fills my every waking hour keeps me from glancing at my phone, distracts me from playing out how I might call him and see if time has healed anything, if the path back to him is as closed as it was when we parted. It doesn't help that both Ellie and Asha seemed so genuinely disappointed when I told them how it ended. Both of them were rooting for us.

To make it easier, I try to think of his flaws, but even those end up endearing him more to me. It's so easy to turn a flaw into something admirable in the people you love. His infuriating stubbornness becomes a commendable strength in his beliefs. The way he makes his decisions rashly and quickly, unyielding to any criticism, becomes the decisiveness of passion, of dedication to his art. Even his 'secrets' make a kind of sense when you realize this is a guy who built himself up from nothing. I wish it was easier to hate him…

"Ah, Willow. There you are."

The voice startles me out of my thoughts and I look up to see our investor Andre walking into the kitchen, politely wrinkling his nose only a little at the smell.

"Oh, hey," I reply, finishing the filet I'm working on quickly and walking over to the sink. "Sorry about the smell. Just prepping for tomorrow."

"It's fine," Andre says, coming to stand beside me as I clean off my hands. "I was just dropping by to see how things were going."

"Good," I say, flicking my hands and picking up a towel. "Though ask me again when I start training the cooks."

Andre laughs easily.

"I'm sure you'll do a fantastic job. You're doing far better than I could have ever hoped anyway."

I take the compliment with a smile and tilt of the head, though it turns out Andre's just preparing me for some bad news. His expression goes gentle as he unlatches his satchel and pulls out a magazine, already folded to a specific page.

"I didn't really want to bring this up, but I just had to know. Is this going to be a problem for us?" he asks as he holds up the magazine so I can read the title while I'm still drying my hands.

Cutting Edge: Why Knife is Still the Best Restaurant in America (if you can afford it)

I skim the article's platitudes and praises quickly and then look back at Andre, shrugging it off with a smile.

"Not at all. Why?"

My shrug seems enough for him, and he puts the magazine back in his satchel.

"I don't know. It's just that this must be the twentieth article I've read about Knife. Sounds like quite the revolution going on over there."

I snort dismissively and turn to face Andre head on.

"The only thing they're 'revolutionizing' is how much people are willing to pay for grilled asparagus on rye. I mean, you could buy half our menu for the price of their soup starter!"

Andre smiles, but his eyes are unsettled, and I can tell the words only make him a little more uneasy.

"Right," he says, concerned still. "I'm just ever-so-slightly afraid we're going to be the 'cheap' version of Knife, you know? They're causing quite a buzz and I just hope we don't end up in their shadow."

I slam the towel over my shoulder in frustration—with the idea, not with Andre.

"We are *not* the cheap version of Knife, because my menu is different, and it's better. In fact, once we get going, Knife will be in *our* shadow, because everybody who eats at Chow will recognize Knife as the pompous, overpriced exercise in food fakery that it is. In fact, you know what I'd love? I'd love to put *my* menu against his—no tricks—and have people taste and see which one they like more. I'd love that, because there's no way anyone could doubt Chow then."

Andre raises his eyebrow and nods.

"I don't doubt you at all," he says. "But there goes that passion again. I was just overthinking it a little, ignore me. Perhaps it's been a little too long since I tasted those mango scallops and chili clams."

I laugh, if anything to release the tension of talking about Knife.

"Well you're my boss now, so you can have them whenever you like—though I suspect we're fully booked for the next three months."

Andre laughs, taps his satchel, and starts walking away.

"It's going to be a hell of a ride. I can't wait."

"Yeah," I say, as he pushes through the nylon curtain. I look back at the pile of fish guts. "Neither can I."

CHAPTER TWENTY-ONE

COLE

Charles is standing in the office when I enter and dump the boxes of dragonfruit and lime in the office.

"Tonight's the night," he says, standing with his hands behind his back, making me wonder if he waited for me like that.

"I know," I say, pulling out a pocket knife and cutting one of the dragonfruits down the middle. "I don't care."

I scoop some of the fruit out and try it.

"You don't care?" Charles says, in the mildly-humored way he asks questions. "Apparently it's the biggest film premiere of the year—there will be photographers here, you know."

I look at Charles as I make my way back behind my desk, putting the fruit down on it—it's good enough.

"Well, Hollywood people are customers just like everybody else," I say nonchalantly.

The truth is, I wasn't even talking about the premiere's private after-party. Something a million times more dramatic and emotionally charged is going to be happening just a couple of streets away from those flash-lit celebrities: Chow's opening night.

"You want some of this?" I ask in an attempt to try and change the subject, offering the other half of the fruit to Charles, who shakes his head.

I continue eating the fruit, taking a couple of bites and then looking up at him, still standing there as if he's waiting for something more, a vaguely concerned look on his face.

"That's strange. Usually you know when a conversation has run its course, Charles," I say, my misdirected irritation about Chow's opening night now coming to the fore.

As if reading my thoughts, Charles' next words are, "That new restaurant a few blocks away is called Chow, I heard. And it's opening tonight."

"Is that so?" I say, leaning back, noticing how he's carefully not mentioning Willow by name.

"I don't know how, but apparently it's causing quite a buzz already. Got a lot of people excited."

I feel my jaw clench. "Mm-hmm."

"But then, I'm sure you already knew that," Charles says, clearing his throat. "Just let me know if you need anything above and beyond the usual, to keep things running smoothly tonight. Since this…after-party…could be stressful for you."

"I'm sure whatever comes up, I can handle it," I practically growl.

Charles seems to take the hint, leaving the office quickly and closing the door behind him.

I cut another chunk of fruit but I can't eat it with my gut tied up so tight, so I get up from my chair to pace a little, try and shake the anxious energy from my limbs.

All I can think about is Chow, and what'll happen when it opens its doors tonight. I picture Willow moving around the kitchen like a dervish, barking orders and exhibiting more kitchen skills in a minute than most people learn over a lifetime. That determined, focused expression on her face—the same one I saw when she cooked for me…

They say if you love someone then you set them free, but I know that's bullshit now. I'm beyond trying to delude myself into thinking I don't love her anymore, but love unfulfilled can burn you from the inside. It can harden into a steel knife that twists with each memory, that digs into you constantly until the whole world becomes a collection of reminders of what you need so badly.

There's a dark, twisted part of me that wants Chow to fail. Not for revenge over the betrayal Willow committed, but so she'll come back. I know it's wrong, and every time I think of her going through the same hardships I went through to build Knife, I want to root for her the same way I rooted for myself when I was attempting the impossible. But then what? If Chow succeeds and Willow gets everything she's ever wanted in life, I'll be just another chapter in her past, a stepping stone toward her happy ending. There's no winning someone back when they're doing so well without you.

I look up when I hear a knock at the door, striding across the office with a frown on my face to yank it open.

"Hello," the young woman behind it says, beaming an innocent smile. It's Maggie.

She steps back and Chloe shuffles forward, the girl looking up at me with her gap-toothed smile.

"Hi Cole!" she says excitedly, running into the office.

I turn back to the woman.

"What's going on? The young chef program is done."

"Yes I know," Maggie says, with teacherly softness. "But Chloe finally competed in the finals of the statewide cooking competition, and she wanted to tell you how it went." I nod, still bemused. "Plus, we were in the neighborhood and I really needed to run to the ladies' room—do you mind? It'll give you two a few minutes to catch up."

"Of course," I say, pointing down the hall, and she zips away from the door, leaving me alone with my former mentee.

"Cole, you'll never believe it! Look at *this*," Chloe says, holding something out toward me.

I look down to examine the bright blue and gold ribbon she's got in her hand.

"Third place?" I say, trying to hide the disappointment I'm feeling for her.

"Yeah! Isn't that great? I'm soooo happy!" Chloe says proudly, looking back at the ribbon and stroking it tenderly. "Thank you so much, Cole. I couldn't have done it without you."

She launches herself at me, hugging my side tightly while I give her a few careful, mentorly pats on the back and try to process the insanity of everything that's going on right now. When she finally lets go I stand and rub my brow.

"Why not first place?" I say. "What happened?"

"Well, first place was *amazing,*" she says, without a hint of envy or anger. "It was this mustard and tar… tarregan—"

"Tarragon."

"Mustard and tarragon chicken—*so* delicious. He deserved it. He was really nice too, and he gave me his e-mail so we could trade recipes! Plus it's not really about the trophy or the ribbons anyway, it's about showing everything we learned, and making friends with the other chefs, and seeing how other people cooked. The competition was the most fun ever."

I suppress the urge to stop her, to look her in the eye like a bad chef and tell her third place is meaningless, that it *is* all about winning, all about the food, all about who's best. That friends and learning don't get you anywhere in this world, that only being better than everyone else will do that.

But she's smiling so much, happiness expressed the way only a child can, without restraint or cynicism. Big brown eyes aglow, glancing constantly at her ribbon to remind herself over and over that she went, she saw, she conquered—and she had a great time doing it.

Seeing that kind of joy so vividly, I suddenly feel like I'm the ridiculous one. Like being disappointed that she didn't get first place is the wrong perspective, rather than the other way around. Twenty years of hard standards, of having it all figured out, of pushing people aside to get to my goal—and all it takes is a kid with a third place ribbon to make it all seem shallow and frivolous.

I laugh gently, partly at the infectiousness of her elation, and partly because I don't even know what to think anymore. Stepping back to the desk, I cut up the remaining pieces of dragonfruit and offer them to her on a napkin.

She gasps, eyes wide. "This is a fruit? It's so pretty!" she says, taking it from me.

"You should try it. Careful, it's got a lot of juice."

"You *have* to come to celebrate with me tonight," Chloe says, still eyeing the fruit as she takes it slowly with both hands like it's a small animal.

"I can't, I'm sorry to say. I'm busy here with a private party."

The supervisor reappears in the doorway. "You guys done?" she says.

"We are," I say. Chloe nods, popping a piece of fruit into her mouth and grinning.

"Come on then, Chloe. Let's leave Mr. Chambers to his work. What's that?"

"Dragon's fruit," the girl answers happily. "Bye, Cole. Thanks again for everything."

"You're welcome," I mutter as they walk away, Chloe still

waving over her shoulder.

A profound, deflated emptiness permeates the office now that her round cheeks and musical voice are gone. A feeling of being proven wrong about something settling deep inside my chest.

When the dinner shift starts there's a sense of urgency and importance more elevated than it usually is on a typical night. Before the first diners even arrive, the prep work is done hurriedly, chefs hunched over their work with complete focus, communication curt and efficient, none of the usual banter that's flung around during the pre-opening lull. This one is different, a calm before a storm, warriors readying for a siege. Everyone is tense, and I wonder if it's my vibe they're picking up on, or if Charles is more of a gossip than I realized.

I perform the final checks and preparations as best as I can, though the crew is well-whipped by this point, and my inspections are mostly perfunctory. I enter the freezer and check for the third time that we have more than enough of everything—if only to distract myself from the growing impression that something is wrong, manifesting itself as a slight feeling of nausea in the pit of my stomach.

"Doors are open!" Ryan calls as he passes the kitchen, and backs stiffen, hands move a little more quickly. The orders start coming within minutes and the kitchen whirrs to life like some giant mechanism in which we're all playing our part. Rich aromas of baking pastries, fresh herbs, grated citrus, and seafood all take their turn assaulting our senses before they blend into one giant masala of heat and energy. The sizzle of meat hitting hot pan, the clang of whisk against bowl, the thud of knife against wood forms a constant backdrop of sound for the chef's dance, the music that we have to sing over in frenetic calls and requests.

And the sense of something awfully, terribly wrong gets bigger and bigger, until it's threatening to make me double over in pain. An hour passes, then two, the orders coming in faster, my senses full but my consciousness somewhere far away—or perhaps not that far.

I fuck up a seared tuna steak, throwing it into a pan that's not hot enough. Ordinarily that would be a major event the chefs wouldn't let me forget for weeks, but this time they're too busy to notice. I get the acidity of a tomato sauce completely wrong, which sets the grill chef behind precious minutes, but the kitchen is too hectic to stop and think about it.

"Chef?" Katy asks, breaking me from my rhythm. "Are you ok?"

"What?" I say, almost offended, without stopping what I'm doing. "'Course I'm ok. Keep your eyes on your filet and stop wasting my time."

"It's just that..." she continues, tentatively. "Well...maybe we don't need that much."

I look to glare at her, and notice a few of the other chefs look away quickly, but not quickly enough to hide their concern. I look back down again at the counter, a truffle in one hand, a grating board in the other, and in the middle a giant mountain of what must be half a dozen fully-grated truffles. More than anyone could ever eat, way more than we need for the recipe, and more than we could even use in a week.

I drop what's in my hands and lean against the counter as I breathe in deep, recognizing once again the feeling that's settling inside of me. Katy quickly turns back to her station and leaves me to try and regather whatever pieces of myself are still functioning.

I whip the towel from my shoulder and turn to the frantic kitchen.

"Can you guys handle everything here? I'll be back in about half an hour."

"Absolutely."

"Yes chef."

"Katy, maybe when you're done with those you can handle the egg whites."

"Sure, boss."

"Good," I say, scanning the place one last time before striding out of the kitchen.

My veneer of composure disappears as soon as I'm out of view. I stumble out of the rear entrance, straight through the parking lot. Down a path I've been walking in my head for the past several hours, a path filled with inevitability, and an answer to what's twisting inside of me.

CHAPTER TWENTY-TWO

WILLOW

It's opening night, and if I stop to think about it I might just seize up and require smelling salts to reawaken. If I didn't feel like the success of Chow was riding on this opening before, then I certainly do now, in no small part due to Tony acting as if we'll go out of business unless it's a massive, blowout success.

It doesn't help that Tony forced me to read an interview with Cole where he was asked about 'upstart restaurants with a mission statement of fresh, simply prepared cuisine'. His response that such restaurants 'had their place' but 'didn't value the artistry of food' as much as he did and rarely lasted—in reality and in memory—stung. It was tamer than his usual, tamer than I would have expected, and I could tell he was thinking of Chow when he answered, but the dismissive judgment only added to my already anxious state. My nerves reach stratospheric levels when I overhear people talking about 'that new place on the corner opening soon' in a coffee line.

I spend the morning with Ellie, Greg, and their two girls, picking them up from LAX and having an all-too-brief brunch with them during which I try to sit still and act like a normal person despite my skin tingling with electricity and my mind buzzing with to-do lists and worst case scenarios.

After eating, I leave my sister and her family with Asha for a whistle-stop tour of L.A. and head back to Chow, checking my watch every twenty seconds, lamenting the fact that I only have five hours until opening at seven-thirty. The kitchen staff are already there, laughing and joking their nerves away, a camaraderie built up over the past few weeks of hard training I gave them. Five chefs, three waiters. Ideally, we had wanted seven chefs, a dish washer, and four waiters, but a combination of high standards, trepidation about initial business, and a lack of time to interview meant that we had to make do for now. With Tony and I doubling up on all tasks, we figured we could get by.

When I arrive at Chow just before three pm, Tony's already zipping between his roles as organizer, table setter, and cook. I blast through the front toward the kitchen and immediately start helping the overwhelmed chefs.

I hear the click of a gas lighter repeat too many times behind me and turn to find Helen frowning at the stove.

"What's the matter?" I say, without stopping my washing of salad greens.

"This stove…it's not coming on."

I finish rinsing and dry my hands quickly as I move toward it, inspecting under the cap and trying it myself.

"The guy told me this happens sometimes," I say, frustrated as I look at the piping behind it, "and that it would clear itself up soon."

I slam the cap back and try again, feeling a release of endorphins as it fires up.

"Thanks, chef," Helen says as I check the clock and see that we're only two and a half hours away now.

I get back to the veggie rinsing, so on edge now that it sounds like there are a hundred people chattering in my head, willing the minute hand on the clock to move a little slower. In the rush to prepare stations, check sauces, and ready ingredients, the time disappears…

"Uh…Willow?"

I turn to look in the direction of the trembling voice.

"Yes, Shane?"

"Are you sure we have enough squid?" he says, as he glances in the ice box uncertainly.

"Of course. We had a delivery just this morning."

I hear Jack's rhythmic knife-chopping stop suddenly, and look up again to find Shane and Jack looking nervously at each other.

"Uh…no. We didn't," Shane says.

"Yes we did," I say, trying to stop the feeling of my heart plunging into my gut. "It would have come before nine-thirty."

"I was here at eight," Jack says. "And we haven't gotten any deliveries today."

I stare at them for a few seconds, mouth going dry, babbling voices in my head getting louder, then drop the salad and push past them on a desperate march toward the storage area at the back.

Nothing.

I yank open the industrial freezer, slimly hoping there was a mistake in storage, but find only the meager supplies left over from training last week.

"Fuck!" I yell. A primal scream that serves only to keep me from combusting with my own anger. I grab the door frame for support and breathe deep, not even the coldness of the refrigerated air able to cool off the lava of my furious blood.

I scramble to pull my phone from my pocket and call the distributor, about ready to tear him limb from limb over the connection, cursing out his entire lineage with every ringtone that he doesn't answer, until it clicks over to his voicemail and I unleash a tirade of war-mongering proportions, gripping the phone as tight as if it were his neck.

The noise in my head is almost unbearable now, a background whine that sets my nerves jangling, my muscles taut. I march back through the kitchen to Tony, who's hurriedly directing the waiters as he rearranges napkins and place settings.

"Tony!" I say, while I'm still crossing the room. "We have a problem."

"You're telling me," he says, rising as I get near.

"The fucking seafood delivery is— Wait. What are *you* talking about?"

Tony's face is a picture of rare concern.

"Well…remember when I said we didn't have to worry about overbooking, because it's not like every single person would show up for their reservation anyway?"

Suddenly it hits me. The voices in my head aren't actually in my head. The thrum and chatter of a crowd…is coming from outside my restaurant. I can see a few people milling about through the glass, but now I move purposefully to the door.

"I honestly didn't expect this kind of turnout, Willow!" Tony says apologetically as he follows me.

I slam through the entrance doors and step out onto the sidewalk, the scene stretching out before me like a punch in the gut.

"Holy shit…"

The crowd is thick, and stretches off down the entire block. It's the sort of crowd that would have been an effort to handle even on a good night at Knife, more like a political protest than a line for a restaurant.

"What the hell, Tony?" I say, hands on my head as I struggle to find where the line ends. "Did you offer people free meals or something?"

"Of course not," he says, shrugging diffidently. "I guess I just underestimated how good I am at promotion."

I peel my eyes from the scene to direct my frustration at my business partner.

"It's not going to be good promotion when we have to turn away two thirds of these people, and the other third has to wait over an hour for their food. We can only seat eighty people, for God's sake!"

"A hundred," Tony corrects me. "At a push…"

"We've got five cooks, and I must be looking at about two hundred and fifty customers." I check my watch. "And it's ten-to-seven. Shit. This is not good, Tony."

I look at him for a moment, with a glint of hope that he might come up with an answer. Some batshit crazy idea for how this could work, the kind of thing he's always been good at, the kind of thing that got us to this point in the first place.

But it doesn't come. And for some weird reason I remember what Cole told me that day at the beach, about trusting only yourself. A slight sadness coloring my frustration as I realize how much I miss him, even in the midst of all of this.

"Open the doors," I say, suddenly purposeful. "Start letting people in."

"What?" Tony gapes, following me back inside the restaurant. "But we still have time—"

"No we don't," I cut him off. "If we're gonna get through this many people we need to start turning them over quickly. *You*!" I point at the waiters. "Push people toward anything that *isn't* the seafood. Recommend the paprika chicken, or the kimchi steak."

The waiters nod and stiffen. I pull my phone out and start looking for seafood distributors, dialing the first one as I push past the doors into the kitchen.

"Showtime!" I call out to the chefs as I tuck the phone between ear and shoulder to start readying the counter. "Orders coming in thick and fast and very soon! Show me what you've learned. Chow is open for business."

What follows is without doubt the hardest shift of my life. Enough orders come in to occupy a kitchen twice our size, and all the while I glue my face to my phone as I call every seafood distributor in town looking for an emergency package. Most just laugh off the request, and others don't even answer at this time of night. The best I get is a box of crab that's good for about three orders.

But even though every member of the kitchen works hard enough to win a medal, proving all my hiring instincts right, and even though Tony puts in a star-quality performance as maître d', head waiter, and occasional dish washer, we're a sinking cruise ship with nothing but buckets to bail.

I don't give up, but a million tiny heartbreaks stretch my hope to its limit. The stove breaks—and this time no amount of cap slamming brings it back to life, leaving us with two burners when even four wouldn't be enough for this hungry mob. Then, in the manic frenzy of the kitchen, the last crate of our most popular craft beer smashes to the ground, causing us to lose precious time cleaning up, and to run dangerously low on alcohol. The seafood dishes have to be reduced to artisanal-small portions, and I overhear the waiters fret constantly over the customers complaining about how long the food is taking.

Even the constant stream of happy diners who pass through to the kitchen to compliment the food only frustrate me, taking up my time and forcing me to be ruder than I'd ever normally be, just to get them out of my hair. When Tony pops back for a moment to happily tell me that some of the customers are ordering multiple entrees, and that a couple of tables seem to be working their way through half the menu, I shriek at the ceiling. The last thing I need is customers staying for hours at our already limited tables. Having folks love our food is great for the long term, but it isn't helping me tonight.

At nine-fifteen I go outside to check the crowd, and see that word seems to be getting around—the line is no smaller than it was before we opened, but now the mood is substantially different. Impatient faces roll eyes at each other, or stare into the distance with glazed expressions due to the length of time it's taking to move forward in the line. I see a few people break off from the middle and walk away, shaking their heads, already mentally composing their bad Yelp reviews.

My breaking point comes soon after, however.

"Uh…Willow."

"Yes, Shane?"

"The seafood's here," he says, and I immediately drop the soup spoon into the boil. "Watch this, Jack," I say, as I march angrily out to the delivery entrance with Shane.

It's the same leathery guy as last time, staring at his folded paper in the same way, while the same companion I remember unloads the ice boxes beside the door.

"Are you *fucking kidding me?*" I yell, the second I see him.

He looks up and smiles, as if surprised. "Is there a problem here?"

I stare at him open-mouthed until I overcome my dumbfounded anger.

"Yes there's a fucking problem! What time do you call this? I'm halfway through my opening night!"

He looks at me as if listening attentively, then checks his paper again.

"You sure? I have before nine-thirty written here." He checks his watch. "And it's only a couple minutes past."

"Nine-thirty *in the morning*," I say, my voice low, hard, and steely with rage now. "Who the *fuck* has their orders delivered at nine-thirty on a Friday night?"

He continues to look at his paper, brows furrowing.

"Ah, I see the problem. My 'am' looks like a 'pm.'" He holds out the paper to his companion who dumps a box and looks. "Doesn't that 'a' look like a 'p' to you?"

"It does," the guy agrees.

"See," leather-face says, smiling at me as if everything is ok now. "Anyway, delivery's here now, so the way I see it, no harm no foul."

"No foul? I'm not serving my customers fish that's been sitting around in your truck all day!"

I launch myself toward him but find myself constricted, Shane grabbing at my hands to hold me back from doing something stupid, or possibly worthy of pressed charges.

"It's fresh enough," the man says, pointing his pencil at the box sitting on the ground.

I shake out of Shane's grip and pry the lid open, stumbling backward as the smell hits me hard. I throw my hand over my nose and glare at the man. "This is *not* fresh. It's not even edible."

He laughs gently. "Easy now. Squid doesn't smell like roses when it comes out of the sea, you know."

"I *know* what fresh smells like, and this smells like it's been out in the sun all day."

The guy gives his companion a 'women-don't-get-it' look, then shrugs back at me, already backing away to retreat to his van.

"Smells fresh to me," he says. "And you paid in advance, so sorry—no refunds."

I launch myself again, but Shane gets there just in time, holding me back even as I flail in his grasp. The two men get into the van and slam the doors and finally Shane's grip loosens, allowing me to kick the bumper as the van revs away.

"You think anybody I know is ever going to use you again when I tell them this?!" I yell at the departing van. "I'll *ruin* you! You just lost a whole load of business!"

I stand there, panting as the vehicle turns the corner. The unmistakable sound of a pile of dishes smashing to the floor tears at the edges of my sanity, forcing me to release my grip on reality, threatening to make my entire being crumble. I bury my head in my hands, consciously struggling to inhale shaky breaths, willing my body to not just give up right here, right now.

"Uh…Willow? Should I—"

"Yeah, just go," I say, sending Shane back into the kitchen with a wave.

I stagger back to the door, struggling to hold it all together.

"Fuck!" I yell, and kick one of the boxes aside, sending rotting cod and melting ice sliding into the alley.

"A real chef's temper you've got there," a voice says.

It's him. Cole. Standing with his hands in his pockets in the darkening alley like some kind of comic book supervillain.

"Oh, great," I say, looking up at the night and laughing. "As if it couldn't get any worse. If you came to gloat, do me a favor and make it quick."

"I didn't come here to gloat," he says, taking a few steps closer.

"Sure you did. This is a fucking disaster," I say, gesturing at the fish, the restaurant, the sound of the impatient crowd rumbling just around the corner of the building. "You got exactly what you wanted."

"No I didn't," he says, looking deeply into my eyes. "I didn't get what I wanted at all."

I tear my gaze from his and point at him angrily.

"If you think this is it, that a bad opening night is going to do me in and have me crawling back to Knife, as if this proves anything, then you've got another thing coming. I'm going to *make* this place work if it kills me."

Cole laughs gently and holds his palms up. "I believe it."

The words draw my eyes deeper into his, wrong-footing me with his sincerity.

"So…what do you want?" I say, confused by his presence now more than anything.

Cole looks down and takes a deep breath.

"That's a hell of a big question. Took me a long time to figure it out for myself."

"And?"

He looks up at me, eyes as open as those days in Vegas, as the night by his pool. Even tangled up in the mass of conflicting emotions that the night has brought on, I feel my heart jump a little at all the warm memories I have of me and Cole connecting.

"What I really want," he says, slow and serious, "is for you to be happy. With or without me."

My lips part, but I can think of no answer. He doesn't need one, however. Instead he pulls his phone from his pocket and dials, bringing it to his ear and looking at me as he talks.

"Charles? Are the premiere guests there yet? Tell them to leave…I don't care. Exactly what I just said. Shut the place down. Give them a bottle of wine and tell them to beat it. Tell them there's a fire hazard, or a health risk…difficult or not, I'm sure you can manage it, Charles…yes. Once that's done I want you to tell all the chefs and waiters to come on over to Chow…right, Willow's place… pack up the vans and bring some tables and chairs, also—"

Cole offers me the phone and says, "Tell him what you need. All of it."

I take the phone, my eyes still on Cole, wishing I could pinch myself without looking stupid. Then I give Charles the long list of ingredients, cutlery, and drinks that we're short of, before handing the cell back to Cole.

"Did you get that? Good. Tell the staff they're getting double overtime for this—and a bonus if they can get here within twenty minutes."

Cole hangs up and puts his phone away, looking at me as I gawp and struggle to come up with words to express what I'm feeling.

"I…thanks…I don't really know what to say, or how to repay you—"

Cole steps toward me, close enough now to put a hand on my arm. He shakes his head. "I'm not asking anything of you—you already gave me enough."

I glance back at the kitchen, take in the sound of desperate chefs fighting over a stove. I let out a sigh.

"To be honest, I'm not even sure it'll be enough to save this. People have already been waiting all evening. And we haven't been able to serve half of what's on the menu."

Cole puts his other hand on my opposite arm, and I realize I'm falling into him again, the hard determination that's made my body tight and wound-up melting at his touch.

"Don't worry about a thing," Cole says. "Nobody remembers the wait when the dish is good enough. And I know your dishes are good enough. Besides, whatever they couldn't order tonight? It's just gonna be one more thing that brings them back next time. 'Cause one taste of you is never enough."

His strong hands move up to squeeze my shoulders as he stares into my eyes, his expression warm and reassuring.

And just like that, I suddenly feel like everything is going to be ok.

Knife's staff arrives like the cavalry, a crack squad rescuing the night from spectacular failure in dramatic fashion. His waiters set tables and chairs up on the sidewalk outside, cheers from the line going up as they shift and find seats, while his chefs lug desperately-needed boxes of seafood and supplies inside. There's even enough alcohol to offer the people who waited in that long line a round of free drinks. Cole even manages to fix the stove, recognizing the problem as a common one with that model, and recommending a superior replacement.

As quickly as the evening descended into chaos, it starts to lift, the atmosphere gathering momentum as tensions seep away both in and out of the kitchen. Soon the anxiously low volume of chatter from the restaurant is a loud, dynamic music of clanging plates and excited voices and the panic-ridden kitchen turns into a smoothly oiled machine, with my rookie staff now ordering Cole's international team about as if there weren't decades of experience between them. When a cop comes past to check that our street side tables and chairs are legal I almost feel it going off the rails again, but a quick conversation with Cole makes everything ok.

By midnight, the restaurant opening is more like the end point of a carnival parade, spilling out onto the street as many diners who couldn't find tables settle for Tony's impromptu idea to serve them takeout. Even the kitchen staff and waiters find a moment to laugh now that we're overstaffed, and I finally get the chance to leave the kitchen and join Ellie and Asha outside, my nieces still tucking into desserts with Chloe.

"I'm so proud of you, Willow," Ellie says, her eyes misting up a little.

"So am I," Asha says. "Though I didn't doubt this place for a second."

"Me too," Chloe says. "The gelato is awesome!"

"You guys really thought I had everything under control?" I say. "Even when there was a line down the block big enough to make the DMV proud?"

Asha laughs. "*Especially* then. Crises bring out the best in you."

"It's true," Ellie adds.

"Well, I didn't do it all myself," I say, looking around to find Cole. "I had a little help."

Taking my glance as an invitation to come over, Cole moves away from a conversation with Tony and comes up beside me.

"Oh my God," Ellie says, looking around. "Where is Greg? I can't believe it's Cole Chambers himself! In person!"

"Well hello again," Asha says, shooting Cole a warning glance.

"This is my sister Ellie, and this is Asha, who you've already met, of course," I say to Cole. "I was just telling them about how you helped me out tonight."

I barely notice the hand Cole places on my back, it feels so natural.

"It was nothing," Cole says, "compared to the help she's given me."

Ellie and Asha beam, on the verge of giggling like schoolgirls.

"Actually," Cole says, looking at me a little seriously, "there was one thing I needed to clear up with you. You ladies don't mind if I steal her for a minute, do you?"

"Really?" Ellie says, a pained expression on her face. "I've got so much stuff I wanted to ask you, though."

"Don't worry," Cole says, glancing at me before looking back at her, "I'm sure we'll be seeing each other again soon."

He turns away, taking my hand and leading me back through the packed tables of happy diners, back through the waiters swinging plates of food through the hallway, through the cooks and smells of the kitchen, out into the alleyway again. It's dark now, and cool, the sounds of my restaurant fading into a distant chorus as the exit door shuts behind us.

"What's up?" I say. "Is this about—"

Before I can finish, Cole spins me around and clutches me to him, pressing his lips to mine. A slow, savored kiss that makes us recognize the hunger we've had to hold back for so long. A kiss that tastes better than any other.

When we finally pull apart, Cole says, "I lied."

"About what?" I reply, a little dazed in the afterglow of the moment.

"When I said I just wanted you to be happy…I meant with me."

"Oh really?"

"Really."

We look into each other until it feels like we're falling, lips closing in so we can come back together again.

"It'll be the last lie I ever tell you, though. I promise," he says, and then our lips meet, and I finally feel complete.

The future's looking up for both of us—I can almost taste it.

EPILOGUE

COLE

It's amazing how much can happen in a year. I guess it's easier when there are two of you making it happen.

I remember every second of it, memories stuck like photos to the walls of my mind. Kissing her at Chow's opening, waking up beside her the morning after and reading her the glowing review in the *L.A. Times*. I remember her surprising me by inviting me over one night and cooking me Basque burgers, me finally giving her the gift I'd kept in my drawer so long: A delicate silver ring inset with white buffalo turquoise from the Grand Canyon. I remember each of the many times either of us stole away from our restaurants during a lull to be with each other, even if only for a few minutes.

And now here I am, standing beside her at the end of the aisle, never more beautiful than she is now, in her crimson red wedding dress (she said she'd spent enough time in white), saying 'I do.' The end of one path, the beginning of another.

It's over before I know it, euphoria making the moments slip between my fingers like water, and then we're running back down the aisle through a storm of flower petals and confetti, cheers, and camera flashes, into the Maybach. Derek says congratulations and we're zipping off to Chow for the reception.

There's booze, and food, and even puppy chow. The guests descend upon the banquet almost ferociously happy, and I remember Willow's joke that half of them only attended for the food. The truth is, though, that we left it up to Tony and Martin—for the first time in our lives, food wasn't the priority. Besides, we'd only have argued about it. Marriage might be about compromise, but when it comes to food we've learnt that neither of us gives an inch.

"Ladies and gentlemen," Tony says, once the guests are all seated at the tables, a space cleared in the middle of the restaurant for dancers. "The bride and groom's first dance!"

Willow takes my hand eagerly and pulls me toward the floor with a giant smile.

"Hold on…" I say, confused. "We didn't even pick a song."

"Yes we did," she beams back.

We move to the center, all eyes on us, and I take her in close to me, the guests fading away to irrelevance, as the world always does when I look at her so close. The music starts. 'Time Is On My Side' by the Rolling Stones. Willow smiles beautifully at me, letting out a little laugh when she sees the recognition on my face.

"This is, like, my favorite song…" I say, completely confused as we start to sway. "How the hell did you know?"

She shrugs effortlessly. "I don't know. I must have heard you humming it or something."

The song…Willow's eyes…that smile… It all blends together into a profound happiness that I'm finally getting used to experiencing with her. Perfect moments just seem to occur when we're together. I steal a soft kiss, and then notice that she's glancing away. I turn in the direction of her gaze and see Chloe sitting at a table, watching us, as joyful as the day she showed me her blue ribbon.

"I was thinking…" Willow says, wistfully. "I should put together a kids' menu for this place."

"You go ahead. I wouldn't even know what to put on it, to be honest."

"Oh…well that's no good," Willow says, her words loaded with a knowing smile now. "Not if you're going to be a father."

I almost stop dancing, only Willow's movements making me sway. I search her eyes for what I think she just said, and they all but confirm it.

"Are you…"

She nods.

I take a deep breath, then smile like I never have before, then laugh, then kiss her the way only a man who's madly in love and as happy as he's ever gonna get can. The knowledge making something deep inside of me fall into place, a sense of meaning that I never knew I was looking to find before, that I didn't know was so important until now, opening up inside of me.

The music fades and stops, leaving us standing still, eyes locked. In my periphery I see the other guests move onto the dance floor, hear another song start, sense the dancers moving all around us.

"I'm wondering if I could love you any more than I do right now," I say, eventually.

Willow kisses me slowly, like a dream. She puts a hand against my cheek.

"We've got plenty of time to find out."

* * *

THE END

ACKNOWLEDGEMENTS

I'd like to thank all the perfectionists I encountered throughout my life for inspiring me in writing this book. Gourmet cooking is one of the most perfectionist professions in the world, and as a laid back slacker, it wasn't easy for me to write it, and it would have been impossible for me to tap into that perfectionism without your inspiration. So thank you!

I should probably acknowledge and thank more people, but since I'm not a perfectionist, I'll just end it here (I have to go to the bathroom).

But I love my wife and my fans and all my friends very much.

Yours truly,

JD Hawkins